Scandalous Ever After

THERESA
ROMAIN

sourcebooks
casablanca

Published by Sourcebooks Casablanca, an imprint of Sourcebooks, Inc.
P.O. Box 4410, Naperville, Illinois 60567-4410
(630) 961-3900
Fax: (630) 961-2168
www.sourcebooks.com

Printed and bound in Canada.
MBP 10 9 8 7 6 5 4 3 2 1

One

September 29, 1818
Cambridge, England

In a single moment, a person's world could alter forever. For Evan Rhys, it had done so twice: thirteen years before, when he found everything he wanted in life, then again two years ago when he at last admitted it could never be his. With that, he had lost his taste for world-altering moments—unless, of course, they promised to be the good sort.

He was not expecting such a moment on this day. And certainly not the good sort.

No, he had decided long ago that an ordinary day was pleasant enough. That is, ordinary for Evan. Since his days encompassed everything from researching in dusty libraries to unearthing the remains of an ancient castle, *ordinary* didn't narrow the scope much.

Today's *ordinary* fell somewhere between the two extremes. As with every other lecture he'd given in recent weeks, the windows were uncovered once the final magic lantern slide was shown. From the lectern at the front of the hall, Evan faced the rows of high-backed wooden benches, filled shoulder to shoulder with the curious public.

"Doubtless you are all devastated to know that was the last slide." A chuckle eddied through the crowd. Evan continued, "I hope you enjoyed seeing these examples of the fraudulent Roman antiquities plaguing today's dealers and collectors—not to mention His Majesty's Customs and Excise. If any of you have questions, I will take those now."

This was his favorite part of a lecture, always, when other curious minds inquired of his.

The first comment came from a plump don in a towering neckcloth. "You discussed the use of these items in smuggling. But surely there is no harm in creating reproductions of antique stone carvings, as long as nothing is smuggled within them?"

"If the carvings are marked as false, no. But if collected or placed into a museum as genuine, then history is forever undermined." Evan's years at Cambridge hadn't given him half the appreciation for history that digging about in the dirt of his native Wales had. "Good news, though: anyone in this audience will now be able to spot the stone common to these carvings. Go forth and lecture. Share your newfound knowledge. But you'll all have to paint your own magic lantern slides. I'm no artist, and creating this set took me far longer than I ought to admit. So I'm not admitting anything."

Another chuckle from the crowd. Good! This was a lively audience. Evan hoped that by keeping their attention, they'd remember his words better. Not that his joking manner could save a bit of history, but...

Well, maybe it could. Who knew what would make the difference between catching a fraud and letting it pass? Misrepresenting the truth of the past was *wrong*.

Nothing had given him a sense of purpose like holding fast to that idea. And by God, he had needed a sense of purpose since that day two years ago, when he left Ireland without a backward glance.

A reedy scholar in academic blacks had the next question. "How can you be sure the stone comes from Ireland, as you insist?"

"The shade and fine grain are unmistakable. I saw it often when I lived there and dug about for artifacts." With more force than necessary, he began replacing the painted glass slides in their padded case.

A female voice then spoke up. "What keeps you from Ireland, if you believe answers are to be found there?"

And the world tipped and altered for the third time in Evan's life, because that was a *familiar* female voice. The voice of the woman he had loved since their first meeting, and whom he'd hoped never to see again.

Never, he had told himself. Yet his head snapped up, gaze roving the assembled crowd until he spotted her.

"Kate...Ka—Ka..." *Kate.* Otherwise known as Abigail Catherine Durham, the Irish Countess of Whelan. Widow of his closest friend; unwitting keeper of Evan's heart.

He was babbling. He was stiff with shock. It was impossible that she should be here in this lecture hall—yet here she was.

He hadn't seen her for two years, but if it had been two decades he would recognize her at once. The stubborn curl of her pinned-up hair, the impish arch of her brow. Her straight nose, her firm chin softened by a cleft like the kiss of a fairy. Her mobile mouth was bent in a *got-you* sort of smile, wry and friendly.

Always friendly, and no more.

He was staring, wasn't he? *God*.

The wooden benches of the lecture hall were arrayed in tight, dizzying rows ever upward. Their occupants were beginning to whisper, a storm of quiet sound that reminded Evan of wind through a grassy slough.

"Um…catastrophe," he fumbled. Kate's twist of a smile grew. "It was a…personal sort of catastrophe. Which has kept me from Ireland."

He cleared his throat, trying to banish the tightness that clutched at it. *Bollocks*. He wanted to speak to her. He *had* to. Time to bring this lecture to an end.

"Since there are no more questions," he said loudly over a scatter of called-out queries, "then I'll leave you with a piece of advice. The best clue that you've found one of these false antiquities is that the head pops off to reveal a hollow inside, where the pieces were joined. But I'd advise you not to yank at the head of every supposedly Roman statue you see, lest you damage a true antique. Use your judgment before you use your hands."

"What should one do if one finds such a carving?" asked a quavering, elderly voice.

"Open it up, if you safely can. If you find smuggled brandy inside, drink it. Then take it to an exciseman, as there might be a reward in it for you." He paused. "If you drank smuggled brandy, probably best not to mention that to the exciseman."

"But we're inland," protested another voice. "They're nowhere close by."

Evan slotted the last magic lantern slide into place. "Write to me, then, in care of Ardent House in Anglesey. I shall be collecting post from there until March, after which time I will reside in Greece."

Not a bit too far away, if Kate could appear in an unassuming lecture hall in Cambridge.

He closed the padded case for his slides, then thanked the audience for their time. For once, he didn't want anyone to linger; didn't want to talk with the lagging curious about painted slides or excavation or the ton's fascination with collecting the past, false or not. He wanted them to leave, and despite his long-held determination never to see Kate again…damn, he hoped she would stay.

And she did. Though he did not look in her direction as the hall emptied, he felt her presence like a hollow place filled.

Usually when a lecture was done, he relished the silent room. The honeyed wood, the slanting autumn light…the faint drift of lemon polish wafting through the air. It ought to offer a sliver of peace—yet now, his heart thumped as if he'd run past the point of exhaustion.

Two years was a long time to be separated from one's heart.

Thirteen years was a long time to deny it existed.

Into the blanketing quiet came a rustle of fabric. Footfalls, light and heavy. Evan fumbled the latch on his slide case. Summoning his most devil-may-care grin, he looked at the row where Kate remained, a man standing at her side.

"Kate. How good to see you." He bowed a greeting, then mounted a few steps to meet her and her companion at their bench.

Kate, her hair a riot of red-gold, was dressed in autumn shades as though she had never been widowed. Evan shot a curious glance at the hulking fellow who stood beside Kate. A new swain? Suddenly, it was difficult to think what to say next.

"Evan." The curve of her mouth was a sliver of sunlight. "You are a master of understatement. I shall follow your example and merely say that it is good to see you too."

For a moment they simply looked at one another. Evan wanted to whoop and jig and pull her into an embrace all at once—and something of this eagerness must have shown in his expression, for a blush painted her cheeks as she replied.

"Ah, I do not believe you have ever met my twin brother, Mr. Jonah Chandler."

"He knows he hasn't. I never went to Ireland." The brother—*thank God, a brother and not a suitor*—leaned forward, hand extended. "Interesting lecture, Mr. Rhys."

"Evan, please." He shook Jonah Chandler's hand, then cut his gaze toward Kate. She was smiling again, the blush faded as if it had never been.

Friendly as ever.

"I'm glad to make your acquaintance," Evan said to her brother. "Especially since you've known Kate since her young and awkward years. You must tell me all about them."

"He wouldn't dare," Kate replied, "for I can match

any embarrassing story he tells about me with two about him."

"Only two?" Jonah frowned. "Your memory is failing."

Evan cleared his throat. "Yes, well. A good memory can be a curse, so no harm done. Tell me, do you share your sister's interest in antiquities?"

"I've been forced to more than once," said the taller man drily. "Not only today. For our birthday a few years ago, she sent me flint."

"Indeed I did," Kate said proudly. "*Ancient* flint. Napped over a thousand years ago."

"That's a good gift," Evan replied. "At least, it is for people who like that sort of gift."

"It wasn't so bad," Jonah said. "It fit into my tinderbox well enough."

Kate huffed, humor touching the corner of her mouth. "I sincerely hope you are teasing."

"Hope all you like," said her twin mildly. "Since I sent you a bolt of silk for our birthday, and you sent me rocks."

Kate rolled her eyes. "Brothers. So ungrateful."

"They are," Evan agreed. "My own brother is extremely so."

Light words had allowed him to regain his composure—and now, he wondered at the heavier question of her presence in Cambridge. "Kate." He hesitated, considering how best to word his question. "I didn't expect to see you this side of the Irish Sea."

She held his gaze with sea-colored eyes. "Did you ever plan to see me on the other side of it, then?"

No. Hell no. For the sake of his heart and his conscience, never again.

"My schedule has not permitted—that is, work has required me to remain in..." He steadied himself on the high back of a bench. "I hope it may not be impossible for me to—"

"Bollocks." Kate folded her arms.

"Sisters," muttered Jonah. "So improper."

Evan ignored this. "Why are you in Cambridge, Kate? Is everything all right in Thurles?"

"Everything is—different." She pressed her lips together, halting further explanation. "I am briefly visiting my father in Newmarket. This was not so far to travel to see an old friend."

He did not miss the dodge of the state of affairs in Thurles, the village near Whelan House in County Tipperary. But he pretended he had. "I'm glad you came here," he said. Which was the perfect truth.

Her smile caught him, as always, right about the heart. "I wasn't sure it was you, when Jonah first told me a man named Evan Rhys was lecturing on antiquities and smuggling. Rhys? I asked. A horse-mad Welshman who laughs at everything?"

"I'll grant you horse-mad." Evan echoed Kate's light tone. "But look how serious I am. I'm even wearing serious clothing. Starch in my cravat, coat tailored, all that." His tidy appearance was the opposite of the way he had often dressed in Ireland: slouching and comfortable, ready for a gallop or a dig at a moment's notice.

"You do look extremely serious," Jonah said. "Serious enough that I'm going to leave my sister in your keeping. I have to see a man about a horse."

Kate groaned. "*Jonah.*"

"It's fine, Biggie. Talk to your friend. In fact, I'll make my own way back to Newmarket. Jerome and Hattie will take you home whenever you like." With a nod, the large fellow eased by Evan and thundered down the few steps to cross the lecture hall, then exit.

"Your brother will be back in but a few minutes," Evan assured her. "There's a necessary on the ground floor."

She chuckled. "I don't know if I'm glad or sorry to tell you that he was being literal. Brothers aren't usually keen to travel fifteen miles to oblige a curious sister. Jonah has a meeting with a professor looking to sell, I think, a carriage horse."

"And is that professor…Jerome, was it?"

"Jerome is one of my father's chestnuts. Hattie is another. They brought us from Newmarket this morning in my father's carriage."

Evan blinked. "Your brother intends to leave you alone for the return journey?"

"Am I alone?" She leveled a blue-green gaze at him.

No. Now that she was here, he would not let her march away so soon. "You were never alone, Kate. Not for years on end."

She went very still. "What do you mean?"

"That there never were such friends as we." Another understatement. He truly was master of them. "You taught me to shoot targets. I introduced you to cheroots. Every evening, you and Con and I shared whisky upon whisky, and we three laughed."

Her head bowed. "So we did. But two years ago,

our three became one. Since you left Ireland the day Con died, I have heard nothing from you."

True, and he had no blithe response to this. "I…"

When he trailed off, she looked down the rows of seats toward the lectern, the case that now held Evan's magic lantern and slides. "Is this work what kept you away from Whelan House for so long? With not even a letter of condolence?" Her voice was brittle with hurt.

A gray feeling touched his spirit. With a sigh, he settled against the high back of the bench before her. "You're not the only one who grieved, Kate."

"So I should have written to you instead?"

He shook his head. No, she shouldn't have. That would have been impossible within the bounds of propriety. Just as propriety—and the loyalty that had so long bound Evan to Conall Ritchie Durham, the late fifth Earl of Whelan—had demanded Evan cut himself off from that family and from Ireland itself.

"It wasn't my place to write to you." He turned away from her, marching down the steps to gather his notes. His slides. The arguments, the evidence he had laboriously created for honesty and integrity.

Honesty, ha. Integrity, bollocks. He'd hidden his secrets, and Con's, for so long that he was as much a fraud as the sculptures he had drawn in inks and paints.

Her voice followed him like a shadow. "Whose place could it be to write, if not an old friend's?"

An old friend, she insisted on calling him, but he wasn't. He was the man who had tumbled for her, swift and sudden as a fall, the first time he met his friend Con's seventeen-year-old bride.

His feelings for her had never altered. Feelings that had become more difficult to ignore over the years, yet more impossible to speak of. The circumstances of Con's death placed them utterly beyond the pale.

Not that he could admit any of that to Kate.

Not that he could walk away from her, either.

Instead, he tidied his possessions, thoughts humming with possibilities. By the time he looked at her, he had an idea in mind. "I intend to stay in Newmarket for a few days." This was true, though the intention was born only that moment. "Might I trouble you and Jerome and Hattie for a ride?"

"That depends." She descended the steps to the presenter's pit. "Are you going to stop talking to me again, and force me to ride in silence as I wonder what I've done and eventually wind up tossing you out the carriage door?"

He considered. "Probably not."

She raised her eyes to heaven. "Bollocks. Again. All bollocks."

"It is, isn't it?" Whatever she thought he meant—anything, everything—it was true. His choices since meeting her had, for the most part, been bollocks.

He busied himself with the fastened latches of his cases. Checking. Checking again. Awaiting her reply, as she stood near him. Two steps away, maybe one.

"It is," she said on a sigh. "Since we're agreed on that much, I suppose you can travel with me back to Newmarket."

There: this was the perfect example of what he'd meant. Riding in a carriage with her to Newmarket was another in his long line of *bollocks* choices.

For how was he to spend three hours alone with Kate without revealing his part in her husband's death?

Two

There was barely any room to sit in the carriage, crammed as it was with parcels. Kate suppressed a chuckle as Evan folded his tall body into a too-small space on the squabs across from her. They had retrieved his belongings from a Cambridge inn, which had only added to the crush.

Strained as the Whelan finances were, she shouldn't have bought so many gifts in Cambridge. But she missed her daughter Nora a bit less when choosing ribbons and fabric to complement the girl's dark hair. She knew her son Declan would think of her when he played with the set of toy soldiers. For the dowager Lady Whelan, Con's mother, an impish urge persuaded Kate to buy a prayer book. A rare Protestant in a land of Catholics, the lady was certain that no one was as devout as she.

Evan was the first to speak—casually, as though most of his attention was directed to finding a place for his left elbow atop the parcels. "You were sly, answering my question about Ireland with no information at all. But I am even more sly, and I pretended that I did not notice."

"You are entirely spoiling the effect of your cleverness by boasting of your triumph." As the carriage lurched into motion, Kate coaxed a hatpin free, then another. Her hat was pretty, the first new one she had purchased since her year of mourning for Con had ended a year before. The first gown in a vivid print, too, with a pelisse of coppery wool that made her red-blond hair shine. Thank goodness for fashion plates and the talented seamstresses of Thurles. They had given her armor enough to return to Newmarket for the first time in five years, to beg a fortune from her father.

Not that she had quite got around to that yet. As far as Sir William Chandler knew, his eldest daughter was visiting because of the race meetings that made Newmarket the hub of English society each October.

Settled now against the back-facing squabs, Evan glanced at her sharply. "Since I've spoiled the effect, I might as well ask again. Kate. Is there some problem in Ireland? Is—how are the children?"

So many times she had been asked this question since Con died. Kate gave the same answer every time. "They're fine." After a pause, she added, "They are staying with Con's mother. They have missed you."

"And you? How have you been?" His eyes dark as chocolate, he watched her with the same careful scrutiny he'd given to his magic lantern slides as he packed them away.

She pulled another pin free, then another, feeling more bare with each one. "I'm fine too." Pulling free her blossom-trimmed hat, she jabbed the hatpins through the plaited-straw brim.

She *was* fine—or as fine as she'd been for years and years of her marriage. Years of financial strain and dawning awareness of her husband's infidelity. But over those same years, she had become skilled at *appearing* fine. And for Con, by God, there was nothing more important than making a good appearance.

"Your words aren't rationed, you know." Evan relaxed against the squabs of rust-colored velvet, sliding one boot forward. "You can use more than three when you reply to me. More than four, even, if you have something of particular significance to say."

The familiarity of his banter made her chest tighten. She swallowed, hard, before replying crisply, "You are fortunate that I was judicious with my words rather than being perfectly frank with you."

"I'm going to regret asking this, but I will all the same. What did you want to say, Madam Frank?"

She lifted her chin. "That you behaved like an utter ass."

Though she had spoken the words lightly, they took on great weight in the close confines of the carriage. "I will grant that I deserve that."

"At the very least. Two years of silence. *Evan.* Didn't our friendship mean anything to you?"

He held out his wrists. "Slap the manacles on me. Whatever punishment you care to inflict, I will accept it."

"I could poke you with a hatpin."

He made a gesture that was not precisely polite. It had the effect of drawing a smile from her before she added, "It's a fair question, Evan. And I'm sly enough to notice that you didn't answer it. You could have come back any time after you chose to leave. After you and Con argued on the day he died."

He snapped upright, drawing his feet in close beneath his seat. Withdrawing into a shell, it seemed. "I couldn't come back after that."

"And why not? Not only *could* you have, you *should* have. What was I to think when you left Ireland without a word of farewell?"

"What indeed? What did you think?"

"I didn't know. I still don't."

The two chestnuts, Jerome and Hattie, pulled the carriage along with smooth strides. For the distance of one…two…a half dozen of their long steps…Kate was silent. Then she added, "Con wouldn't tell me what had passed between you, only that you'd argued. He was upset. Terribly upset. So shaken that he should never have ridden out. And—"

"My God." Evan rubbed a hand over his jaw, the chiseled line of his mouth. "You think it's my fault that he died."

Her head snapped back. "Not your fault. It was no one's fault. His fall in the steeplechase was an accident. Everyone said so, from housemaid to magistrate. The cinch on his saddle split, and…and he fell. Badly."

"Maybe *fault* is not the right word. What of blame? Do you blame me?" His dark eyes were steady and fathomless.

She held his gaze. "No. I don't blame you for that. If I fault you for anything, it is that you called me friend, then and now, but you never showed it when that friendship was tested."

He made a dry sound, like a laugh gone cold. "You cannot know how I was tested."

"I cannot, because you never told me. Not a single word. All I know is that you and Con argued, and you left, and that was that. You threw our whole family away like rubbish."

"There is no such thing as rubbish," he said quietly. "Only pieces that antiquarians will one day discover and come to understand."

God. He was so…so *Evan*. "That," she replied, "is not adequate. I need more from my life than the hope that someone will try to piece it together hundreds of years from now."

Through the carriage roof, Kate could hear the occasional cluck or halloo of the coachman. Sir William's traveling carriage was built on spacious lines, like Chandler Hall and his stables. Every surface was brushed clean and gleaming.

The conveyances in the carriage room of Whelan House's stables were neat but patched, oiled but aged. A few years ago, there had been many more. A few years ago, everything had been different.

Was it wrong that, despite her crushing debt, she was happier as a widow than as a wife?

Was it wrong that she didn't mind if it was?

"What has it been like for you?" Evan's question seamlessly followed the ones she posed herself. "These past two years?"

"Like running down a hill, hoping I can reach safety before a rolling boulder crushes me."

"That is an alarming analogy."

"I thought you'd like it," she said. "Because of the stone. Pretend it's an *ancient* rolling boulder."

He shook his head. "Still alarming, though now the

alarm bears historical significance. What has got you running, Kate?"

She waved a careless hand. "Nothing much. Administering an earldom for my ten-year-old son. Constantly playing hostess to my crying mother-in-law."

Evan looked to heaven. "Ah, good old Gwyn. I've known her since Con and I were at Harrow together. She's always been the epitome of calm and selflessness—if one is speaking in opposites."

"If I ever called her 'good old Gwyn,' she'd probably have an attack of the vapors. She prefers I call her 'Countess.'"

"Pure love and sunshine, that one is." Evan toyed with the carriage window's shade. *Frrrrip.* It rolled up. *Frrrrup.* It rolled down, casting the interior of the carriage into half-shadow. "Did she want you to come to Newmarket? If I make my guess, she'll spend the whole of your time away on a fainting couch declaring how exhausted she is."

"She didn't want me to travel, exactly, but she saw the need for it." Kate chose her words with deliberation, skirting the line between truth and polite fiction.

"You needed to see your father, you said. Is he ill?"

"No." She arranged her hat beside her. She should have brought a hatbox, maybe? Or her lady's maid? She was out of practice with fashion.

Evan leaned forward, the late-afternoon light from the carriage window throwing his features into sharp relief. "It's a financial matter, then. Isn't it? Con must have left you in a bad state."

"Ugh. You are always so *noticing*," Kate said. Evan had a scholar's curiosity, not only for chips of flint and

Roman vases, but also for the heart-deep workings of a household. No subject evaded his curious mind. "Yes, Con left a financial ruin behind him. I have sold what I could, but I owe...so much. The magistrate, Finnian Driscoll, has bought up all my debts—"

"Con's debts."

"Well, Con doesn't plan to pay them," she retorted. "So I must, on behalf of the earldom, lest I am forced to sell off all the Whelan lands that are not entailed."

Frrrrip. Up went the shade again. "Is it as bad as that?"

"Worse. I have only until the end of the year before Driscoll calls in all the debts." Three months before a family heritage hundreds of years in the making was lost, all due to Con's fondness for gambling and spending.

"Con was my friend," Evan said. "Closer to me than my own brother. But he was also a damned fool, and I told him so many times."

"He laughed it off. He always did." Kate could almost smile at the memory—almost. "That was a particular gift of his, laughing off anything he didn't want to hear."

Con had been fond of carriages, the flashiest and highest-perched and quickest imaginable. They had seemed irresistible to Kate once. A rich man's toys, a treat in which to ride. When a few bad harvests made funds more and more meager, there was less money for toys and treats of any sort. Yet Con had never been used to denying himself what he wanted, or to waiting for it. This was one of the reasons he and Kate had wed at such a young age.

Kate and Con had met at a fortunate time. He,

returning to Ireland by way of Newmarket with Arabian stock he hoped to breed with Chandler mares, and she, wanting an escape. Her mother had died three years before, her father was endlessly traveling, and she was far too young, at seventeen, to care for her siblings and run a household.

Con, four years older and flush with the newfound power of attaining his majority, had wanted her rich dowry. She had wanted to run off with him, for he was handsome and blithe and confident. By post from Spain, Sir William had given his permission for Kate to wed a man he'd never met.

If there was a flaw in the logic of a woman who married to escape the thankless care of her siblings—well, seventeen was young. Too young to think beyond the next *yes*, the tussle of passion, the excitement of going somewhere new.

For rich years on end, the young earl and countess had been a team, pulling in harness, supporting one another. Theirs had been a good arrangement for a while. Then, with the coming of poverty, it had not been. Then there had been Con's other women, some staid, some as flashy as Con's favorite carriages.

Kate had pretended not to know. But there had probably been other women all along.

"I want to help you," Evan said. "I will help you come up with the money somehow."

Ouch. One of the hatpins had jabbed her through her skirts. She hadn't realized it stuck out so far through the brim. "No. I don't want that. I plan to ask my father to lend me the money needed. That's what I need to speak to him about."

The corner of Evan's mouth turned down. "Why do you not want my help?"

She fumbled to explain. "Because...I don't want you to be obliged to me. I don't want our friendship to be a burden—if it still exists at all, after two years of silence."

And Evan's parents might be wealthy, but he was not. There was no way he could scrape together even a fraction of the debt owed.

"Of course our friendship still exists," he replied. "Surely we know each other as well as anyone does."

"Maybe," she granted. Maybe this was true. Though no one besides Kate herself knew of the spark that had lit her hopes for years, the hidden wish that her life might be different. She had hidden this wish from Con behind dutiful pleasantries.

She had certainly got what she wanted, deprived of husband and income and friend all at once. Perhaps she ought to have specified the sort of *different* she would prefer.

"This could be a good thing," Evan said. "Your time in England, away from Whelan House."

"How do you mean?"

"No one can make demands on you now. You can just be..." *Frrrrup*. "Kate."

"Leave that shade alone or I shall tie your hands together." This was an easier response than *who the devil is Kate?* For thirteen years, she had been wife, then mother, now widow. At the age of thirty, she could not remember a time she had not been someone else's rock.

"I know what you're thinking," Evan said.

"That you're reaching for the shade again? Correct.

Please, Evan. Stop. Go…go ride with the coachman if you are burdened with an excess of energy."

Frrrrip. One last time—Kate hoped—the shade opened, revealing a square of clear sky and horizon distinct as a pencil line. "I like the sound it makes." Evan took a handkerchief from a pocket and wiped a bit of dust from his hands. "And no, I was thinking that *you're* thinking that Kate has to be all things to all people, and so how could that possibly be a respite?"

"How did you—" She slammed her mouth shut. After a moment, she said, "You are shockingly incorrect. That's not at all what I was thinking."

"Hmmm." He stretched out his boots, hooking one foot over the other. "Right. Well, even if it wasn't… despite the other people and tasks that lay claim to her time, Kate was once my friend. Can she be again?"

A flip, simple answer was at the tip of her tongue—and then she noticed his hands. The handkerchief was stretched between whitened knuckles, and he had dug his blunt nails into the linen.

The tightness of his grip made her throat close.

There were many ways one might help, weren't there? And there were far too many things for which one might grieve without looking for more. She could keep opening the wound of Evan's absence, his long silence—or she could accept his apology. His company, as long as it lasted. The comfort of his laughter. The honesty in his dark eyes.

When she thought of the matter like that, she was able to turn her back on the hurt of their separation. To look ahead, and to answer him truthfully.

"Yes. I want my friend again, Evan. I have missed you very much."

Three

I want my friend again. It was all Evan had thought he wanted to hear. Now that she spoke the words, though, *friend* seemed a smaller idea than it used to.

Maybe because it was so *good* to look at Kate. He felt he hadn't seen anything properly since he'd left her side, or experienced it vividly, and being with her now was like coming awake. How could *friend* describe someone who made one feel awake and alive?

Kate had always been a woman of great energy and ingenuity. She *did* things, packing the everyday matters of household and family into tidy tasks to be maintained and solved. Every problem, no matter its size, received a careful look and a determined effort. To Evan, troubled with grayness of spirit, her belief that every problem had a solution was irresistible.

They would find a solution to this too. To every *this*. To her debt, and to his stubborn love, and to where to put this damned parcel that kept jabbing him in the ribs, once they reached Newmarket.

"When we arrive in Newmarket," he decided, "I

will buy you a measure of whisky. Consider it my thanks for conveying me from Cambridge, and a reminder of all those evenings we sat together. You and Con and me, drinking whisky and talking about the estate, or laughing over odd bits of history."

She curled against the wall of the carriage, a sweet, rounded figure in rust and cream. "May I tell you a secret?" Her sea-blue gaze was mischievous. "I am fascinated by history, but I've never liked whisky."

"Truly?" This took him aback. "I've never seen a lady toss it back with so much gusto."

"Exactly. I had to. When I met Con, he called me a 'pretty girl.'"

"How…awful?"

She tucked an arm behind her head, making a cushion of her own limb. "It is when one is seventeen and wants a handsome Irish noble to see one as a desirable woman. 'Pretty girl' is a sexless compliment. I wanted to impress him."

"Whisky would do it. He'd a taste for it from his schoolboy years." A taste for it, but no head for it at all. Evan could not count the number of times he'd unfastened his friend's collar so Con could be sick. "What of the target shooting? The cheroots? Were those for Con's benefit too?"

Humor touched the corner of her mouth. "Not those. You must allow me to have a few vices of my own."

"I will, if you'll allow me the same."

"Of course. Men must be allowed their vices."

Her tone was light, but Evan knew all that she had left unsaid. Con was as profligate as a tomcat, and as carefree, and everyone in the household—no, the town—was aware of it. To him, vows were cheerfully made and easily broken when a greater pleasure crossed his path. How many times Evan had cursed him for this over the years, he couldn't now recall. But Con only laughed—until their final fight, when at last Evan had touched Con's sense of honor, and their friendship was irrevocably broken.

It was a friendship formed in roguery, when the Irish aristocrat and the rough Welsh boy met at Harrow. Con tackled the world with a buoyant confidence, as though whatever he wanted was his due. Such certainty was irresistible to Evan, seeking relief from the habitual grayness inside. He was only too willing to paint it over with minor misdeeds and laughter—like helping Con hoist a sheep through the window of a professor's lodge, or nipping from the secret bottle of wine in the house matron's chamber.

Upon a trellis of such events, then, did their friendship cling and grow.

For his years of school and the years since, Evan drifted between Wales and Ireland. He did little with his classical education save for idly digging up artifacts and translating the occasional bawdy poem from or into Latin.

Con's death had changed many things. One was the way Evan passed his days.

Yet he could not wish that a single evening had been spent differently.

"I am glad you joined Con and me on so many evenings," Evan said to Kate. "Even if your seeming enjoyment of the company and conversation was polite pretense."

"You give me too much credit for politeness. I could never have fooled you for evening upon evening. No, I liked the talk of the children, the horses. I liked hearing about the antiquities you'd found. Oh!" She sat up straight. "Is that why you give lectures now? Because you want new people to hear your stories?"

He had never thought of the matter like that.

In truth, it had happened by chance. Circumstance. The fortunate realization that he had become part of a tapestry of knowledge larger than his own life.

Ever since boyhood, Evan had found the world to be gray about the edges. He had been safe. Comfortable. Maybe even loved, best as his determinedly elegant parents knew how. Yet the gray feeling dug into him with idle claws, a glum lassitude that made nothing seem to matter.

If he spoke of it to his family, he was gruffly reminded of his blessings. So he stopped speaking of it. He laughed and joked, was glib and wry. The flaw was not with the world outside—it was within.

Studying antiquities mended the flaw, if only temporarily. He liked being regarded as a man of substance. Someone other than the rogue at whose escapades Kate used to laugh as she settled into the curve of her husband's arm.

"Yes," he decided. "I do want that. To me they are more than stories." He edged a boot forward, knocking her foot with his. "And I am madly arrogant and need new audiences to praise me all the time."

"I shall wear myself to a thread applauding for you.

Only let me get free of this infernally close carriage first, so I can clap with the proper fervor."

She pulled her hat onto her lap, trailing her fingertips over the silk blossoms. A pucker formed between her brows. "Are you really going to live in Greece in a few months?"

"Six months," he replied. "Yes, as soon as sea passage is safe. The ambassador to the Ottoman Empire has invited me to study artifacts *in situ*. Ever since Lord Elgin—how shall we put it? Helped himself to marbles from the Parthenon?"

"That is a polite way of stating the matter. Lord Elgin would be most pleased."

"Right, well, since that time, pillaging antiquities has become a favored pastime of the *ton*. I'd almost prefer to see false Roman sculptures in museums over genuine Greek statues in English parlors."

"You have a bold idea, then, that the past can be known even if it is not stolen. You are a revolutionary, my friend."

"I believe that's the only way it can be known. I don't want to leave Great Britain merely for the sake of traveling. I only want..." He considered how to explain. "I want to do something that matters."

She laughed. "Women understand that urge quite well. The law of the land makes it all but impossible for a woman to achieve anything in her own right, yet we want it no less."

"Everything you do matters." He meant every word, and deeply, but knew they were not enough. "Mother. Countess. Daughter. Friend. Daughter-in-law to Good Old Gwyn."

"You may try to make it sound important, but it's only one thing after another." She pulled a face. "So—are you lecturing in Newmarket? Is that why you're on your way there?"

"Not exactly." Before seeing Kate in Cambridge, he'd intended to visit his parents and brother in Wales before beginning a new excavation...somewhere. Winter was a poor time to dig for artifacts in the frozen, bleak ground, but for the time being, autumn still held sway. There was a chance of excavating in the Paviland limestone caves for a few weeks yet, to do something *real* with the months before he left Great Britain.

Or he could stay with Kate. The decision was easily made.

"I would never expect to travel to Newmarket during the month of October and think to talk of anything but horses," he said. "No, I'm going there purely for love of the turf."

Well. For the love of *something*.

Born into the horse-mad Chandler family's tradition of Thoroughbred racing and breeding, Kate accepted his reply without question. "Where will you stay in Newmarket? Have you hired a room?"

Inwardly, Evan cursed. It would be impossible to find lodging when much of the *ton*, and half of the rest of England, was flooding into Suffolk to attend the races. "I haven't, no. But I'm not unused to camping. The grass of Newmarket will be far more comfortable than the floor of a cave, and I've slept on those many a night."

"Nonsense."

"No, it's true. Cave floors are not unpleasant in themselves. It's the bats that cause all the problems, not the rocky floors."

"Ridiculous man. That's not the part that's nonsense. No, you cannot sleep on the ground. Where would you keep your magic lantern while you slept in the outdoors?"

"I would—huh."

"I thought so. It would be a great pity to risk spoiling slides that were painted with an unspeakable amount of effort. You'd be welcome to stay at Chandler Hall. My father's great barn of a house has plenty of spare rooms."

"Thank you." He wasn't fool enough to demur. "I would be delighted to. I won't even roam the halls at night like an angry ghost."

"The servants will be relieved not to encounter your spectral presence in the wee hours of the night." She smiled. "I can venture to speak for my father, you'd be welcome even beyond the length of my own stay."

"What's this? You lob a mysterious comment with wholly inadequate context. Do you mean that you are returning to Ireland soon?"

"I must. I traveled too late in the year to make a long stay in England. The Irish Sea is hardly a warm bath at the best of times, and if I remain here much longer, it'll become impassable."

"What a coincidence of timing!" Evan hitched a booted foot across his other leg, settling into the comfortable squabs. "I planned to travel to Ireland myself. To, ah, investigate the source of the false artifacts."

"Did you?" She leaned back, regarding him with great skepticism. "I am not certain I believe you."

Since the idea of the journey had been half-formed and largely fictitious before this carriage ride, he wasn't sure how strongly to defend himself. "It's the honest truth." *As of this instant.* "But I wanted it to be a surprise."

"Bollocks," Kate said. "You're making up this journey, aren't you?"

"No. I fully intend to travel to Ireland."

She narrowed her eyes. "Is it because you feel sorry for me?"

"Hell no." He could say that with perfect honesty. "If I ever tried to feel sorry for you, I'm confident you'd show me how well you could shoot targets."

"And don't you forget it." A grin began to spread over her features. "You were planning to come to Ireland?"

"Eventually." *Someday. When I couldn't stay away any longer.*

"Why?"

To see you.

No. Not to see her. To be in Whelan House with Con's widow was a reminder of all that was lost, and all Evan still couldn't have.

But if he could find the source of the false artifacts…if he could identify the source of the goods used for smuggling…well, that would be something real too, wouldn't it? When he left England and Ireland for good, at least he would leave them a bit better off.

"I want to solve everything," he said. "Everything that needs solving."

Her light eyes crinkled at the corners. "Ambitious,

aren't you? Well, perhaps we can travel together. If we're both leaving on the packet from Holyhead—"

"Naturally."

"Then I can adjust my ticket, if there's a difference between our departure dates."

"I doubt there will be." Considering he hadn't yet procured tickets. "I'll sort it with your maid once we reach Chandler House."

"It will be good to have you in Ireland again. The children have missed you," Kate said. "Do you remember how they called you uncle?"

"I remember. Even more clearly, I remember how they climbed on me as though I were furniture."

"I hope you were honored. That's how they show affection—or it was, when they were younger. You were like one of the family."

Like one of the family, but not truly a part of it. He had a designated bedchamber in Whelan House, and he went to it each night after watching Kate follow her husband upstairs.

He was *like* a brother to Con. He was *like* an uncle to Nora and Declan. But their real uncles were Kate's brothers Jonah and Nathaniel, whom they had never met. And Evan's true brother lived in Wales and thought him a spoiled wreck of a person.

Bollocks.

"I remember," he said again.

After this, there were more memories to share. Laughter, sometimes for no other reason than that one needed to laugh. More than once, a silence cradled them between recollections; then the words wandered on again like twine unspooling.

After a while, Evan shifted Kate's flowered hat and took the seat beside her as they chatted. She didn't bat an eye; she only bade him to take care in moving her hat. This close, she smelled of something sweet, like a baked bun. Warm and comfortable, familiar as his own self.

And they talked on. Yes, he agreed. No, he had never played such a prank, and frankly, he was insulted at the…oh, all right. Yes, it had been his idea. No, he wouldn't teach it to the children. He would set a good example as an uncle—or nearly so. Yes, it would be good to visit Whelan House again.

It was true. All of it, true. Yet it was not the whole truth.

Con had bent the rules of society to suit himself. Evan had learned their shape so he could skate about their edges. Most importantly the rules of friendship, because Evan was fairly certain that a man ought not covet his friend's countess.

When Con died, none of the rules mattered anymore, except the rules that applied to Kate. Evan kept his distance from her, because she deserved better than broken rules to go with her broken heart. And because, in the midst of his own grief, he wasn't strong enough to watch hers.

Through the carriage window, he caught the faint, drifting scents and sounds of autumn. The earthy smoke of stubble burning in a field, the savor of meat roasting. Piping music and distant laughter of villagers at a fete. The pale afternoon light faded, then melted into gold and pink and red.

After a while, Kate settled against the squabs. After

another little while, her body went soft and heavy against his in the slack of sleep.

Their reunion was too new, too sudden, for him to do anything but wish they belonged like this. So Evan cradled her head against his shoulder, breathing in the scent of her hair and wishing…wishing.

Four

To Evan's pleasant surprise, Sir William Chandler was unfazed to encounter an unknown guest at breakfast the following morning.

The first two to arrive for the meal, they had a chance to become acquainted. The baronet shook Evan's hand with a courteous "A friend of Kate's husband is always welcome here."

"Thank you, Sir William. I am relieved not to be booted from your doorstep. Although—I was first a friend of Kate's *late* husband, but it was not long before I befriended Lady Whelan as well."

Not that such details mattered to the baronet, but they mattered very much to Evan. He would have given all the silver plate on the sideboard—if it were his—not always to be spoken of in the same breath with Con.

From a wheelchair of great bulk, directed on satin-smooth wooden wheels, Sir William looked up. "Late." He repeated the word with a shortened *e* at its heart. Steely brows lifted with curiosity. "Is that a Welsh accent I hear, Mr. Rhys?"

"It is, yes. I thought I'd pounded it out flat during my years of schooling. But I was born not far from Holyhead, on the Isle of Anglesey."

"About as Welsh as Welsh gets, then."

"So think the people of Holyhead. Though in their opinion, I'd be more Welsh if I spoke the language with greater fluency." The elite of Wales—of which Evan's parents were decidedly members—preferred to ape the English rather than their own neighbors. Not until Evan began an excavation near the Rhys tenants' cottages did he pick up more than a stray word of the old language.

Sir William's expression went soft. "The Cambrian tongue, all l's and w's. It's pleasant to the ear. I once knew a woman who spoke it." The baronet lifted the cover of a dish. "Kippers. Salty as the devil's tongue. I'm not fond of them, but they'll fuel you for a good morning's work."

"How can I resist a recommendation like that?" Evan served one of the small fish onto his own plate.

Clearing his throat, the baronet added, "I wonder if you know the woman of whom I speak. Anne Jones? Oh—what are the chances? I realize not all Welsh people know each other."

"You might be surprised." Evan regarded the kippers dubiously, decided against taking another, and then replaced the lid over them. "As a matter of fact, I know no fewer than three people named Anne Jones. What age is the lady of your acquaintance?"

"Forty or forty-five years old. Very pretty. A criminal genius."

At the matter-of-fact tone of these last words, Evan

set down his plate with a *clack*. "Is she? My felicitations, Sir William. As a member of the Jockey Club, you meet the most interesting people."

"I met her some years ago. In Spain. Not, ah, in my capacity as a member of the Jockey Club. Perhaps you've heard of *Tranc*? Sometimes she adopts that name instead."

The Welsh word for death. "How melodramatic. No, I can't say I know her. The Anne Joneses of my acquaintance are a matron of some thirty years and half as many children, an innkeeper's wife of near your own age"—which Evan guessed at near sixty—"and the baby daughter of one of my parents' tenants."

"It is a good name," Sir William decided. "Which is why it's used so often. Someday I'll find the right Anne Jones again."

"You called her a criminal genius. Did she steal something of yours?"

"A daughter, I think." The baronet returned his attention to the sideboard. "Not one of the ones you know. I might well have another daughter, but all I know of her is that she was born in December 1805 and is presently in London. Under the protection of Anne Jones."

That would make the unknown girl much younger than the grown Chandler offspring. Nearly the same age as Kate's daughter Nora.

Somehow, Evan suspected Kate knew nothing of her father's preoccupation. *Men must be allowed their vices*, she'd said. Yet one never thought of one's parents as sharing the vices of the younger generation.

Evan retrieved his plate. "You have material enough

to write a novel, Sir William, if you should ever turn your attention away from the turf."

"You have no idea," the baronet replied drily. "A life such as mine could fill many volumes."

And that was the end of those intriguing subjects: criminal genius, hidden potential children. With a pragmatic turn of attention that had Evan feeling a step behind, the baronet served himself from the row of dishes in deliberate amounts. A footman standing to one side of the large room took the plate after Sir William had served his meal, carrying it to the head of the table.

If Evan made his guess, breakfast was taken in the same room used for dining: a great echoing chamber of simple, smooth lines. Chandler Hall was startlingly new, built—as Kate had told Evan—within the past decade to display its owner's wealth as well as accommodate the baronet's wheelchair. Despite a soaring rotunda, the chambers of Chandler Hall spread out on a single story, with floors of glossy polished stone and doorways cut on generous lines.

Evan took his place at the long table. When Kate appeared for breakfast a minute later, he greeted her.

She was dressed in a morning gown of riding-habit green, which made her hair and eyes bright by contrast. "Jonah will be here in a minute, Papa," she said as she took a seat across from Evan. "He checked on the new horse, then wanted to tidy up."

"New horse," Sir William grumbled. "As though one needs to buy a carriage horse during a Thoroughbred race meeting."

"It was a good bargain for precisely that reason."

The gravelly voice of Kate's twin accompanied his weighty footfalls. "Besides which, I had to buy Bassoon. Kate left with the carriage and stranded me in Cambridge."

She twisted in her seat. "Slander! You told me to take it. After, I might note, you'd removed extra tack from it. Before we set out, you were preparing to ride home."

Jonah grunted, but a faint smile softened his features. "I didn't think you'd spotted the extra tack."

"I have two children. I notice everything. For example, you said you would tidy up after visiting the stable, but there's still straw dust on your boots."

Jonah cursed.

"And Papa asked for coffee instead of tea, which means he plans a long day at the racetrack."

Sir William cursed.

"Though that's not much of a guess," she added, "the day before a race meet begins. As for Evan, he—"

"No, no. Don't you turn your gimlet eye in my direction." Evan pointed his fork at Kate. "I never denied your infallibility. By the way, you look lovely this morning. Did I mention that?"

"—is far too polite to tell you that what he likes for breakfast is a nice Irish porridge with treacle." She waved at his plate. "Toast? A kipper? Pitiful English fare. See, he's hardly had a bite."

"That is because I only just sat down." He eyed Kate, then decided to admit the truth. "As much as you like Irish whisky? That's how much I like porridge."

"Whisky for breakfast? Tut, tut. Our little drunkard," Jonah murmured, sitting at his sister's side—not far away enough to dodge her thrown elbow.

"I didn't realize." Her head tilted, a considering posture. "All those mornings at Whelan House..."

"Had much in common with the evenings?" *If you could keep us company with a tumbler of whisky, I could certainly choke down porridge for a chance to sit at your table.*

"Yes." A faint color rose in her cheeks as she turned her attention to her plate.

It was no more than a hint of pink, but it was enough to banish any grayness that had clustered about Evan that morning.

❧

On so many mornings, Kate had played the perfect hostess with tolerable skill. She had never guessed her favorite guest—practically part of the family—hated every bite of breakfast he took.

Was that the price one paid not to be alone? Sipping whisky that burned one's throat? Slurping porridge that lay in one's belly like a swallowed blanket?

Surely not. Surely it didn't have to be that way—especially not going forward, when Kate ran Whelan House as she wished.

With advice and lamentations aplenty from the elder dowager. Good Old Gwyn.

Kate spooned up some of her porridge, cooked by the kitchen staff at Chandler Hall for "the Irish countess." Boiled over a fierce coal fire, it didn't taste like the oaty breakfast she enjoyed in Ireland. That porridge was simmered slowly over peat, thickening until it clung to a lifted spoon.

She ate her breakfast anyway. *Take that, Evan.*

Before she could speak again, the door to the room

opened. "Good morning, all! No, thank you, James," said a quick-spoken female voice to the footman. "I've already eaten, and so has the baby."

The newest arrival was Kate's sister Hannah, youngest of the four Chandler siblings at twenty-six years of age. "Lady Crosby," Kate greeted her with feigned formality.

Hannah had married the previous year, the scion of the dreadful Crosby family that lived nearby. What exactly was so dreadful about them, Kate didn't know. Their dreadfulness was simply imparted to her as an essential bit of her upbringing, along with letters and math.

Since arriving in Newmarket a few days earlier, therefore, Kate had taken every opportunity to tease her sister.

Hannah groaned. "Stop calling me that, Biggie. Even though I'm a Crosby now, I'm still Chandler enough that the name sits ill in my ears."

"Crosby, Crosby, Crosby. Congratulations all the same." Kate rose from the table and enfolded her sister in an embrace—mindful of the infant supported across his mother's chest in a cunning sort of sling.

Hannah was a sunned and stretched version of Kate herself, with golden-brown hair and freckles and the lithe build of a natural horsewoman. For years, she had served as Sir William's secretary. Of the four Chandler siblings, she resembled Sir William most closely in his determined pursuit of excellence on the turf. To them, victory was everything.

Kate gave her sister one more hug. "May I hold baby John?"

"Please, yes. Take him." Hannah extracted her plump little son, handed him to Kate, then freed herself from the sling. "There, it's good to be out of that harness. A bit like a horse myself, am I not?"

"I've always thought so," said Jonah.

"And that's why the baby's name is *not* Jonah." Hannah put out her tongue. "I did think the sling was clever. It keeps the baby steady and allows me both hands to drive over."

"What of your illustrious husband?" Sir William said through teeth that were almost not clenched.

"Preparing for tomorrow's races. I believe he'd like to live at the racecourse this month. Golden Barb is running well, and—"

"Not that damned horse again." The baronet stabbed at a kipper with his fork.

"Yes, that damned horse. Stab all you like. He's going to win, see if he doesn't."

Fortunately for Kate's comprehension, Hannah had recounted the story by letter. For Evan's benefit, Kate explained, "Last year, an unscrupulous groom switched one of my father's horses for one of Sir Bartlett Crosby's. For a time, Golden Barb had—how many people wanting to own him?"

"Everyone wants to own him, because he's a champion," said Hannah.

Evan's brows lifted. "Sir William, I think your life could fill an entire library."

"Oh, we have a visitor!" Hannah rounded on Evan. "Good morning, sir. Are you a friend of Jonah's?"

"I don't have any friends," Jonah said. "Too much trouble."

"You haven't changed at all, my dear twin." Kate shifted the drowsy baby to one hip. "Hannah, this is Evan Rhys, a friend from Ireland. Or should I say Wales?"

"I am a man with no country," sighed Evan. "Or maybe I possess all of them. I haven't decided which would be preferable."

"You are Con's friend!" Hannah exclaimed. "The scoundrel. I mean, the charming scoundrel."

"Charming scoundrel?" Evan set down his fork, as though tasting these words. "Yes, that'll do. I can live happily with that description."

Con's friend. Why wouldn't he say he was *Kate's* friend?

But then, she hadn't exactly said it either, had she?

"Now that everyone knows everyone else," said Sir William, "I'd like to visit the stables. Kate, you ought to come along and meet all the horses. You'll be leaving after this week's meet, won't you? Got to get back for the Thurles steeplechase."

In October, Newmarket played host to two horse-racing meets, each a week long, and only a week apart. This was the highlight of Sir William's autumn. He could hardly fathom that one would miss a race—unless it was to attend a different race.

"No, Papa," she said. "I'm not basing my travel plans around the steeplechase, but the behavior of the Irish Sea."

"Even the sea wants to bring Irish people home for the steeplechase," decided the baronet. "Now, imagine how well you could run it with one of my horses. With Pale Marauder? Thoroughbred speed, solid bone—you'd lead the pack."

"Is that the same horse who false started eleven

times at the Derby last year?" She tickled the baby's belly, and he rewarded her with a gummy yawn.

"Only ten false starts," Sir William replied. "But he's much calmer this year. Sometimes."

"Pale Marauder's legs would snap off the first time he tried a jump," Jonah said. "Thoroughbreds aren't built for pounding races."

"That is disgusting," said Hannah. "And so is... whatever you're eating, Jonah."

"That's not my plate. That's Kate's breakfast."

"I knew I couldn't be the only one who disliked porridge," muttered Evan—though Kate wasn't sure whether anyone heard him except herself.

And the baby, who yawned again. He smelled sweet and clean, a well-washed new little being. Plump pale skin and the slow-blinking eyes of one who hadn't quite brought the world into focus. She kissed him on his fuzzy little head—only to be rewarded with a spot of drool on her bodice. With a smile, she drew out her chair again and sat, arms full of infant nephew.

Around the table, the others were still debating the steeplechase. "Thoroughbreds want to *win*," said Hannah. "Which carries them over any obstacle. Even if their legs snap off, which they won't."

"Not *off*, but they could break," said Jonah.

"*You* could break," Hannah huffed. "What do you think, Mr. Rhys?"

"I think I don't want you to tell me I could break." Evan put a hand to his heart. "Such an insult would positively...unhorse me."

"That is the worst joke I've ever heard," said Kate. "If you can call it a joke."

"Kate," said Sir William. "We look to you to defend the honor of Irish horses."

"Must I?" She tucked the baby's head beneath her chin, letting him settle against her front. "What if I like your horses best?"

"You might as well be honest. The title will fall to Jonah, but I have willed each of my offspring the same amount of money."

"Thus dies primogeniture," said Jonah. "How will I keep the others under my thumb?"

"Did you think we would allow that? Not a chance." Kate laughed. "Besides, you are far too benevolent to serve as dictator."

"Should I put forward Welsh horses as the best?" Evan said. "Not for a share in your will, Sir William. Merely to muddy the waters."

He had taken to the quick, cheeky pace of the conversation with an ease that pleased Kate. How did he do it? She had required days in Newmarket to settle in, to feel herself not an interloper with people who had known her all their lives.

"Welsh horses are the kindest," Kate said. "They are imps, full of good-natured mischief."

"My countrymen—er, beasts—thank you."

She lifted a staying hand. "But they'd never win a race. They aren't terribly quick to act."

Evan narrowed his eyes. "You underestimate them, Irish lady. Given the right motivation, they might surprise you."

"The baby prefers Arabians," piped up Hannah. "Who will speak for them?"

Everyone ignored this. "Biggie. What do you think

of the horses of Ireland?" Sir William looked to Kate—really looked—as though he wanted her answer.

He was not talking only of horses, she knew.

She could never resist an entreaty coupled with the old family nickname Biggie. Taking another whiff of the drowsing, powder-sweet baby, she considered. "Irish horses are best for what they're bred to do: throw their hearts over every obstacle. They're less costly and far hardier than Thoroughbreds. There, do you like that?"

Sir William rubbed at his chin. "Go on."

"Ah…that's all I have to say. Why?"

"I'm glad you're proud of Ireland. You've lived there a great while, yet I never knew if it felt like home to you."

Oh. So many curious eyes on her now, from footman to friend and every relative imaginable. "It…can feel that way. Yes. I'm proud of our horses. But I wouldn't love them so if I hadn't been raised among horses here."

"Chandler blood will tell," said Hannah.

Sir William counted his remaining bites of breakfast, then folded his serviette and rolled back from the table. Kate recalled this ritual from her last visit: he calculated and balanced his own nourishment as carefully as he did that of his racehorses.

"I'm off to the stables." He directed his wheelchair toward the doorway with easy, practiced movements. "Daughters, care to accompany me? You too, Rhys, if you want to see what a real champion looks like."

"The kippers have made you mischievous, sir," Evan said.

"He's that way no matter what he eats," Jonah replied. "I'll be after you in a few minutes, Father. To see whether Bassoon is still faring well."

"I should not come with you," said Hannah. "That would be treachery. I'd spy on you and tell Bart all your secrets."

Sir William regarded her over his shoulder. "And you'd tell me all of his in return?"

"You know I would. Fair is fair."

"As if Crosby knows anything I don't," he shot back before exiting the dining room.

It was today or not at all. Kate *had* to speak with her father. She'd been hesitating, waiting for both of them to grow comfortable with each other again before she inflicted her request for a fortune to save her family's lands. Acting proper. Smiling. Helping.

But what had propriety got her? A husband who strayed. A lifetime of debt. An empty bed. A friend to whom she could not write. Propriety was nothing but a burden.

Damn propriety, then. She should have damned it long ago, seizing every opportunity that came her way.

When she looked at Evan, something knowing in his gaze made her feel warm—almost as though her whole body were blushing. Whether he realized it or not, he had caught her in a secret decision, and that made him a part of it.

She kissed baby John on his head, letting him drool all over her gown. Then she stood, handing him back to her sister. "I need to speak with our father, Hannah. Be good to our guest. Not that I am any less of a guest here than he is."

"You could be." Hannah settled the baby into her arms. "You could come as often as you liked, Biggie. Any time."

To this place? Kate had never lived in Chandler Hall, built years after her marriage on the wide, smooth lines needed for Sir William's wheelchair. Here, cheer and money seemed inexhaustible.

She thought of Whelan House, short on both, and the memory was a pinch between her brows.

Maybe she'd have returned to Newmarket more often if the family home had been like this when Kate was seventeen. If her father were here instead of traveling the world and piling up a fortune, and her sister were happy.

If that had been the case, maybe Kate wouldn't have wed so young.

Maybe Jonah wouldn't have married a woman who promised the moon and stars, only to vanish after their wedding night.

Maybe Nathaniel wouldn't have been rootless, and Hannah wouldn't have been left alone.

If. Maybe.

These were fruitless words. The only phrase she should allow herself was...what now? She could damn propriety, but there was nothing to put in its place.

Yet.

Yet was a word with far more possibility to it. An idea would come. And maybe it would involve Evan Rhys, who knew with uncomfortable, familiar, delightful accuracy her every worry.

"I'll see you later," she told Hannah and Evan.

Knowing this was true was a pleasure, sweet and

sincere. But that knowing look Evan had cast her… that *damn propriety* that seemed written all over her skin…there was something more than friendship in the nature of that exchange.

What it had been instead, there was no time to consider right now. She sped in the direction of the stables, where she intended to beg her way out of debt.

After all, she was an Irish horse now. When an obstacle arose in her path, she would batter at it until she had achieved victory.

Five

"Does she know you love her?"

Evan was now alone in the dining room turned breakfast parlor with Hannah, Lady Crosby, and her sleeping blanket of baby. As peaceful and silent as little John was, so his mother was alert and sharp-eyed.

Though Lady Crosby's question caught him off guard, Evan did not pretend to misunderstand. "No. Considering how many times your sister has mentioned I was like a brother to Con, she has no idea."

It was a cruelty that she valued him so much and wanted him not at all.

As if in agreement, the sleeping baby released a stream of spittle.

"I wondered about that." The young baronetess snatched up a serviette and dabbed at her soiled gown. "It's possible she *does* know you love her, but she doesn't want you to say anything about it. Because that would spoil your friendship."

"Lady Crosby, I did that well enough already."

"Call me Hannah, please. And how did you spoil the friendship?"

Evan pressed at his temples. "I should have tallied the number of times she mentioned yesterday that she'd had no word from me since Con died."

"You never even *wrote*?" Hannah goggled at him, then slapped the serviette back onto the table. "Never mind, never mind. I'm sure she said a great deal on that subject."

"You are correct."

"Yet you are staying in our father's house, and after the race meet you'll travel to Ireland together. Is that something not-friends do?"

"Travel alone with a woman he can never have?" Evan said drily. "That's not something any man in his right mind would do."

"'*They are in the very wrath of love*,'" murmured Hannah, patting her son's back. The baby released a great belch of air. "That's from *As You Like It*. My brother Nathaniel's favorite play, because there is a Rosalind in it, and that is his wife's name. I learned quite a bit of the play. For several months I had nothing to do but sit about and read Shakespeare and grow an enormous baby."

"Well done," Evan said. "The baby is most…er… enormous. In a way that's just right for a baby."

Hannah granted this, then asked, "If you do love Kate, how long do you intend to wait before pursuing her?"

Evan shrugged. "Forever."

"Too long. We Chandlers regard ourselves as invincible, but that is not the same thing as immortal."

"I know that." Twice he'd feared that Kate would die when she was brought to bed of Con's children.

Kate, whom he teased into laughter when she was

focused on the *next-next-next* of a busy wife's, mother's, and countess's life. Kate, who helped Evan remember that there would always be a *next*, and that gray wasn't the only color in the world.

"She said she wants my friendship," he told Hannah. "And I'd rather be her friend than mean nothing to her at all."

"Why don't you let her decide if those are the only two choices?"

"Are you the voice of the devil, Hannah Chandler Crosby?"

She winked. "That, I'll leave to you to decide." Pushing back her chair, she stood. "I'll take John home now before he soils my entire habit."

Evan took to his feet as well. "Babies emit a great many fluids. I am constantly impressed. I don't know how they manage it."

"You're not the only one who wonders that." Hannah jounced her son to one hip. "If you could hand me my sling?"

Evan did so, and Hannah settled the baby again. "Will I see you at the racecourse tomorrow?"

"Naturally. I wouldn't miss race day," Evan said.

"And have you decided whom you'll bet on?"

"I wouldn't bet against a Chandler horse," he replied. "But I'm not sure how much I'm able to stake."

"You have one day to determine the answer," said Hannah—and with that, she and the baby were off.

One day. Hmm.

The lady had given him much to think over. Mischievous Welsh beast though he might be, it was time he acted.

Over the years of his hidden love, he had grown accustomed to thinking in impossibilities, of all he might lose should he risk what was precious. But there was another way to think about the matter as well.

He wondered what unexpected victory he might win, if only he strove for it.

Sir William was waiting for Kate in the doorway of his study as she exited the dining room.

"Come, join me in here, Biggie."

Biggie. The nickname ought to have been horrid for one who always hovered on the edge of plumpness—or slightly over it—but it always cheered her. As a toddler learning to speak, Jonah had made a mash of his twin's first name, Abigail. Throughout childhood, their parents and younger brother and sister—Nathaniel and Hannah—had adopted the nickname as an endearment.

Abigail Catherine Chandler by birth; Kate Durham, Irish Countess of Whelan by marriage.

Kate had missed being called *Biggie*.

"Papa, please—call me Kate. I am a grown woman now." Yet she felt anything but, perched in the little chair next to the great table her father used as a desk. Here to plead her case.

The desk was cluttered and piled with the accumulated business of a great house and a great stable, a stud farm and a string of racehorses. Sir William kept no stable master, and since his daughter Hannah had wed and her replacement, Rosalind, had married

Kate's younger brother Nathaniel, he hadn't had a secretary either.

Kate wasn't the only one overburdened at present.

"Kate, then. What is weighing on your mind? Not that I'm not pleased to see you, but you haven't returned for a race season in years." His features were as stern as ever, but his hazel eyes were not unkind.

"I need money," she blurted. "By the end of the year, or I'll have to sell all the Whelan land that's not entailed."

Stripping her son of his inheritance, and that of those who would follow him. Turning the welfare of tenants over to whatever stranger would pay the highest price.

Or not a stranger at all. Finnian Driscoll, the magistrate of Thurles and holder of Con's debts, would buy the land. A large and friendly man, he was well-liked by the villagers.

In the shock of new widowhood, Driscoll's attention to Con's creditors had eased her burdens, leaving her free for the immediate needs of her family. But there was such a thing as too easeful. In the end, the things he did *for her own good*, *just to help*, *to make things easier* had the effect of taking all choice away.

The idea of the lands falling away from Declan's control into Driscoll's hands made her stomach twist, repulsed.

Sir William sighed. "I thought it might be something like that. Come and walk with me."

Kate glanced, startled, at his wheelchair. Her father's smile was weary. "In a manner of speaking."

Glass-paned doors led from the crescent-shaped

study onto a smooth gravel path. Kate stepped out after her father, pulling the doors shut behind them, then tipped her face upward to the morning sun.

It showed its face here more often than in Ireland, where it often hid coyly behind dim drizzle. The trees were dressed in every bright shade of gold and bronze, and the breeze was cool and gentle as she fell into step at her father's side. Her feet made pleasant little crunches in the smooth white gravel of the path, and Sir William rolled his wheelchair along with almost idle movements of his sturdy hands.

"To what end do you need the money?" he asked.

"Repairing the house. Buying winter fodder for animals and seed for spring. Maintaining the land's drainage for tenants." For what did she *not* need money? "Con left many debts, and crop yields have plummeted since the year he died." A year of dreadful cold, in which summer hardly warmed the earth before winter fell again. Kate had been glad to leave behind 1816, though each year since had brought its own challenges.

Sir William's hands clenched on the sleek wooden rims of his chair. "I should have met Whelan before I agreed to let you wed him. It was a difficult time."

This was an understatement. He had contracted palsy and was near death in Spain. An aristocratic marriage for Kate had likely seemed the best way to see to her welfare.

"I had met him, Papa, and I wed him anyway."

At this distance in time, she could speak the words with a flip of carelessness. Conall Ritchie Durham had many gifts, among them charm, handsomeness, and the ability to make a wealthy innocent feel like the most precious and special creature on earth. She had fallen for him swiftly, enraptured.

He'd married her for her money, of course. Oh, he'd been fond of her too. But would he have pursued her without her dowry? Never.

Realizing that *never* had taken years, difficult years. Years of lavish spending that gobbled the dowry and the income from the estate. Con was not one to bother himself. *Don't worry about it. You focus too much on minor details. Let me cheer you up.* But "cheering her up" invariably meant more gifts they couldn't afford, such as horses and gowns and lavish orders of smuggled luxuries from France.

So confident was Con that creditors never dunned him, letting the debts mount. *Don't distress yourself, Katie. I'll take care of it.*

But he didn't. Instead, he had been killed, and there was a new way of life to which she had to come to terms.

Poverty. Scraping, shabby-genteel poverty and the fear of losing her son's livelihood.

"How bad is it?" Sir William asked.

She scuffed her boot heels through the gravel. "Bad. I need thousands of pounds." She named a figure that still shocked her, even after careful calculations.

And I do not know when I shall ever be able to pay you back. Years from now, maybe. If the land recovered well after the biting winter of 1816. If harvests were good for seasons on end, and the repairs to Whelan House went well. If, if, if.

She sighed.

Sir William halted as the path split, one fork leading to the stables and the other running into a wood. "I hoped you'd lay your burdens down in Newmarket, once you decided to visit."

"You should know better than that, Papa. A parent and a noble can never forget the ties that bind them to home."

She didn't want to, truly. Her children and her responsibilities as countess were heavy burdens to carry alone. But it was better to carry them alone than to hope for the contributions of a helpmeet who, instead, added rocks to her pack.

Besides, she loved them. She loved Nora and Declan better than herself. She loved Ireland as the place of their birth. One would perform great feats for love that would seem impossible otherwise.

Sir William looked toward the stable, the lines of his face deep-carved by slanted morning light. "As it so happens, Kate, I cannot lend you the amount you need at present. I've invested heavily in broodmares from Arabia. They cost the earth, but in a few years, their offspring will be well worth what I've spent. Their stamina must be seen to be believed." Wistfully, he traced the wooden rims of his chair.

Though Kate's feet were firmly planted on gravel, the ground seemed unsteady. "I understand," she said.

She did. Buying horses and racing was what Sir William Chandler did. It was what made him—what made them all—Chandlers. It was how Sir William had built the family fortune and earned the title of baronet from a grateful Prince Regent who needed strong and true cavalry horses during wartime.

Her father looked at her with eyes that understood too much in return. "What will you do, Biggie?"

She drew herself up. "I've been asking myself the same thing for years." She tried for lightness. "Somehow I've always found the answer."

"How will you find it now?"

"I don't know," she said. "But I'm a Chandler, and tomorrow, I'm going to the races. I'll pick up my troubles after that."

"That's my girl." He reached for her hand and gave it a quick squeeze.

There was nothing more to be said, was there? So she walked with him to the stables and stayed in the company of the horses, warm and sure, until she could almost forget the ever-present uncertainties of her life.

Six

The day of a horse race began before sunup, as Kate knew from groggy experience. Even before her maid had laced and buttoned her into her gown, Jonah and Sir William had been thundering around, alerting the whole household as they prepared to leave for the track.

Lagging a few minutes behind them, Kate gulped a cup of strong tea laced with milk and sugar. Beneath the soaring ceiling of Chandler Hall's central rotunda, she bumped into Evan. "Ready to walk to the track?"

"Ready as I'll be without another five hours of sleep." He looked like himself again, Evan as she remembered him. Homespun and carefree, clad in well-shaped buckskin breeches and boots worn until the leather was supple as cloth. Wool coat and starched collar and cravat, all worn with touchable ease.

She reached toward him, fingertips brushing his sleeve. It was real. After all this time, he was part of her life again.

She drew back her hand, hoping he hadn't noticed her silly little gesture.

Evan patted a coat pocket. "Half the servants of Chandler Hall are sending me off with their wagers."

"Not all of them?"

"The other half will be at the track to place their own bets."

Kate frowned. "I wonder why they did not ask me."

"They wanted to ask me because I'm so handsome." With a cheeky grin, he swung his hat atop his head. "Also, they didn't want to bother you. You've gone into rogue housekeeper mode, you know—making up menus and telling the servants how to make certain dishes and checking on the horses fifteen times a day."

"Only ten," she murmured. "Though it ought to be fifteen. My father sorely needs a housekeeper and stable master." *Rogue housekeeper.* The epithet made her smile. "A rogue housekeeper is the only type of rogue I'll ever be, I suppose."

"I don't know about that. You look ready for anything today."

"Do you think so?" She gave a little twirl. She had garbed herself in a riding habit and tidy plumed hat, a military look that made her want to square her shoulders and march forth.

Horses, crowds, anticipation. There was something in her blood that woke to the chaos of race day. Something she had not even known was sleeping.

"I have become a little interfering," she admitted. "But you know I like to keep busy."

"I know. I do too."

This was true. She remembered that about him. How many evenings had unrolled like silk as she talked with Evan before a parlor fire? While she settled into contented stillness, he whittled wood into sleek shapes and tossed the shavings into the flame. She looked at his hands now, callused and tanned, marked and scarred.

He drew on a pair of gloves, and she was sorry to see his skin covered. "Shall we?"

She pulled on her own gloves, then rested fingertips on his proffered arm. "I don't know which horse I'm going to bet on." An odd flutter had taken up residence within her chest. But why? She had nothing at risk today.

"Bet on yours," he said. "I certainly plan to."

A rain during the night had left the ground spongy, but the chill dawn was clear and crisp. As Kate walked with Evan to the twin racecourses—so flat, yet they dominated the town—streaks of daylight-blue began to split the sky.

Strings of horses were walked toward the track, while carriages of all sizes and all levels of tonnishness were pulled by yet more. Silk-clad jockeys staggered by with their arms full of tack, heading toward the weighing room.

"Shall we try to find your family?" Evan asked. "If we can. I see Newmarket is full of early risers."

Already, throngs on foot and in carriages gathered about sellers of race cards. Bookmakers who would later make their way to the betting post threaded through groups of spectators, their expressions avid and ears listening. Boys hawked newspapers. Broadsheets from the notable London horse dealer Tattersalls fluttered to gain notice.

"Only wait until it's time for the races to begin,"

Kate said. "The whole road will be blocked by carriages and wagons, and we'll hardly be able to shoulder through the grounds. For now, my father and Jonah will be in the weighing room, probably." Jockeys had to hop onto a giant balance before and after the race to have their weight recorded. Older horses were required to carry more weight than the youngest colts and fillies.

Sir William was racing two Thoroughbreds today: the infamous Pale Marauder, a swift but temperamental colt prone to false starts, and a two-year-old filly named Celeste. Kate had curried and crooned to the filly the day before. Moon-gray and light on her feet, Celeste would have her maiden race today.

For years after his legs were paralyzed, Sir William had been confined to his own lands. But after a trip to London, then Epsom, the previous year, he'd discovered that his wheelchair could be stuffed into the traveling carriage, and that losing the use of one's legs was no reason to miss a race meet.

"Will they find a place from which to watch?" Evan asked.

"One place? I doubt it. They'll try to watch from everywhere. If you keep to one spot, you won't see more than a sliver of the track."

This meet's races would take place on the Rowley Mile. An arrow shot of manicured turf, the straight track was lushly green from autumn rains and deceptively simple in form. Kate had walked the white-railed line time and again as a teen. Here a bump, there a dip, and just when the horses were wrung and exhausted, a great hollow that had caused many a beast to stumble. Then a rise to the final post, an uphill climb on which all but the greatest of heart flagged and fell back.

Evan scanned the crowd. "Yet I do think I see your sister. Isn't that her, tugging a bay through a puddle?"

Kate followed his gaze, spotting Hannah and a jockey in red-and-white striped Crosby silks leading a saddled bay. The colt had no liking for wet earth, evidently, for he stamped his hooves in the great puddle left from the night's rains, bobbing his head with annoyance. Hannah laughed and said something to the jockey, and on they walked. To the parade ring, maybe, where bettors and competitors alike eyed the horses preparing to race.

"That must be her champion, Golden Barb," Kate said. "We always used to hiss the Crosby horses. Now that Hannah has married into the family, we had better behave ourselves."

"If a strange hissing sound comes from beside me when a Crosby horse appears, I promise I won't look about for the source of the noise."

"So generous," she said.

"I know it." Evan tucked her hand more securely in the crook of his arm, edging her past a heavyset man who appeared to be deep in his cups. "Such is the mark of true friendship. Your family is delightful, by the by."

"They can be, can they not? That should not be surprising, as I'm one of them."

"Did I indicate surprise? I am certain I did not."

"No, you didn't. You were a perfect gentleman."

"Good for me. I managed it for once."

"Well done." Kate skimmed the growing crowd in

vain for the black-and-gold silks of the Chandler stables. Once there had been a time she knew her father's racehorses as well as she knew her own siblings.

"I am the one who's surprised," Kate added. "It's not the same family within which I was raised. Not even the same house."

She remembered her father as always traveling, always absent. Now he'd made a community and placed himself at its heart. It was sweet to see, but odd in its unfamiliarity.

The changes were all to the good—except maybe those Jonah had gone through. Who could be certain? He could not be coaxed to speak of his wayward wife, even to Kate. Instead, he had passed the years between Newmarket and the Chandler stud farm, where promising young horses received their first training for a life on the turf.

Kate had been trained in the same way, but she'd been less obedient than one of Sir William's foals. Alone of the four Chandler siblings, Kate had found the people involved in the world of the turf more interesting than the horses. Because of this, she had been eager to leave Suffolk County; to meet more people and spend less of her life at the races.

At the moment, she was not sure why. A spark of excitement sang lightly over her, following her contours like a skimming hand, setting her to shivering.

"You are cold? We ought to get you indoors."

Kate was about to exclaim hotly when she recognized the spark of mischief in Evan's eyes. "Rotten man. You couldn't pull me away from the track today with the promise of a million pounds."

"I don't think anyone will give you odds on that." Evan touched her nose with a gloved fingertip. "Biggie."

The touch tickled, and she batted his finger away with a laugh. "Unless you're a Chandler, you will lose a fingertip for calling me that."

"Delightful, did I say? I misspoke. 'Prickly' might be a better term." Again, he touched the tip of her nose—lightly, this time wordlessly.

Kate's breath caught in her chest. "It might be." She hardly knew what she was saying. She tipped her face, letting his finger skate across her cheekbone, then trace the curve of her cheek and jaw.

A damp breeze blew, chilling cheeks grown suddenly warm. "I—" Now, what could she say?

I like it when you touch me, because you are you.

I am afraid when you touch me, because it is new and unexpected.

She swallowed her confusion. "Will you share an apple with me?"

This was not such a *non sequitur* as it seemed. Food sellers were setting up their goods, and the scent of roasted apples and cider sweetened the air. The warm fruit scent married with the earthy smell of horses: sweat and manure and the clean grass they ate, along with the oil and leather of their tack.

Overhead, the sky was fully blue now.

Evan dropped his hand, doffing his hat to her. "If the lady asks me to share an apple, I can only accept. But from where did she get it? I hope it was not given her by a serpent."

"As I haven't bought it yet, you can make certain of that," Kate said lightly.

With Evan at her side, she threaded through the growing crush, following the scent of roasting sweetness until she reached a gap in the crowd. Here a ring of stones marked the edge of a low fire built of wood scraps and rubbish. Next to it stood a rangy chestnut horse harnessed to a farm wagon. Around the edges of the fire walked a man in rough homespun and a floppy farmer's hat, collecting pennies from the crowd, while a stairstep of wheat-blond children held sticks on which apples were skewered. The red skins browned and split, spitting juice onto the flames with a *hisss* and a heavenly warm scent.

"We'll have one," Evan said, handing a coin to the farmer. The man nodded at the smallest of the children, whose apple was the brownest. Stick and all, the lad handed the fruit to Evan.

"For you, Eve." As soon as they had stepped back from the ring of stones, Evan handed Kate the stick. "It's safe to eat. No serpents in sight."

"With this many horses about, they'd all be trod flat." As Evan turned to converse with another vendor, Kate sank her teeth into the apple.

Sweetness flooded her mouth, then a gentle tartness. And heat, sizzling heat! Oh, the juices within were almost boiling. Opening her mouth, she fanned it with one hand as the other held the staked apple. *Please, don't let me encounter anyone I know.*

Evan turned back to her, all wicked mirth. "Did someone bite into the apple right away? For shame, Eve. You'll lose your tongue that way."

"Iss hur-fect," she said, still fanning her mouth. "I all-aze do this en I eet."

"Perfect. Right. I remember the dinner parties you used to host, in which turtle soup was scalded and so were the guests' mouths."

Her grimace would have been much more quelling had she been able to close her mouth.

With some difficulty, Kate managed to swallow the piece of apple. "It's good. Would you care for a bite?"

"I can't take it from you. My hands are full of race cards." This must have been his second transaction: Evan had got hold of the cream-colored papers on which were detailed horses, owners, trainers, and riders for each race.

"I...could feed you a bite."

His grip on the race cards tightened. "That is true. You could."

Which was not a *no, don't be ridiculous.*

Which might as well have been a *yes.*

She scooted closer, into the lee of Evan's frame, and held up the apple to his lips. He sank white teeth into the hot fruit, regarding her with unfathomable eyes the same shade as flame-licked wood.

Her cheeks went hot again. It was intimate, this feeding of a man with a plump forbidden fruit. She had not expected it of herself, or of him. She had not known it would be so difficult to look away, or to know what to do once she had shared an apple with him.

She felt naked, bared to her old friend in all her uncertainty. And with that bareness came a flicker of lust, uncurling warm and pliant as if waking from a long sleep.

"You were right," he said, still looking at her. "It's quite good."

"I…thought so." Breathless. Inane. But they were friends of long enough standing that he did not look at her oddly. He only smiled, as though whatever she did was right.

Then handed her a race card from the shuffle in his hands. "The first race of the day will soon begin. Would you and your apple like to move to a better vantage point?"

"There could hardly be a worse one," she teased, the heat still high in her cheeks.

This was not an answer, precisely, but he took it as such, and she followed after him as he shouldered through the crowd. The racecourse was a crush such as Kate imagined a *ton* ballroom would be during the season, a crush such as she had not known since attending races as a girl.

Most of the steeplechases she'd known in Ireland were informal affairs, horse against horse, rider against rider, all against the unfurling of the terrain. From pub to church steeple or the reverse, there was more distance and fewer people.

Here the turf was tidy and circumscribed, and the crowds clustered at every inch. A half dozen races would be run that day, with the same number each subsequent day of the meet.

On race day, the stratified world of English society was stirred up and blended. Not mixed, precisely, for even here each group kept to its own. The Jockey Club had its own stand. The inner circle was a precious few pence more expensive. Some people sat atop gleaming carriages and breakfasted from hampers. Some ripped bites from slabs of brown bread and shared nips with dogs that inevitably wound through the crowd. The poor drank milk so thin it was blue, while the wealthy quaffed wine aged until it was garnet-red.

But the race cards were the same in every hand, as was the color of the money that slipped from fist to fist. Bookmakers wouldn't turn down a coin, no matter its source.

That was familiar. So was the shape of Evan at her side, unyielding. Now, too, was the roasted apple she brandished at the end of a stick, like the world's least terrifying sword. It was hers. Theirs.

He spoke to a bookmaker, making the bets for the servants at Chandler Hall. Then they followed the line of the racecourse, looking for a thin spot in the crowd. Kate hit a few people with her apple—mostly by accident, but it proved an effective way to gain them standing room. They crammed into a spot along the rail just past the treacherous dip in the Rowley Mile course. Once situated next to the track, Evan shuffled through the race cards.

"The two-year-old fillies are first to race," he noted.

Kate peered over his arm to skim the card, then she poked through the others. Today's other races were for two-year-old colts and for seasoned racers. There was a handicap race, plus two races staked by nobles who wanted their name on everyone's lips. A new set of horses and jockeys would tramp to the starting line every thirty minutes, then run their hearts out for glory.

"My father's filly, Celeste, is to be in this race," Kate realized. "She's carrying eight stone. Do you know the odds on her?"

"Five to one when I placed the wagers. She's the

second favorite. Her maiden race, isn't it? She must have trained well."

Kate agreed—though there was no denying the horses knew the difference between an ordinary gallop and a race. It was in their blood, the desire to run, to win. That vivid urge set them straining against the bit, lined up and waiting for the starter to free them.

"I would have bet on her no matter what," Evan said. "I told her yesterday I would, when I visited the stable."

Kate snorted. "And did she understand you?"

"She made the same noise you just did, so I believe she and I are on remarkable terms."

"You do have a way with ladies."

"Have I? How delightful."

A *yuuup* rose above the low din, and the crowd nearest the starting line roared its excitement.

"They're off!" Kate clutched the rail with her free hand. A swell of primal excitement buoyed the crowd: calls from many throats, following the horses down the Rowley Mile as they ran. Closer and closer came the sound, and before Kate was ready, a flash of black and gold whipped by on the back of a swift gray. Then white and blue, crimson and black, checked and patterned in a blob of color, the brightly clad jockeys on horses bunched so closely it was impossible to pick one from the next.

And then they were past, and she was leaning over the rail to see up the final climb—but so was everyone else, and there was nothing but a sea of hats and shoulders before her.

It wasn't until the call went out from the finish that

she realized the filly Celeste had won. A champion the first time she competed.

"Good girl." Kate's eyes prickled with moisture. "Good girl, Celeste."

Oh, to win so quickly. To know what one wanted, and to run one's heart out trying to reach it.

Kate had done so, for years and years. But in the end, maybe, she hadn't chosen the right goal—to be the ideal wife and mother and countess. Daughter. Friend. Landowner. Widow.

It was too much to hope for. Yet how could she strive for anything less?

She turned to Evan, who was marking his race card with a stub of pencil. "The staff at Chandler Hall will be pleased with that race," he said. "They'll all get a few extra shillings in their pockets."

"How did you do?" Caught in faraway thoughts, Kate was relieved her voice sounded almost normal.

"I put a pound on her, so now I'm a wealthy man. Once I settle up at the end of race day, I can buy you all the apples you want." When he looked up from the card, his ready smile vanished. "Is something amiss?"

"Not at all. I'm perfectly fine. But I don't need any more apples." She took one last bite. The roasted fruit had grown sticky with juice, the flesh mealy as it cooled.

She was ready to let the stick fall, and the apple with it. But no; why let it be wasted? A treat such as this could tempt another. Turning, she scanned the crowd until she caught sight of the farmer who had sold her the apple—and of the raw-boned horse that had pulled the wagon of fruit to the race meeting. After a quick word to Evan, she shouldered her way through the throng toward the chestnut. Good creature. He stood calm and steady amidst the bustle, yet never got a taste of the fruit he carried. She tugged the apple from the stick and fed it to him on a flat palm, then handed the roasting stick back to one of the blond children.

There was one more role she played: horsewoman.

With an effort of thrown elbows and sheer will, she threaded her way back to Evan's side. "What is the next race?" With both hands, she clutched the rail. "I'm ready."

It was minutes on end before the festivities of the first race were completed, the purse awarded, and the fillies walked from the course to cool down. Somewhere, Sir William was celebrating—but not too much, for there was always another race.

The judge's stand would be drawn further along the track now, the starting line advanced. The second on the schedule was one of the stakes races, with a plump purse collected from the entry fees of the stables that entered horses. Kate recognized the names of many owners, and even those of some jockeys. Racing was a tradition for generations on end, passing from parents to children.

Clouds covered the sky in coolness, and a light mist speckled Kate's face. "The jockeys won't like this," she observed.

"Probably not. But the horses won't particularly care."

The crowd had never seemed to quiet once the first race was finished, yet somehow, the noise grew again. The great wave of sound crashed, as sure a marker of the race's beginning as the flick of the starter's flag.

Kate was ready this time, watching the track with wide eyes. A minute's gallop brought the race before her: browns and bays, a chestnut and a white. The silks of the straight-backed jockeys flowed past in a colorful river, as the horses' long legs ate the ground with a quiet thunder of hooves. And they were past, then, and another race was safely gone, and—

No! As the last horse streaked by, he stumbled in the hollow of the course. The colt's quick strides went ragged, a lunatic shuffle and buck to keep his footing.

The jockey fell heavily to earth. It was impossible to hear the thud of his form over the crowd, gasping as one, but Kate knew the sound it had made. She had heard it two years before, when Con fell to his death before her eyes.

She pressed a gloved fist to her mouth, strangling her startled cry. The jockey was clad in buff and blue, and he lay still on the turf.

Buff and blue, the colors Con always wore at a steeplechase. Buff breeches, blue coat. He had lain still too, kicked and surrounded by merciless galloping hooves.

It wasn't supposed to happen here. It was supposed to be over, done, wept for, and left behind.

There was an arm around Kate's shoulders, a quiet voice in her ear. *It's all right. He's all right. See, he's already getting up. The horse is all right too. Everything is fine. Everyone is fine.*

Determined, she swallowed the tightness in her throat, thinking of now. Now. She was here, and Celeste had won, and most people who fell were fine, and she was fine too.

She trembled, lost between past and present, until the warmth of the voice melted the ice about her. On and on it spoke, and finally, she realized it was right. The jockey had been shaken, but he hoisted himself upright and waved to the crowd. Shouts of delight, whistles, catcalls, and lewd offers followed. A stew of sound, relieved and grateful, happier to see the man rise safely than if there had been no fall.

He was fine. He was a stranger to her. Kate's life would not alter again, heaping burdens on worries on uncertainties. She must pull herself together.

"He was last," she said in a voice that hardly shook. "No one ran him over. That surely saved his life."

"This must be the only time a jockey was grateful to hold last place," came the reply in that blessed warm voice, and she realized it was Evan's. Steady beside her, he had taken her into the shelter of his arm and talked to her until she came back from Ireland.

A hand was rubbing her back. Evan's, of course. He had dropped all of the race cards in a scatter about their feet, the better to comfort her.

The better to take her, almost, into his arms.

She ought to step back, to assure him that she was fine, but she could not manage it. The sky still wept a chill mist, and she shivered as though she would never stop.

"Do you want to leave?" Evan asked. He tipped her face up, searching her features with his dark eyes. "I will see you back to Chandler Hall at once."

"No." She drew in a deep breath. Lifting her hand to his, where he caught her beneath the chin, she laced her fingers with his. And by God, she kept her chin up. "No. I don't want to leave."

But something within her had been startled loose. Shaken free. It was something that would not let go of Evan's hand now, something that wanted to press into his side more tightly, to take the comfort he offered.

To take something new, and damn propriety, because there were so many ways to fall. Who better to fall with than a friend, who had held her so tightly?

She didn't want him to stop holding her.

She rose to her tiptoes, speaking into his ear in little more than a whisper. "Tonight..." Her lips were dry, so she moistened them. "Tonight, I want..."

Could she say it? Could she even imagine it?

She could, and she spoke the words with a leap of faith that left her heart pounding. "I would like you to come to my bedchamber."

His whole body jerked. "For what purpose?"

She dropped to the flats of her feet. With their laced hands, she bumped him in the belly. "For God's sake, Evan. I asked you to my bedchamber. What purpose could I possibly have in mind?"

He was still now, and quiet as he studied her. "You are most beautiful," he said, "when you yell at me. While propositioning me. In the rain, with the feathers of your little hat hanging over your face."

Her heart thumped. "So...what does that mean? You don't like my hat, or you are interested?" She swallowed. "Or both?"

"I lack the proper interest in your hat. But in you, I am interested." He drew her hand across his belly, wrapping it within his coat. "I am decidedly interested. I am so interested that I will pretend to watch the remaining races, but I will be thinking of your intriguing proposal. When you took my hand in yours. Where you might put your hand next. Where—were you saying something?"

"Uh," she replied with incoherent anticipation. He enfolded her in his arms, in his coat, and she felt armored for anything that might come to pass.

"Right," he answered. "Couldn't have put the matter better myself. Now, since we're to stay and watch the other races, who do you think will win the third?"

Seven

Before Evan could so much as knock at Kate's bedchamber door that night, she opened it.

"Come in, come in," she hissed, grabbing the lapels of his coat and yanking him through the doorway. "I've been listening for your footfalls this past quarter hour."

"I'm glad the footmen don't wander the corridors at night, or this could become awkward."

"Says you," she huffed. "You're the third person I've pulled in here."

His mouth fell open.

"Only joking." She winked, easing the door shut behind him and turning the key in the lock.

Now that he got a full look at her, he realized he was distinctly overdressed. He still wore his clothing from supper, a clean and reputable set of garments. Kate, however, was garbed in a dressing robe of cobweb-fine white linen that revealed the lines of an equally translucent night rail beneath. Her feet were bare.

Some sort of greeting was required. "You look..." *Delectable. Edible. Ravishing.* "...comfortable," Evan concluded. "If informal, but under the circumstances, that's to be expected."

"Oh, I am. Gloriously comfortable." She sounded anything but. Her hands fluttered, touching her hair. Though still pinned at the back, it had come down in front and curled about her face in eager spirals. "No stays tight around my—well. You cannot imagine the relief."

"I cannot, that is true. But if the pleasure of having stays removed is anything like the pleasure of removing them, then I felicitate you."

He took a step forward into the room and realized there was a carpet beneath his feet. The first one he'd seen in Chandler Hall. It was of prodigious size for a bedchamber, patterned over with vines on a background of deep cream.

Similar gentle lines dominated the room: candles in sinuous branches, a large bed with turned wooden posts and sweeping curtains of rich damask. The coverlet was pulled enticingly back at one side. A high-built fire licked its chops, warming the room.

Kate had set the stage for seduction. Like a play, it all seemed rehearsed. "The rogue housekeeper has been here," he observed. "She has made the room…"

"Comfortable?" Kate paced the length of the carpet, then back, tugging the sash of her dressing robe tight.

Her agitation was welcome, for it was so genuine. Kate, fussing. Kate wanting everything perfect. As though she cared about the impression she presented to him.

Damn. That was a lovely thought, the sort of thought that made him want to settle in and bask. It felt like sun after a long spell of cold.

"Yes, comfortable," he replied. "To say the least. I am so comfortable, I will sit here and bide a spell."

Before the hearth were arranged a velvet-covered settee with a low back and tightly scrolled arms, along with a small table on which two tumblers shone with golden liquid. Evan crossed the room to examine them. "Is that whisky? You shouldn't have. Unless both tumblers are for me, in which case I will have to assume you have improper designs on me."

This was meant to make her smile, but it only increased her fluttering. "Oh—no, I didn't. Don't. That is, it's not whisky. I couldn't give you whisky. My father keeps no spirits in the house except for brandy and the red wine often served at dinner. It's a fine brandy."

She was speaking quickly, like an over-cranked musical box—and then she wound down.

"I've no doubt of the brandy's quality." He paused. "Kate, is all this for my benefit?"

"Why, what do you mean?" Seating herself on the red velvet settee, she hitched one leg up and spread the dressing robe about it. Then she lowered her leg again, crossing it over the other. Each time, pale flesh shone new and enticing through the shifting fabric.

The more she fidgeted, the more he wanted to gather her up in his arms and hold her. Settle her. Kiss her into calm and pleasure.

Lord. He was going to die in this room.

Already it had been a long day; agonizingly, sweetly long. They had stayed at the Rowley Mile's rail for the day's remaining races, though Evan couldn't have sworn whether horses or dogs or monkeys ran the course.

No one else fell. He knew that much. One fall was bad enough.

Or had it been a blessing in disguise? Kate had been shaken, badly, at the sight of a prone body on a racecourse. But Evan could recall nothing so determined as the way she lifted her chin and decided to stick out the rest of the schedule.

Perhaps she saw nothing when she looked at the track. Perhaps she was in the Ireland of two years ago, remembering Con's fall. But she had stood beside Evan and let him hold her, and he helped her not to be alone. Whether or not she knew it, she did the same for him.

"I was thinking"—she spoke again, still wildly rearranging herself on the settee—"that this could be the perfect arrangement. Two friends who care for each other very much, giving each other pleasure."

The breezy explanation was perfunctory, so much so that it took him aback. From the end of the settee, he peered down at her. "Is that what this invitation meant to you?"

"What else should it have meant?"

"I don't know that it *should* mean anything at all." He sighed, tucking himself beside her at the end of the settee. "Kate. If you want comfort, I'll comfort you, as innocently as you like. I'm good at brushing hair."

Thunk. Her just-hoisted foot slid to the floor. "I don't need my hair brushed."

"I could let you hold my hand, then. It can be comforting, holding a hand."

Her shoulders hunched. "I don't need my hand held either."

"Good, good. As delightful as that can be, it loses

its savor after a while." He trembled on the edge of honesty, then tipped. "You seem—is this—are you trying to recapture some old closeness? Because I don't think we—"

"God, no." She laughed, a shaky, startled burst. "I don't want to recapture anything, Evan. If I did, you'd be eating porridge, and I'd be sipping whisky, and... well. The whole day would have gone differently." Her whole body seemed to flush. She was pink and cream, warm colors all over.

Not unaffected, then. He could draw her out. "The day of races?"

"The day of...everything. Today, I decided I was ready for a change."

"You were thinking of this sort of change," he said. "Us. Alone. Tonight."

"I was." She tied her dressing robe about her more tightly. "I could not stop, once the idea seized me. Damn propriety and all that sort of thing."

"Then why not untie the robe instead?"

"Well...about that. Now that you are here, I have started to...to think about what we might do."

"That sounds delightful." He grappled with the weighty bolster at his side, tugging it free and flinging it over the arm of the settee. "Though from the million pauses in your speech, I wonder if it strikes you the same way."

"It...does. But I am so aware that you have seen me only in clothes—"

"As opposed to what? Mermaid skins?"

She sputtered. "Is that even a real—never mind... *No*. You know what I mean. This will be different."

"It will only be as different as you want it to be."

"Maybe. That's what I was hoping. I want different." She swung her feet, bare toes tapping the floor before the hearth. "Evan, I thought it would be easy. Being different with you. But now…I'm nervous. Are you?"

"No."

For the sake of graciousness, he probably should not have replied so swiftly. But nervous? Not in the least.

Nervous was waiting not once, but twice, to hear whether she would be safely delivered of a baby, or whether she would lose her life in childbed. *Nervous* was waiting, five years ago, for her ship to return her across the Irish Sea from her last trip to England.

Nervous was how he felt when her life was at stake. Now? He felt newly born, in all the frailty and triumph that the phrase implied.

"I'm not nervous at all," he said.

"That's because you've never had babies," she blurted.

"Er…true. Biology forbids the matter. But how is that relevant?"

"My confinements—they changed me. My body became squishy and…and lumpy."

"Hold a moment." He put a hand on her knee, halting the agitated fidget of her leg. "Let me understand. You're nervous not because we're about to—what word would you like to put to it?"

"Enjoy each other?"

"Enjoy. I like that. All right, you are nervous not because we're about to *enjoy each other*, but because you think childbearing has made you *lumpy*?"

"Well. Yes. I mean, it's a bit of the first too, but

mostly the latter. You're so..." She trailed off, waving one hand while the other clutched tightly at the dressing robe.

"For the sake of my frail pride, I shall need you to finish that sentence. I'm what?"

"Fit. Tall. Not lumpy."

"Part of me is lumpy. One lump, really, but it's a long one."

This won from her a chuckle. Good. A few more, and he might have her loosening that grip on her dressing robe, at least enough to *enjoy* herself.

He folded his arms with mock sternness. "Is this the most convoluted way possible for you to tell me you like the way I look?"

"It...hmm." She leaned away, the better to allow her gaze to roam him.

As she did so, her movements slowed, calmed, stilled. Top to toe, she studied him, lingering. His face, the line of his shoulders, the planes of his chest. He had never felt so *seen* as when Kate took the moment, long as a caught breath, to look at him with new eyes.

"Over the years I have known you, I grew used to the way you look," she said. "I liked it because I liked you."

"Your use of the past tense fills me with anticipation." Evan put a hand to his heart. "What of now? Will she let my hopes fly, or will they be cruelly dashed?"

"Ridiculous man. I'm looking at you all over again, and there is nothing about you I do not like."

His fingers clenched, a quick fist of celebration. Yet he managed to remain glib. "You cannot be looking carefully, but I'm not about to correct you."

"*I* cannot? See, that is what makes me nervous. You're always looking at ancient statues with perfect bodies. All smooth and—and slender."

He had to laugh. "Are you comparing yourself to a statue? Do you honestly think any man would prefer a statue to a real woman?"

In truth, he'd been comparing all women to her since the moment he met her. An idle lover here, a quick liaison there. At first he had chosen to be with women who looked as much like Kate as possible: strawberry blond, lush of form.

That made his longing worse. So he sought spare-figured brunettes.

That made his longing worse.

For a great while, he'd made do with his hand and his imagination.

She shrugged, her hands a play of awkwardness. "I want you to think I'm perfect."

"Dear heart, I have known you long enough to know you're nothing of the sort."

With an indignant noise, she turned toward him on the settee and clouted him on the arm.

"What is this?" he asked. "You can call yourself lumpy and wobbly, but I cannot so much as say you are imperfect?"

"Right. It's impolite. And I don't think I used the word *wobbly*."

"Come here," he said. When she paused, he added, "Just as a friend. Come here."

He turned on the settee to extend a leg along its length, then held out his arms until she scooted over. Nearer and nearer, tentative and stiff at first. He trailed a hand down her arm, a slow easeful stroke of fingertips. Then back up, then down. Petting her until she relaxed into the angle of his body with a little sigh. She smelled sweet and spicy, like cinnamon over a pastry.

"Now, my friend," he murmured, "I shall tell you how very imperfect you are."

"Careful. I have an elbow right beside your seductive bits."

"All of me is a seductive bit. And if you elbow me, this interlude will come to a quick end." He caressed her arm, feeling the fine texture of the linen she wore, the soft contour of the limb beneath. "You are far too beautiful for this garment. That's one flaw."

"What? I thought it was pretty. What would be better?"

"No garment at all."

She choked. "Bollocks."

"That can be arranged."

She tilted her head, sinking against his chest languidly, her curls pillowed on his shoulder. "What of my other flaws?"

"Your hair is ridiculous."

"Oh—"

"Not in its color, which is of a shade to make you look ladylike and wild at once. Not the curls, which make me want to twine my fingers through them." He suited his action to his words, easing a U-shaped pin free as he did. "No, it is ridiculous that your hair is confined in pins. Let it be loose." He paused. "Unless *you* like the pins. I mustn't order you about, after you have so thoughtfully poured me two tumblers of brandy."

"No, I don't need the pins. I always take them out

at night. But it seemed excessive to greet you with unbound hair."

"If I can see you without stays and not faint from the shock, I can manage the sight of your hair."

He was wrong about this—wrong indeed. For as she eased herself upright from his chest, turning to face him, he was undone by the sight of her. Curves outlined by firelight, breasts lifting against the fine linen as she tugged pin after pin loose. With each hairpin she laid on the seat between them, another winding curl fell free. Tangled in wild spirals, all shifting shades of light brown and pale red and blond. Her hair fell down her back, danced against her collarbone, whispered over her cheek.

"You are so beautiful." He could not help but speak the words. Not to speak them would be to lie.

"Right." She pulled a face. "So beautiful that I ought to strip this not-pretty-enough garment free?"

"No." He reached out, touching a curl that caressed her neck. "So beautiful. That is all."

"But..." Her strong brows knit. "I don't understand."

"We'll do what you wish."

"What about what *you* wish?"

"You invited me to your bedchamber. Even if I do nothing but touch your hair and look at your beautiful curves through that wispy robe of yours, I will have more than I could have wished for." She yelped and crossed her arms over her breasts. "You are not perfect, Kate. But you are just right."

Eight

As Evan watched, her arms sank, baring her heart. "You mean that."

"I mean that, yes."

The fire snapped, the only break in the long silence that followed. Evan waited, the next step belonging to her.

"I asked you here," she said, "because you are my friend. And because of all the roles I play, for all people, the part of *friend* is the one with the greatest room for…" She caught her lower lip in her teeth, considering. "Whatever is needed. And it is the only one that allows me the joy of laughter."

Maybe Evan wasn't the only one for whom life became gray sometimes.

"I would give you a laugh every day if I could," he said.

"I would do the same for you."

There were many ways that they could enjoy each other, and one lay within this moment. "I cannot remember if I have coaxed you to laugh yet today, so let me make sure of it right now." With a quick dart forward, he tickled her side, then sat back.

She pressed her lips together, squelching a smile. "Not enough to win a laugh. Sorry."

"I failed? I can't have that. Let me try again." He tugged at her arm, and when she lifted it, he poked her beneath it. All down her side, *poke-poke-poke*, as though he were dotting her with spangles.

Her nose wrinkled, the beginnings of a laugh. "You are ridiculous, Evan."

"I aim to please. Now, where are those lumpy bits you were so concerned about?"

Shaking her hair forward so it hid her face, she pointed at her midsection with a tentative finger.

Quick and delicate as the steps of a butterfly, he danced his fingertips across her linen-covered belly. She shifted and shivered as he touched her, and he had to use restraint not to fill his hands with her and kiss her senseless. "Where else?" he asked.

Her thighs. First one, then the other, they received the ticklish dance too, until her feet twitched with a new agitation, and he thought he might perish from wanting her. "Now. What else? I want to be thorough."

"My arms," she said. "They are as plump as columns."

"I'm the antiquarian. I'll be the judge of that." He made a pincers of his thumb and forefinger and tweaked her arms lightly. "Sorry. Nothing like columns, my lady." Catching up her hand, he turned it over. The underside of her forearm was exposed as her sleeve fell back, and he traced the sensitive line of it. "This is, I am sorry to tell you, nothing less than the arm of a beautiful woman."

"You shall make me laugh after all," she said.

"That's the idea." He pressed a kiss to the inside of her wrist, a slow movement that made her fingers clench. Merciless, then, he had at her: every bit that she had covered, every bit that she had worried about. Poking, tickling, teasing, until her mouth relaxed. Curved. Until she loosed a throaty laugh as she squirmed closer and closer into his embrace. Until her flesh was a vehicle for delight.

Whatever he did to her, it affected him the same way. Pleasuring her, he was buoyed with pleasure. Caressing her, his fingertips took joy in the touch.

And then, when her laugh had gone quiet and her eyes met his gaze, his touch changed. Softened. Slowed.

She wanted them to enjoy each other? He would make sure of it. He would make sure she enjoyed him so damned much that she would never forget him or this night. He would make sure one night wasn't enough for her.

On the soft velvet of the settee, with firelight tracing her from springing hair to clenching toes, he lavished her with touch. The neglected bits, like the tender skin behind her knees, where a brush of his fingertips had her wriggling. Through light, abrading linen, the sensitive bowl of her navel. The bits she called lumpy, which to him were curves. Curves from running and dining and bearing children and growing older. Curves that shaped and reshaped her body and showed how she had lived. Curves to fill his hands and tempt his tongue.

He nibbled along the swell of her hip, the side of her breasts. Near the center of her pleasure, tantalizing, each touch and caress a pleasure in itself.

She wiggled and twisted under his touch. "You seem as though you want me."

For years. You. No one but you.

Of habit, he replied lightly. "Ha, I have fooled you completely. I am not enjoying myself at all."

She shifted against him. "But your cock—"

God. He got stiffer just hearing her say the word. "It's always like that. You should see it when it's hard."

"I should, should I? Let's see if we can make it so." Curving into him, she reached for the fall of his breeches.

He swallowed. "If you touch me..."

She did so, a caress that rocked him even through the layer of buckskin. "Will this be a threat or a promise?"

She looked so mischievous that there was only one possible answer. "It will be," he said, "a kiss."

At first, it was a press of lips to lips: chaste, almost friendly. Not that he had ever kissed her thus, outside of his imagination, though many was the time he'd given her a peck on the cheek or forehead.

His imagination had never touched the reality. Even this simple, light pressure was enough to squeeze at his heart. *Careful...be so careful. You are within reach of everything you have wanted.* What could he do, then, but reach for her? Catching her shoulders, he leaned back and pulled her atop him.

"Mmm," she said, which was encouragement enough to continue. He parted his lips to sip at her, so warm and delicious. A quick brush of tongue that she matched, then a deeper one—more and more each time, each kiss, as they clutched at one another. This kiss, the next, the next: all were a way to make love with lips and tongue.

They clashed and joined, kissing and kissing, until Evan was hitching up one leg and surrounding her in an embrace of his limbs. She rolled her hips against him, thighs parted.

"I'm being cut in half," she gasped, "by the tie of my robe."

"I'll take it off you. Problem solved. Here, you can take something off me too."

Freed from the knotted sash, she knelt upright and let the robe slip from her shoulders. She was clad only in a shift now, simple and diaphanous.

"If you insist," she said, and entered into the play of the exchange. Reaching to dip her finger into the nearer tumbler of brandy, she trailed it down his profile, chin, then jaw. "What a mess I've made. The rogue housekeeper must make things right."

Leaning over him, she kissed the brandy from his forehead, from the line of his nose. She lingered on his lips, as though she found him worth savoring.

When she lifted her head, Evan was in a scatter of anticipation. Fumbling for blithe words, any words. "You are forever altering that phrase for me. I shall not be able to hear of a housekeeper without stripping free my cravat and collar."

"Stripping free of a few articles of clothing. Now, that's an idea." She worked at the knot of his cravat.

The position was a ripe one, with her breasts right where he could touch them. As she kissed and licked at the spirits on his jaw, he grazed her with gentle hands, then between the knuckles of each caught her nipples through her shift and pinched at them lightly.

Her hips bucked. "*God*. Do that again."

He complied.

The result was impressive. They undressed in a tangle of garments and hands, of questing mouths, and the tickle of her loose and flowing hair. Clothes were flung over the back of the settee, and had to be drawn back from a landing spot perilously close to the hearth.

Once bared, Evan asked, "Would you like to move to the bed?"

She nodded, a jerk of the head that hinted at the return of her agitation. "I haven't done this in a long time. When I found out Con was…"

Evan shut his eyes. *Con, you fool.* "Not true to you?"

"He was in so many other beds. Eventually I forbade him mine."

His heart shifted out of place, beating awry. "None of that matters now. I would not be scoundrel enough to judge you for anything you'd done or not done in the past."

"Would you not? That is more than I can say of myself."

"The rogue housekeeper is always her own harshest critic." He busied his hands until she was pliant and gasping.

"Now *you* will ruin that word for *me* if you keep touching me like that."

"Ruin it? I rather think I shall remake it." Drawing her to the bed, he tossed back the folded coverlet to reveal a smooth expanse of crisp white sheets. When they settled onto it side by side, the mattress beneath was pillowy and yielding.

"Let me enjoy you now," Evan said.

"You want to enjoy me even *more*?"

"You are not a maiden. Do I need to remind you what more there could be?"

"Yes. No, you don't—but please do. I...I...don't know what I'm saying." Laughing, she covered her face.

"As long as it starts with yes?"

"It does. Yes."

When she lifted her arms to take him into her embrace, he felt new. For a long moment, he held her in his arms, inhaling the scent of her spicy sweet perfume, the musk of her desire. Nudging a knee between hers, he then slipped a hand down—over the line of her belly, to tickle the curls below. She dug her nails into his shoulders, opening her legs to him. "Yes."

Yes. He slipped a finger through her slickness. She was ready, wanting—her body as much as her words.

He painted her with her own excitement, easing a path for his fingers. Stroking the nub of her pleasure, piercing her with one finger, then two.

"Yes," she said again, clutching for his hips. The invitation was unmistakable, and he'd no wish to decline.

He positioned himself above her, and with one sleek glide, he filled her to the hilt. A moan broke from both their throats at once.

Face to face, they looked at one another: wide-eyed, disbelieving, delighted. "God, I have wanted this," he confessed. Revealing too much, maybe, and he stopped further words by kissing her deeply.

"Guh," she replied when they broke for breath, which he took as a good sign.

Bracing himself on his elbows, he slid free, then thrust home again. They quickly found their rhythm, the intimate push and pull that made sensation spiral to pleasure, to delight. Clenching his toes against the gathering wave, he played her body with mouth and tongue, with everything he had and was, until her breath turned to gasps, then to a soft cry and a quaking climax.

Gritting his teeth, he withdrew from her. "Best to be safe," he managed.

At once she reached for him, wrapping her hands around his slick shaft. "I will do it," she said. Pumping him swift and hard, she brought him off with shocking ease. As the orgasm claimed him utterly, she caught his seed in her hand.

Spent and sated, they lay panting. "I…enjoyed that," Kate managed.

"Likewise," Evan said.

One of the greatest understatements of his life.

Chivalry prodded him from the bed first, to retrieve a handkerchief. He dipped it in the pitcher on her washstand, then returned to the bed and cleaned her hand with the damp cloth. "What else? I have another handkerchief."

"Nothing else. I want to stay like this for a while." She stretched like a cat in the sun.

It was erotic and innocent and lovely, and he lay on the bed beside her and could not look away. She was glad, wasn't she? That she had taken him to bed? At least for now, she was glad.

She could not know this was the closeness of which he had dreamed for years. He could not tell her his true feelings. Not yet. The weight of his love would be a burden, when she already had so many to carry.

"Did that truly please you?" She sounded saucy as ever, but there was something careful in the set of her features.

"You have always pleased me," he said quietly.

One brow lifted. "Bollocks."

"*That* didn't please me. Such doubt. You malign my honor." He reached for her hair, then spiraled a curl about his index finger, as though in so doing he could hold her fast. "Perhaps we have changed in these past two years, after all."

Not only her, in abandoning the proper *shoulds*. He had too. He wasn't in the habit of being so honest. His conversation was of the sort that skimmed the bright surface, lest he go too deep and tap into the grayness.

"If this is what change brings, then I am glad for it," she said. "Are not you?"

"More than you know." For a minute, an hour, an untellable amount of time, he remained at her side and settled into the rhythm of her breath. At last, he forced himself to wrench free, to slide from the bed.

As soon as his feet touched the floor, she spoke. "Will you not stay with me?"

He looked over his shoulder. "I shouldn't."

"Because?"

He hesitated, then turned back to face her, bare in a way that had nothing to do with being nude. "Many reasons."

Reasons ranging from protecting the servants' sensibilities to protecting his heart. Though it was difficult to give a damn about those reasons as she hitched herself up onto one elbow, imploring him with eyes the shade of the Irish Sea.

"You are right." She blinked, then looked down to trace a shape on the sheet beside her. "I ought to be prudent and let you go. But I would rather hold you longer."

And that was that for his heart, as surely as if he'd taken a spear for her. Clearly, he would never recover from his wanting of this woman. He could not deny her what she asked, especially when it was something he wanted as well.

"Let me put out the candles, then."

After he snuffed them in their branches, he returned to bed. She rolled away then tucked herself against him, back to belly, like the nesting of spoons. His upper arm she took over her body in an embrace. A cage of Evan, protecting her.

A shield of Kate, colorful and strong.

Breathing in the scent of their entwined bodies, he fell asleep.

Nine

When Evan woke, he was alone in an unfamiliar bed.

The disorientation of nighttime wakefulness seized him for a moment. The fire had gone cold, and outside, blackness blanketed the thin draperies at the windows. The softness of the mattress pulled at him as he struggled to sit. A faded, sweet scent tantalized his senses. Where was he? What had happened?

Memory came back in a flood: Kate's bedchamber. Chandler Hall. It was…some hour of the night, or the morning, early enough that the maids had not yet entered to lay the fire.

Where was Kate?

As his eyes adjusted to the dimness, he noticed his clothing still flung over the settee. Hers was gone, such as it had been. Those filmy gowns didn't cover her well enough for her to roam the house.

Finally, finally, he had been with her in almost every bare way—of mind, of flesh. He had not shown her all his heart, but *God*, it had been a good night.

He should have departed when he'd felt the urge,

instead of allowing himself to be the one left behind. A matter of self-preservation as much as wisdom, for as he slid from the bed, his thoughts began to fog. *What happened? Why? What if?*

He pushed such questions back with cutting logic as he gathered his clothes. Maybe he would find Kate in his own bed. Maybe she had startled awake, unused to another person in bed with her, and gone in search of a cup of tea. There needn't be anything amiss.

It was for the best that he leave now, though. He needed to get himself out of here before he was seen.

Quickly, by touch, he tugged on his clothing. Shoved his feet into his boots. At every second, he expected Kate to enter the chamber again.

But it didn't happen, and he instead found himself skulking through a night-dark passage to reach his own room, so he could mess up the bed as though he'd been sleeping there all along.

She wasn't in his chamber either. In fact, he didn't see her again until entering the dining room for breakfast, where he found her alone.

"Another day of races," Evan realized. "Your father and brother are off again. How can they stand it?"

This last question covered a multitude of frustrations. Kate lifted a dish cover with such calm, he wanted to snatch it from her hand and send it crashing to the polished stone floor. How could she look so fresh and unaffected? How could she greet him without the slightest blush?

"I don't know," she replied. "One day is enough for me."

"Is it? Was it not so pleasurable that you wish to go again and again?"

The serving spoon clattered from her fingers. "Indeed it was...pleasurable." The flush on her cheeks revealed her understanding of his meaning. "But I have so much to do here, and preparing for the journey back to Ireland—I couldn't think of going to the track again."

"You're already somewhere else, even as you stand before the sideboard and take..." He peered into the dish. "Ham? Well, well. No Irish breakfast for you today?"

"It wasn't enough of an Irish breakfast to put the servants to such trouble." She replaced the lid with a determined *clang*. "Of course, you must go to the races again. If you wish."

"Going to the races isn't nearly as pleasurable when one is alone."

He managed to keep his tone flip, even as he parsed her every word and movement. She was all of a bustle, not meeting his eye. The rogue housekeeper at mealtime. Where was the friend and lover of the night before?

"Do you never rest, Kate?" he wondered.

"As little as I can." She took her plate to the table. "If I don't wander, my thoughts do instead."

"I know what *that's* like," Evan muttered.

Without paying much heed, he piled food on his plate from the various serving dishes, then sat at the table across from Kate. "Where did you go this morning? If you wanted the room, I would have left it. I offered to do as much last night."

Her knife skidded across her plate, chopping the slice of ham in two. “No, no. I didn’t want you to leave. I couldn’t sleep, and so I tidied my things and went to Father’s study for a while. He needs help with his papers, and—”

“All right, all right.” He held up his hands. “That’s my answer. You got up at an ungodly hour of the night and left your own room because you were being sensible. Very well.”

She cut her food into little pieces, pushing them around on her plate. A tower. A circle. A heap. A mess—all scattered with her fork. “I was afraid. Of—of what it meant, that we’d done something we’d never done before.”

“It meant we wanted to do it.” He squinted. “Is this difficult? It doesn’t seem difficult. You invited me to your room. I said yes. You asked me to stay with you. I did.”

“And all that was agreeable of you. With you.” She hesitated. “Maybe I haven’t changed as much as I assumed I had. Propriety is a habit of long standing with me. And I’m, you know, *me*.”

His eyes felt grainy from lack of sleep. “I know it well.”

“I’m just…so many things already. I can’t think of becoming something else too. Countess and mother and terribly proper widow, and…” She trailed off, looking confused.

Gray trembled at the edge of his vision, and he rubbed his temples. “Here I had hoped for the opposite: that yesterday was something for you. For your own pleasure, not regarding anyone else.”

He knew this for an untruth as soon as it had passed his lips. He had hoped that *enjoying each other* would wind her closer and ever closer to him.

"It was a great pleasure, but—" She shook her head. "It's too much. I can't—that is, it was..."

"If you don't finish a sentence within the next three seconds, I'll throw my toast at you."

"You are my only real friend," she blurted.

The silence that followed seemed especially silent.

"It's true, Evan." Her sea-colored eyes were full of entreaty. "I left England behind for Con. I acted the perfect wife and mother until the roles felt natural. But who would be my friend, Evan? Not the people of Thurles, who saw me as an interloping Englishwoman. Not the servants. I always had to...to be countess-y around them. Only you were a true friend."

"Only me," he repeated. How could this be, bright and warm as she was? It was no wonder that she had been hurt by his long silence.

No wonder, too, that now she had drawn back from change.

"You said—this time in England might be a respite for me, from all the things I have to be." She blurted this, not meeting his eye. "And I am grateful. As I would now be grateful if we could go back to the way we were. Exactly as we were."

This brought his temper to a simmer. "Which *were* do you mean, Lady Whelan? Would you prefer the *were* in which I sat like your lapdog while you settled into the arms of another man? Or the *were* in which we had nothing to say to each other for months on end?"

Her head snapped up. "How terribly unfair you

are. I always had something to say to you. You are the one who went silent." Flags of hot color stained her cheeks. "And that's not what I meant, wanting you to sit with me and another in a trio. No—neither of those *weres* you suggested! I don't want that. There was always more to our friendship than that."

"Was there?" He ticked on his fingers. "So you don't want anyone else, and you also don't want me. You don't want anything to change between us, nor do you want our friendship to go back to the way it was."

She attempted a smile. "You could throw toast at me if you like."

"I will decline that honor for now." Desperate to move, to leave, he folded his serviette and slapped it onto the table. "Lady Whelan, I am off to the races."

If Evan had thought Kate had been the rogue housekeeper before, it was nothing compared to the frantic level of activity she maintained through the remainder of the week. It was clear that she'd have run away if she possibly could. But since he was a guest in her father's home, he made himself as unobtrusive as possible. During race week, there was much to do: drink and wager, walk the horses, even flirt and dance a little at the nightly revelry in Newmarket.

If he did a great deal of all those things, he could almost not notice the *shush* Kate's skirts made when she whipped around a corner to avoid him. He could almost not conjure the sound of her bedchamber door closing as she left him slumbering, fool that he was, in her bed.

By the time race week came to a close, they had returned to a tolerable state of friendliness. It was the sort people displayed with a person they didn't know well and wanted to treat with courtesy.

It was a poor substitute for the easy intimacy they'd shared.

But imagination was a poor substitute for reality. Fruitless love was a poor substitute for having one's affections returned. Evan was familiar with poor substitutes.

He and Kate, along with Kate's lady's maid Susan, left Newmarket on a Monday. The waxing moon was still faint in the sky as they made their early-morning farewells.

"It's good to see you happy again," Jonah told his sister gruffly, engulfing her in a great embrace.

"Close enough," came Kate's muffled voice from within his arms. She wiped at her eyes when he let go, and everyone pretended not to notice.

Jerome and Hattie, the staid chestnuts who had drawn Sir William's carriage from Cambridge to Newmarket, would now take the travelers to Holyhead, the port on the Irish Sea.

This first leg of the journey back to Ireland was over land, a great stripe across England and Wales. A week's travel at the best of times, the roads were uncertain in autumn when rain made them soft and pitted.

A week in a carriage, jostled about with Kate and her maid. This would be...interesting.

Evan shook Sir William's hand and thanked him for his hospitality. The baronet nodded. "Take good care of my horses," he said. "Jerome and Hattie are the best-tempered of creatures, but Jerome is stubborn about his meals. If he's hungry, he won't go another step. And Hattie..." The baronet looked around Evan, where the chestnuts were being harnessed. "Check her shoes each day. They come loose more often than any female's shoes I've ever seen, and I include humans."

"I will see to it," Evan said. "And I'll make sure your daughter is safe too."

Sir William's hazel gaze was narrow. "That, I took for granted."

The trunks were loaded, a hamper was stowed, and the travelers climbed within. Kate and her maid sat on the forward-facing squabs. Evan seated himself across from them. The coachman put up the steps, closed the carriage door, and took to his box. With a cluck to the horses and a jingle of harness, the carriage began to roll.

Thus began the journey to Wales.

Evan had expected it to be a silent and awkward journey, but within a few minutes he realized it would be nothing of the sort. Because of the presence of Kate's maid, a young Irish woman named Susan, they could speak of nothing private.

This was for the best. Words had served them ill since the night they'd spent together. So as the women made pleasant chat about the scenery, speculated about the next week of races, wondered if they had forgotten this or that...Evan began to seduce Kate again.

He did it subtly, so that she thought his gestures an accident at first. Small touches of the toe of his boot against hers; a secret smile directed her way when she met his eye. A joke to put the maid at ease when the jolting of the carriage made Susan queasy; a pair of apples retrieved from the hamper for the horses to crunch. A midday stop at an inn, ostensibly to stretch his legs, where the ladies used the necessary and he bought them hot buns and strong tea.

Yes. Evan was going to seduce Kate by being absolutely necessary to her well-being. By making traveling with him a damned delight.

And it worked. By the time they halted for the day at a clean and cozy inn, Kate was having trouble meeting his eyes, and her cheeks were constantly pink.

They only became pinker when the trio disembarked from the carriage, and Evan considered how to arrange their rooms. "You're not wearing black."

Kate looked down at her garments, which were all sorts of pleasant autumn shades. "Correct. Is that a problem?"

"You don't look like a dried-up, bereaved widow. How could it be proper for us to be traveling together? We'll have to be…something. Brother and sister."

At once, they made a mutually horrified noise.

"Husband and wife?" Evan suggested. A man could hope.

Kate blushed, then lowered her voice. "I think it best we not share a bedchamber again. What about uncle and niece?"

"Ruthless woman. I am, what? Four years your senior?" Evan considered. "If anyone asks, we are cousins."

After arranging lodging for the night, Evan and John Coachman saw to the horses with the help of the inn's ostler. Yes, Hattie's shoes were nailed on properly. Jerome had his nose in a manger as if he hadn't eaten for a week. When Evan stroked their forelocks, both chestnuts gave him a *whuff* of warm breath, their ears relaxed with the simple pleasure of contented animals.

"Good creatures," he said, scratching behind the ears of first the gelding, then the mare. "Thanks for your steadiness today. I wish I needed only warmth and food to be happy."

Hattie bumped him with her nose, as though admonishing him.

"I know. I should be."

Should, should. Even here in a warm stable, with contented horses and the low talk of stable hands about, the gray feeling hovered. It waited, always, for the inactivity that meant a gap in his armor. Then it sank upon him, dissolving certainty into questions. *What should I have done? Why did that happen? What if I had done this? What will happen next? What will I do if?* Until the very acts of everyday living took on a weight so great as to make them impossible.

Almost impossible.

"I'm tired," he told Hattie. "That's all."

She bumped him again with her nose, the *whuff* more of a snort this time.

"You don't believe me?"

She blinked long-lashed eyes darker than his own. Then, with a shake of her head that sent her chestnut forelock into a tangle, she turned her attention to her hay.

"You're right. I'm talking bollocks." He had to smile.

The battle between thought and external cheer was ceaseless, but only because he would not surrender.

Instead, he went inside the inn to see to Kate's comfort again—and when she blushed as sweet and pink as a rose, to see her and Susan to their chamber and bid them good night.

"Sleep well," he told Kate.

If his wishes were granted, her dreams would flutter in his direction, and in the morning her waking self would see him anew.

Ten

KATE COULD NOT REMEMBER WHEN SHE HAD ENJOYED a journey so much.

Yes, the roads were dreadfully rutted and bumpy, jolting the travelers all about. But on their second day in the carriage, Evan had made a game of things. Whoever bounced the highest off the squabs got to pick a surprise from the hamper, which he had filled at the inn with biscuits and dried fruit. By the time they halted at midday, both Kate and Susan were groaning with sweets, far too full to do their meal justice.

That afternoon, one of the wheels stuck steadfast in mud, and not the combined efforts of Jerome and Hattie could pull it free. The wheel only sank further, setting the carriage at a crazy tilt.

"We'd best see what's going on," Kate said. Evan hopped out of the carriage, then helped Kate and Susan clamber down.

The coachman climbed from his seat to look at the buried wheel. "Aye, she's stuck good and proper. Need something to dig with, I reckon."

"We don't have such a thing!" Susan's light eyes

were wide. "What'll we do, Lady Whelan? How long will we have to stay here?"

Susan was so young, and she had been drawn so far away from the village of her birth. Kate put a calming—well, she hoped it was calming—hand on the maid's arm. "We've got something we can use, surely. We just have to think of it. Even if we have to get Hattie to throw a shoe, we could dig with that."

The coachman crossed himself. "Never say it, Lady Whelan. That mare's the worst for throwing shoes."

Within the harness, the mare tilted her head to regard them with reproachful eyes.

"Sorry, Hattie," Kate murmured.

Evan frowned. "I have a little trowel in my trunk. A brush and pick too, though I doubt those will be of help."

"Your antiquarian tools," Kate realized. "How fortunate."

"It would be more fortunate if I were carrying a spade with me, but we'll make do."

John Coachman helped Evan wrestle free his trunk, and he pawed through it and came up with a small case.

When he unfastened it, he cursed. The little digging tool was hardly longer than his hand. "I could swear it's got smaller since I packed it. This was made for delicate work, not excavation."

"Then let's be delicate about digging out the wheel." Kate gathered her skirts about her ankles and crouched beside him, near the stuck wheel. It was buried almost to the axle.

"My lady, you let me work on that." John Coachman

pulled her to her feet with more vigor than solicitude, then hesitated. "But we can't leave the horses on their own."

"They're not going anywhere. This stuck wheel has seen to that well enough," Kate said. "But I'll see to them."

As she stepped aside, she let the weight of her skirts brush against Evan's body. He looked up, curious, and she did not know whether she ought to grin or to pretend ignorance.

She only looked at him, and it was difficult to look away.

The air was heavy with mist and the scent of wet grass, and as she crossed to the well-trained horses, a light rain began to fall.

Susan dogged her steps. "What can I do to help?"

"Dear Susan." Kate considered. "Would you like to look for rocks that the men could use to smooth the path of the stuck wheel? Or would you like to get into the carriage and stay warm?"

"I'd be a fool not to want to get into the carriage, and I'm no fool." A thin young woman, Susan's lips were already losing color. "But I'd be an arse if I didn't help, and I'm not that either."

"That you're not," Kate agreed. "I would welcome your help, but you must get into the carriage if you start to shiver."

"I will, my lady." The maid set off, kicking at the wet grass.

Kate stood before the team, lightly holding their heads and talking soft nonsense to them. They were so large and powerful, these chestnuts, but they loved the sort of gentle voices and patient treatment that a mother lavished on her infant.

"Who's a good boy," she crooned, petting Jerome's head until he closed his amber eyes and hung his head with contentment. "You're like a big puppy, aren't you?"

Hattie stomped—just once, just hard enough to draw attention. "Keep your shoes on," Kate said, then turned her attention to the mare. One at a time, she talked soft nonsense to them, occasionally peeking around the side of the carriage to follow the progress of the work.

Susan had found some fist-sized stones to jam into the softening mud. Evan was using the sharpest of them to carve free the wheel, while John Coachman took to the other side.

Wet and cold and stuck, they ought to have been utterly miserable. But the trace of dewy rain on Evan's features was like a glow, and at the sight of him, Kate had to bite her lip against a swell of emotion. How had she borne the journey from Ireland without him?

She had borne it because she knew no other option. She had borne it because she had never expected to see him again.

Sometimes she wondered at all she had managed to bear over the past years.

"Now!" called Evan. "Walk them forward, slowly!"

Kate clucked to the horses, tugging lightly at the pole and pole straps between them. "One step now… after me…"

Broad gray-brown hooves lifted and stamped into the earth. Powerful necks strained against the harness collars. "Come on, dear ones, follow me." Kate backed away, glancing over her shoulder to make sure the road was clear. "Another step."

The carriage swayed, its alarming angle deepening, then lurched upright again—and halted.

"Wait here." Kate held out her hands to the horses, who looked at each other with as much doubt as equine faces could hold.

She raced around the side of the carriage. "What happened? Are we still stuck?"

Evan stood, mud-spattered from forehead to boot. "No, the wheel's free." He wiped at his face, smearing the mud. "See here? Between the digging and the stones, it's rolled up onto solid ground. Until the rain makes a swamp of the whole road, that is."

John Coachman groaned. "Did Hattie lose a shoe?"

"Definitely not," Kate said. "She stomped her hooves at me, and all her shoes were on."

"I'm getting into the carriage," Susan decided, "even if it never goes anywhere again." She climbed in and huddled on the floor.

John Coachman climbed atop his box again and took up the reins. "Come on, now. Let's get into the middle of the road." He chucked at the horses. Hattie shuffled her hooves, but the carriage stayed stubbornly still.

"What the devil?" Kate bent over, skirts trailing on the dirt as she looked at the four carriage wheels. "They're fine."

When she straightened up, Evan was grinning, his teeth white against his earth-smudged skin. "It's Jerome, I'd wager. Your father told me he was an awful brat about his meals. If he gets a treat, he might walk on."

"Geldings," huffed Kate. "*Such* brats."

"They have much to feel bratty about," said Evan, with a gesture that made Kate redden.

She turned away, hiding her laugh, and asked Susan for the hamper. "If we didn't eat all the biscuits…ah, he might like this." She pulled a plum cake from the depths of the hamper and broke it in two.

Why not? Hattie pulled the same weight.

With the encouragement of the plum cake held out of reach, the horses extended their heads—then took a step, then another, and another, and soon the carriage was rolling. Kate scrabbled backward, skirts tangling about her ankles. With a whoop of glee, she let the team nibble the cake from her outstretched hands, then hitched up her skirts and bolted for the carriage door. Evan hopped inside, then hauled her in and pulled the door shut behind them.

They plumped onto the squabs, each sighing. In the dim of the carriage interior, the three wet, muddy, bedraggled people looked at each other—and as one, they laughed.

"We smell like a farmyard." Kate looked ruefully at her gown. The cloth was rumpled and stained, probably beyond saving. A shame. She had few pretty clothes that had escaped the black dye of her mourning year.

"We're wet as ducks!" Susan exclaimed. "John Coachman's got his nice oilcloth, and we've got…"

"We've got brandy." Evan reached into his coat pocket. "I took it from my trunk before we stowed all the tools again." He leaned forward, shaking the silver flask. "Go on, take it. It's fine Chandler brandy. All the best people use it."

Use it, he said, and she remembered how she'd trailed it over him. So awkward, so eager. As hesitant as a virgin to whom everything was new.

The memory caused a pulse between her legs. When Susan offered her the flask, Kate demurred. "I'm warm enough already."

Going *back to the way we were* had been a silent and tentative business. She should have known there was no going back once people became lovers. But how might they go forward?

For the rest of the day, and for the days of travel thereafter, the carriage rolled on, but she never came up with an adequate answer.

For the final two days of the journey, Evan felt his birthplace drawing nearer, along with the inevitable visit to his family. Wales was embraced by the sea, the touch of the water about the land always felt, even if not seen. The sea made it seem small and stretching at once, close to infinity and crushed by it. This swoop of dissonant feeling was what Evan liked best about it. A man had to be jarred free from his own grayness when he saw the blue of the sea.

Their destination, Holyhead, lay at the far reach of Wales on Holy Island—a nub of land off the Isle of Anglesey. Anglesey was itself cut off from the Welsh mainland by a river. The gap between the lands was not much wider than a man could fling a pebble in spots—if he had a wind in his favor and a strong throwing arm. The river was shallow when the tide was out, but with a quick current. Travelers were wiser to take a ferry than to try fording the river, especially if they traveled with a magic lantern and its fragile slides.

And so, with more plum cake and soothing words, they coaxed the pair of chestnuts to draw the carriage onto the flat surface of the ferry. The crossing took place without incident, unless one counted Jerome sneaking Hattie's bit of plum cake with a swipe of his long tongue.

As they traversed the breadth of Anglesey, Kate's face was pressed to the carriage window. "I have never been to Wales. I've always sailed from Liverpool in the past. I didn't know it was like this."

"Like what?" Evan couldn't help but be curious how it appeared to her eyes.

"Well—it's got a bit of everything, hasn't it? Mountains and marshes, new farms and ancient standing stones within sight of the road. The sea all around, close enough to feel it."

"When I bring myself to return here, such are the thoughts that sustain me," he murmured.

She turned a keen eye to the unrolling land about them, hilled like a folded fan where Newmarket was flat as a sheet of paper. "It's not unlike Ireland, is it? Not Tipperary, but the Irish coast. It's all wild and green with a sense of its own great age."

Thus she had used to speak, animated and bright of eye, during those long-ago slow evenings of peat fires and whisky. He looked out his own window, trying to see the landscape with the eyes of one who had never seen it before.

"You are right," he agreed. "It's not unlike the Irish coast we'll soon see. Though here, more than in the rest of Wales, the people speak Welsh."

"I don't know a word of it. Does your family speak it? Will they expect us to speak it? They are expecting our visit, are they not?"

"They are," he replied with a fair appearance of calm. "I wrote to them a few nights ago when I was sure of our arrival date. And no, they could not speak Welsh, even if they wished to."

Which they didn't. Rhyses took a perverse pride in not fitting with their surroundings, as though this showed mastery over it.

At the hour when daylight transformed into sunset, the carriage turned into the drive of Ardent House. The building was of rare construction, two stories of red brick that beamed against a moody sky from the end of a graveled drive and neatly clipped lawn. The structure was of perfect symmetry, quoined in stone, roofed in slate. Each of the main windows was pedimented and swagged, while small eyebrow windows lifted the roof as if in judgment.

A thousand years from now, antiquarians might uncover the ruins of Ardent House and deem it a structure of great beauty, built for effect rather than usefulness.

The Rhys family was the same—except for Evan, who never took to red brick as he ought. Evan, whose eyebrows tended to lift with mischief or knit with doubt, thus spoiling the symmetry of proper manners.

"I must warn you," Evan said to Kate as the carriage

drew to a stop before the front steps. "They're nothing like your family."

"God help the world if there were many families such as mine."

"You say that with a laugh," he replied. "But there is little of laughter in this house." That was the mildest and simplest way to put the matter.

"Oh." She sounded surprised. Thinking, maybe, of how she'd thanked him for giving her room to laugh. *I would give you a laugh every day.* Such a wish was a gift. "Thank you for the warning. I'm quite prepared to meet your family."

Bleak humor tugged at the corners of his mouth. "That makes one of us," he said.

Eleven

To Kate's delight, they had arrived in time to share dinner with the adults of the family: Evan's parents, his elder brother, and his sister-in-law.

"Don't look so pleased," Evan warned her when he retrieved her in the corridor outside their guest chambers.

The pair had been given time to tidy themselves from travel, and Kate had donned one of her favorite gowns: butter-yellow, with tiny topaz beads edging the short sleeves and neck. She noted that Evan had dressed formally too, donning his lecturer garb of a traditional man of fashion. She preferred the slouching grace of the clothing he wore for outdoor work.

"I cannot help but be curious about your family," she replied. "They made you, after all. What sort of people could they be?"

"Here's an early look." With a flick of his hand, he indicated the walls. Portraits in oils, pencil sketches, light watercolors, all in heavy gilt frames, marched alongside them. Painted-silk paper showed through the gaps. Luxury, history, tradition—all were on display on the first floor, above the main receiving rooms.

"Look at this Elizabethan fellow. Are those jeweled earrings? If I'd known you came from such elegant stock, I would have been kinder to you," she teased.

"On a second son's allowance? You mustn't allow yourself to become too fond. Every family has its black sheep," he replied.

"Surely not you."

"I am more of a gray. Just wait, my dear friend, and you will see."

He seemed not to relish this visit, but it was the best location from which to leave on the following morning's packet across the sea. So. She would help. She'd make him laugh three times before the evening was out.

When they entered the dining room, Kate quailed for a moment. No table ever groaned—elegantly, of course—under the weight of more gleaming silver. The greetings of Mr. and Mrs. Rhys, a handsome silver-haired couple dressed in the height of fashion, were of as crisp an accent as Kate had ever heard from the tonnish crowd at Newmarket.

Evan's older brother, Owen, was a bluff, stocky version of his younger brother. A solid wall wrapped in cravat and bespoke superfine, he escorted Kate in to dinner. Evan paired Owen's wife—Elena, Kate heard Evan call her. The younger Mrs. Rhys was a tall and sturdy woman in beautiful silk, with a lovely, placid face.

As Kate took her seat at the long table beneath a gleaming chandelier, she became aware that her plain short sleeves and lightly trimmed skirt were three years out of fashion.

But despite Evan's lukewarm introductions, they all seemed pleasant. Eager to see Evan, certainly. Willing enough to meet his friend's widow.

"You look charming, Lady Whelan!" exclaimed the elder Mrs. Rhys. "I'd not have thought to see that color again since it went out of fashion in 1815. Dear me, I've missed it. I've never seen it worn so well as on you."

Oh. Maybe this was what Evan had meant by *wait, and you will see.* "Thank you?" Kate asked with some doubt.

"And how went your latest lectures, Evan?" Mrs. Rhys served a whole roasted squab on a plate of petal-thin porcelain. "London and—where was it? Oxford?"

"Cambridge." Evan was taking a little of whatever dishes surrounded him.

"Oh, Cambridge. Well, that is all right too."

He turned his head to fix his mother with a curdled gaze. "I know it is. I was happy to speak at Cambridge."

"That's fine. You mustn't dwell on it—you know how you get."

"I don't recall. How do I get?" He was everything polite and curious, but Kate noticed his knuckles were white as he held his cutlery.

"Honestly, dear! You know. So *morose.*" Mrs. Rhys sliced through the flesh of her squab. "Tut! Antoine has left these on the spit too long. The heart is shriveled almost beyond recognizing."

Evan let out a bark of laughter. "Surely not *that* shriveled."

That laugh didn't count as one of Kate's three. It hardly counted as a laugh at all.

Evan, morose? That was one of the last words she'd use to describe him. Evan, irreverent: that would be far more expected.

"I like the squab," said Owen. The pile of tiny bones on his plate indicated that he had already consumed two. "Don't you, Mrs. Rhys?"

"Yes, Mr. Rhys," said his wife in a soothing, low voice. "But I know you enjoy them even more, so I wouldn't dream of eating any." With this, her husband served himself a third squab with a belly-deep sigh of gratification.

Elena Rhys's quick, clear glance to Kate across the table indicated that the lady was not so docile as she seemed. Kate suspected that she did *not* care for squab, but she had found a way to do as she pleased while keeping peace.

Hmm. This might be useful for Kate's next encounter with Good Old Gwyn.

"Even if it *was* in Cambridge, your lecture was a service." For the first time, Evan's father spoke. "You ought to be proud of that. Keeping the silly English from snapping up worthless fiddle-faddle."

"Helping them recognize it, rather," Evan said. "They're no sillier than any people who haven't had the opportunity to learn their own history."

"So stuffy!" hooted Owen. "A younger son hasn't any responsibility. You ought to be roistering around the world. Where's your sense of fun?"

"I left it in Cambridge," Evan replied. "It's in a box with my magic lantern slides."

"I don't know about that," Kate said. "I think you had your sense of fun with you in Newmarket." This was a prod, and to him it would not seem subtle. *I'm here, and I think you're marvelous.*

What of it? They were friends, and she had always thought him marvelous.

"As Welsh," she added to his parents, "no doubt you have a great admiration and understanding of the genuine Roman artifacts that originate on your soil. None of that English fiddle-faddle for you, correct?"

This gave rise to a gratifyingly awkward silence.

"You are English by birth, are you not, Lady Whelan?" asked the elder Mrs. Rhys.

"Indeed. My father is a horse breeder in Newmarket." *And a baronet*, she could have added, but she did not. When she'd been born, being a horse breeder—a wealthy, successful, and well-connected one—was William Chandler's sole honorific.

"But now, you're a countess," said Mr. Rhys. "Well done. It is an Irish title, but those still count for something, eh?"

Oh, for God's sake. She would take up the reins of this conversation and crack it into a gallop. "A little something." Kate sipped at her glass of wine—a fine dark red that tasted of plums and spicy herbs. "We have roofs and walls enough. You cannot imagine how glad I was to meet your son all those years ago. He told us…" She lowered her voice to a confidential volume. "…that one could create a pit for night soil, instead of flinging chamber pots out the window each morning." Another shocked silence followed. Kate sipped at her wine again.

Evan cleared his throat. "You mustn't make me out to be a genius of innovation. Con was familiar with the notion too, from his years at school in England."

Kate shot Evan a quick look. A *they don't even guess that I was joking* look. A tiny shrug, a smaller shake of his head. *No, they don't.*

So she decided to amuse herself.

"True. The flower beds have suffered for it, but the gardeners are happier. And when I say gardeners, I mean the trio of little black Irish cows that we use to tend the lawn."

"Very clever of you," Mr. Rhys was the first to reply. "Use what you have, eh? That's being resourceful."

"Exactly. One does what one must. The cows make the devil of a mess—pardon my language—when they come into the kitchen. Which is a ring of stones with a spit, but you know, the earldom must have its indulgences." A broad, knowing wink. "We cook over an open fire, and their hooves—you cannot think how quickly they can stomp out a fire."

"But surely you can cook in ash," said Owen helpfully. "Potatoes and...and whatnot."

"And porridge. Oh, yes. We make do."

Kate said this last with a pang. She liked both porridge and potatoes, and she missed the simple, hearty fare. It was filling and warm—though it did give Kate a figure that was more padded than she would wish.

The others were eating up her words as eagerly as their dinner. So she sauced a final remark.

"I am glad to have the chance to speak about Ireland," Kate said. "Just as I am to learn about Wales. This is my first visit here. Can you credit it? I admit, I once assumed Wales was all colliers and shepherds and rocky tors. But even before I saw it for myself, I met Evan Rhys and realized that I must be wrong. He was cultured and rough and funny and considerate, and so I understood that the Welsh are a people of great variety. As are the Irish. And the English. And, no doubt, every other civilization on this planet. No, thank you, Mrs. Rhys, I won't have a squab. But that asparagus looks fine. Thank you, I will take some."

And she speared it on her fork and ate the whole stalk, end to end, without cutting it.

"Good lord, Ev," said Owen. "She's a lecturer like you."

"I am a countess," said Kate, with her mouth full.

Evan's look was appraising. Through the candle wink on silver and crystal across the table, it was hard to interpret the shadings of expression. But she thought, maybe, that he was glad for what she had said.

She was glad she had said it. She could have said much more to his credit.

"Evan," intoned Mr. Rhys—setting Kate's outburst behind. "Do you plan to lecture more in England this season?"

"I cannot say. I don't know how long I'll be in Ireland. I need to gather more material. And in March, I'll be off to Greece."

Right, right. Kate must remember he'd come to Newmarket for the races, and would now travel to Ireland to look out for the source of the false artifacts. Their very friendship had an end date, three months after the date by which Kate needed a financial miracle.

Quickly, she drained the rest of her wine.

"Maybe you'll meet a nice Irish lass while you're there." Owen winked at his brother from across the table and sucked with gusto on a wishbone. "Someone who doesn't mind you traipsing about after ancient thingummies. Eh, Lady Whelan?"

"I agree wholeheartedly," Kate said. "Ancient thingummies do not appeal to a great many women. Most prefer their, ah, thingummies to be modern and firm."

Evan laughed. Good! That was one.

"But the discerning sort of woman," she added, trying to catch his eye, "thinks of a thingummy's source. And if she admires the source, nothing else is of consequence."

Elena Rhys held a serviette up to her mouth, covering a coughing fit.

Owen Rhys, however, had more to say. "That's fine for a fairy tale, but in truth the discerning sort of woman prefers an older son. Still, Evan is of good family. How should he have reached the age of thirty-four without finding someone to take him?"

"I don't know," Kate said. "It is difficult to imagine why someone did not snap him up long ago."

"We thought he might take the daughter of one of the country squires," said Mrs. Rhys. "But he never came up to scratch, and so she wed someone else. Samuel Jones, a farmer. She could have done better for herself. Now she's thirty years old and has fourteen children."

"I thought it was fifteen," was Evan's only contribution. He seemed unbothered by the discussion of his marriageability—but Kate was not so indifferent. Why, if Evan should wed, that would bring an end to their friendship. Another Mrs. Rhys would surely not understand its nature—even if she did not find out about their single, ill-advised liaison.

Which had been the greatest, most shaking pleasure Kate had taken in years, and she must not allow herself to think of it at table.

She pressed a cooling hand to her cheeks, but not before Evan noticed the rising color. In his dark eyes, something wicked kindled that was not the reflection of candlelight.

Then his brows knit. "I just remembered..." He shook his head. "Anne Jones."

"Yes, dear. It's too late for that," said Mrs. Rhys.

"It was too late fourteen years and fourteen children ago." Her husband chuckled.

"Not that, not that. It's the name. Kate's—ah, Lady Whelan's father mentioned that he knew someone by the name of Anne Jones, but it is not that one. Do you know any others?"

The two sets of husbands and wives looked at each other. "Which one?" they said all together.

"The butcher's wife?" asked one. "Or the innkeeper's?"

"The vicar's mother?" asked a second.

"Oh! The dressmaker's assistant—the one on the street. You know the one, with the terrible gowns in the shop window."

Judging from the laughter that succeeded, apparently in Wales it was considered extremely funny to discuss the commonness of the name Anne Jones.

Evan's voice cut through the chatter. "The one I mean is forty or forty-five years of age. Prettyish."

Kate shot him a questioning look. He made a gesture of surrender with his hands. "I don't know any more. It's the description your father gave me. He, er...knew her some years ago."

Ha. That meant only one thing: a paramour. When a man dropped an *er* into a simple sentence about a past acquaintance, he was giving himself time to think of how to shield a listening lady from a more scandalous word.

Con had, er…known a lady in Thurles since before their marriage. He had, er…seen to her welfare when that lady developed smallpox—and then, shortly before his death, the longtime mistress had, er… delivered a son.

Such long-standing devotion was almost honorable. Er.

Kate cut her food into ruthless tiny pieces. "I have never heard the name."

"There is a Mrs. Jones of about that age who runs a foundling home near the English border," said Mrs. Rhys. "I cannot speak to her prettiness—"

"Oh, yes! Quite pretty, she is," interjected her husband, causing his wife to frown.

"I know of her because she travels through to collect the orphans of the parish." That lady spoke on in a determined rush. "She takes them off to her foundling home and finds work for them, and they needn't then be a drain on our parish resources. It keeps everything so nice and tidy."

"Does she have any children?" Evan asked. Odd.

"I know of none besides those she cares for in her foundling home. Quite as though they were her own. She says so." Mrs. Rhys shaved the thinnest possible sliver of breast meat from the squab.

The remainder of the meal wore on in similar fashion. Kate ate more than she ought and drank more wine than she should, because it prevented her from talking. She didn't find so much humor now in the role of Provincial Countess.

Evan was right. There was little of laughter here, at least of the sort in which she could share.

After the meal, Owen and Elena's children were brought down to greet the company in the drawing room. A half dozen dark-haired, bouncing boys and girls, they ranged in age from two to ten years. When they saw Evan, the older ones ran to surround him, and the younger ones toddled after their siblings on fat little legs and embraced him about the knees with fat little arms.

Kate's heart gave a squeeze. Oh, she wanted to snatch up those littlest ones and hug them, tight, tight. She missed that innocent age, when life was nothing but the present moment, and a child could be made happy merely by finding something interesting on the floor to shove into his mouth.

She missed all the ages through which her children had passed.

She felt a gaze on her, and looked from the children to meet Elena Rhys's hazel eyes. The other woman smiled, and as she clapped her hands to summon her children back to the nursery, she brushed past Kate. "You'll be good for him," she murmured, then lifted her voice in a placid, polite good-night to the company.

And whatever did that mean? *We're friends, nothing more*, Kate wanted to call after the younger Mrs. Rhys—but friends, nothing more, did not take each other to bed, and Kate did not know what name she ought to put to her relationship with Evan now.

When Evan excused himself, Kate did the same, pleading the excuse of travel fatigue. She followed him from the drawing room, letting the door shut behind them. They were in another rich corridor, this one tapestried and lit by beeswax candles in cut-crystal globes.

"I see why Good Old Gwyn doesn't faze you," she said.

He had gone a step ahead of her, but at the sound of her voice he halted. "Indeed." He touched one of the tapestries, a stitched-silk depiction of a saint's grotesque martyrdom. "I had hoped things would be different with you here. A new person, changing the shape of the old familiar interactions."

"How could I change anything when I don't even know what a privy is?"

"Or an indoor kitchen?" His smile was saturnine, all candlelit plane and shadow. "You were wicked. I can't think of when I've enjoyed a meal more."

"Wicked? A provincial charmer such as I?" She batted her lashes in exaggerated fashion.

"You were, in relation to me. You needn't defend me to my family. It won't make any difference to them."

"Did it make a difference to you?"

"It wrung my heart." Ah, the rakish charmer was back as he laid a palm over his chest. "It made my evening whole. It set me to swooning."

She cuffed him on the shoulder. "Don't tell me what you think, then. I know I was rude, but I cannot be sorry."

His hand fell to clench at his waist, but he said nothing.

"I liked meeting your nieces and nephews too," Kate added. "I hadn't realized you had so many. You don't need Nora and Declan at all."

He laughed. "Nonsense! As though children are interchangeable." That was two. With every laugh she coaxed from him, she felt the distance between them lessen.

A distance she had put into place. She knew that.

"Besides which," Evan added, "yours are my only godchildren. So they must always be special to me."

"It was not creative of us to name you godfather to Declan after having you serve so for Nora. But you gave such wonderful presents, how could we not?" she teased. "I didn't mean to imply that children are all the same. Only I didn't realize you have so much family of your own."

"Hmmm." He traced the line of a silken spear. She liked watching the movement of his hand, so strong over ancient thread so delicate. "You are wondering why I spent so much time in your house?"

"Not in an ungracious way. More in a curious way. If I could see my family so easily by crossing the Irish Sea, I would—"

"Do nothing differently at all, I'll wager. If your heart lies across the sea, there's no difference between a day's travel and a week's. You'll follow it."

"And where does your heart lie?"

He picked at a loose thread, turning an embroidered stab wound into a river of blood. "Oh, you know me. It's buried in the earth hereabouts. Wales is full of old Roman ruins and standing stones that date back even farther. Dig awhile, and you never know what you'll find."

"Yes," she said. "I have been thinking the same about you."

"Ah, Lady Whelan. You'll have me blushing if you keep that up."

So easily, she became the one blushing. She didn't know why—what—oh, she was a muddle of fiery cheeks and *back to the way we were* and confusion.

"Will you show me around this place?" she asked. "Not the rich and elegant bits, but something people don't usually see."

"Such as?" He caught her eyes, looking down at her with cool curiosity.

"Whatever makes you want to come back to Wales. Whatever..." She swallowed. "Whatever holds your heart here."

"Ah." His strong features took on a wistful cast. "For that, we'll have to go to the stables."

"Then lead the way."

Twelve

SHOW ME WHATEVER HOLDS YOUR HEART HERE, SHE had said.

The answer wasn't in Ardent House. That was for damned sure.

Evan felt better as soon as he and Kate were outdoors with lantern in hand, crossing the manicured lawn toward the stables. He smiled, and what a feat that was. It was always more difficult to smile here.

The rich tapestries reminded him of the grayness he ought not to feel. The silver plate scattered over the table was merely grayness made to shine as though it were worth something, but it wasn't. Grayness wasn't even real. So had said his brother and parents time and again.

Count your blessings.

Think of those less fortunate than you.

I'll give you a reason to be sad.

Why are you so ungrateful?

And tonight: *You know how you get. So morose.*

He had been born to great good fortune, and there was no reason for his life to be anything but bright.

Constantly being reminded of the fact was not, however, helpful.

The stables were built of the same red brick as the manor house, slated over and pedimented and columned. But once one entered, the feel was entirely different. True, within the winding building, stalls were divided by columns more finely carved than those in many a house. But the ceiling was high and airy, and during the day sun would spill through windows nestled beneath the eaves. Perfect for bringing light to things no one else cared to see.

He turned right once they had entered the great doors, ready to show Kate his collection—but instead of following Evan, she headed for the nearest horse.

"One of the Welsh cobs about which I've heard so much! Oh, she's a lovely creature. May I pet her?" She tugged off a glove and extended her hand, flat of palm, for the horse to examine and sniff.

He hung the lantern on a hook, adding to the row of lights hung by the active grooms. "If you wish. This is Lady Alix. Despite the loftiness of her name, she's got the good temper of her breed." Always glad for company, the mare shuffled forward in her stall and shoved her muzzle into Kate's shoulder. Of middle age, Lady Alix was as playful as a filly.

"Lady Alix." Kate petted the small horse's neck. "Are you a countess? I wonder if you are better behaved than I am."

"I am sure she is. But then, one can take a riding crop to a naughty horse."

Kate choked. "And not to a countess? The bawdy books in our library have been lying to me?"

"Bawdy books..." Evan trailed off, shaking his head. "You will be the death of me. I never know what you will say."

"Usually something about horses."

That was that. A shame, for the subject had promised to take an intriguing turn.

"On that subject," Evan said, "I am thinking of bringing this lady along to Whelan House, so I needn't constantly steal your horses." A sturdy bay animal with an unfashionably long tail of coarse black hair, she was surefooted and pleasant. If any horse were to handle a crossing of the Irish Sea with tolerable calm, it would be she.

Lady Alix had nipped up the glove Kate had removed and dropped it on the stable floor. "You know the stables are open to you, Evan. Always." She bent to pick up the glove. With a hint of a smile, she draped it over the mare's stall door.

"I know. But I want to—well, to pay my own way, in a manner of speaking. I'll cover the cost of her travel and her board."

Lady Alix nosed the glove onto the floor again. He wasn't sure whether that was a sign of approval or not.

"Others have taken enough from you, Kate," he explained. "I don't want to be another in that number."

He expected her to argue, but she didn't. "I know what you mean." Idly, she picked up the glove again. "I would travel with a carriage and team of my own too, if I had a bit of money. It is wearing to rely on my father's kindness. The loan of his carriage and horses is too much for comfort, not enough for salvation."

Lady Alix extended her head, nipping at the

glove in Kate's hand. "You've made a friend," Evan said. "She'll play with you for the next hour if you let her."

"Another time, my lady." With one final pat to the horse's neck, Kate stepped back to Evan's side. "We came here for you to show me something. Whatever you'd like to."

He'd like to sink to one knee and take her hand in his. He'd like to show her the heights of pleasure, the breadth of sweet comfort. He'd like to show the words *if* and *maybe* and *exactly as we were* to a high cliff and shove them over.

But they were in the stables for a different purpose altogether, and Evan felt too raw after dining with his family to do anything more than nod his understanding. He retrieved the lantern. "This way. The stall at the far end."

He led her down the row, murmuring greetings to horses and stable hands alike, until they reached a loose box at the end. This was used as a catchall for bits of tack in need of mending, for extra supplies and—Evan suspected—a bottle from which the grooms nipped on cold evenings. It was also the place where his crates were stored.

He unlatched the stall door and motioned Kate within. "Have a seat on…ah, that saddle, I suppose. I'll show you some of the artifacts I've found."

She plumped sideways on the discarded saddle and stripped off her second glove. "Why are they in here rather than on display?"

"They're not pretty enough to be displayed indoors, and they're not fine enough examples to be sent to museums. But I found them, and I can't throw them back into the earth."

"No, of course not. And waste the chance to learn something of them?"

"Exactly." He hung the lantern, then slid open the lid to one of the crates. "We don't have time to go to one of the digs, or I'd show you my favorite finds—the foundations of ancient structures."

"You mean the houses people lived in?"

"Those, and their privies and rubbish heaps. Both are places people toss things they can't use, or that they want hidden." He sifted through the packing sawdust. "The chase of history is a sort of voyeurism."

"How scandalous you make it sound. I should have paid more attention during your lecture. What is the most intriguing item you've found?"

"If I've the right crate, you'll see it in a moment. Oh, here's a nice little piece." Handing a metalwork brooch to Kate, he explained, "That was probably a dolphin once upon a time, before the earth crushed it. The Romans were besotted with dolphins."

"Were they? This has become so distorted it looks like a gasping fish. I'd like to see that become all the rage in London ballrooms next year." She gave it back, and he dropped it into the crate.

"There are better examples in the British Museum in Bloomsbury. Not only brooches, but all sorts of items. Those flints you loved so much you had to send some to your brother. Broken pots. Unbroken ones. Carved bone…aha, speaking of which—you wanted an intriguing item? Here's one that might amuse you."

As Kate took the foot-long piece from him, her mouth dropped open. "Is that a winged..."

"Phallus, yes." He grinned. "From what I can tell, it's a decorative piece. It isn't, say, a flute."

Kate choked.

"Nor could it be used for...intimate purposes. Its hollow structure is too fragile."

"I would never have thought of such a thing. Now I cannot help but..." Kate was a lovely shade of pink. When she ran her finger down the length of the animal bone, Evan felt a prickle down his spine. "Someone took great pains to carve it in detail. Why does it have wings, do you think?"

"I would dearly love to know the answer. Could it be a supernatural being?"

"Considering Roman mythology? I would not doubt it. I know little of history, but do know the Romans had a bawdy sense of humor." She turned the piece over and regarded its underside. "Look. Bollocks, Evan."

And Evan laughed.

He laughed because a countess was sitting on a broken saddle, showing him the baubles on a bone carving more than a thousand years old. He laughed because that countess was Kate, and because she had been interested in what he had to say after a long chill-mannered meal in which every approval came tied to advice and conditions and *why don'ts* and *you oughts*.

For God's sake. Sometimes a man just wanted to dig up an ancient cock sculpture and show it about. Was that too much to ask from life?

And he laughed at that too.

Kate looked up from the carved bollocks, beaming.

"Oh, excellent. I was determined to make you laugh three times this evening, and I was one shy."

He accepted the ancient phallus from her and tucked it back into the crate, aware of the ridiculousness of the action. "I laughed twice this evening?"

"You did, and it was because of me. I was so funny and witty."

"You were, yes. You were a delightful brat at dinner. But why did you set your will to the goal of making me laugh three times?"

"Because I went two years without hearing you laugh, and I have missed the sound."

This admission, simple and frank, was like a knife slipped beneath armor. He sat down, hard, on the lid of the crate. "Why, because of how it makes you feel?"

She toyed with the stamped leather decoration at the front of the saddle. "No. Because of how it makes you feel. If you're laughing, then for the duration of the laugh, all is well with you."

He opened his mouth, but was not sure what to say. How could she be so warm of heart, yet keep him as her only friend? How could *exactly as we were* serve?

"Thank you," he finally said.

She met his eyes. "Your happiness has always mattered to me."

They sat in the dim stall for a quiet minute, surrounded by the muted sounds of grooms talking, of horses snorting or thumping about in their stalls.

"Thank you for showing me what you found," she said. "Before I attended your lecture, I never knew the hunt through the past was more to you than a hobby."

It was warming, to be understood in this way. Yet

he demurred. "Until I take up my post in Greece, I won't receive pay. Maybe it is only a hobby."

"No. At the very least, it's a passion. A calling, even. You could always make the past come to life for me. Even with whisky in hand, I loved to listen to you speak of what you'd found."

He could hear her talk of this all evening. All night. Forever. To be listened to and known, in any small way, was a gift. "What did you like most about it?"

She leaned back against the wall of the stall, stretching forth her legs. She still wore her dinner gown and fragile slippers, not suited for the stable.

He knew the shape of the feet within those slippers, the legs beneath that gown, and he almost groaned for wanting to touch her again.

Heedless of how she set him to burning, she considered. "I ought to say, maybe, that they were people much like us. Which is true, and the artifacts you find like combs and chamber pots make it plain."

Mustering his thoughts into sensible order, he agreed. "The Elgin marbles might make such ordinary objects look dull, but they're equally important to history. Maybe more so, because they show who was *here*, on the land we now walk."

"But they weren't really like us at all, were they?" Kate leaned closer now, her gaze earnest. "They were explorers and soldiers from Rome, and if they were here they were far from their homeland. They were always at war, always pushing. So maybe what you find—it shows what we could become if we are not careful."

This was an unusual insight. Unsettling, too. "Are you afraid for us?"

"For England? She does not care what I believe or fear."

"For us." He stepped back from that admission. "For yourself."

"I am, a little. It's easier to stay home than step out into the world. But I do wonder...what could I become, if I were willing to conquer?"

He reached for her, brushing her fingertips with his. "I fear you would be invincible."

"Oh." Her fingers clutched at his. "Evan. You are not perfect, but you are just right." She didn't meet his eye as she said that—except for a quick sidelong glance. Almost shy.

"Wise words," he said. "I think I've heard those before."

She squeezed his hand, hard, then withdrew hers into her lap. Laced her fingers together. "I'm sorry for the way I've treated you," she blurted.

Ah. They were to talk of it at last.

Manners would instruct him to deflect the apology with pretended misunderstanding. Evan declined to use good manners.

"What, chatting with me as a friend and brushing me with your skirts like a lover? Pulling me toward you, then pushing me back again, so I never know what to expect?" Somehow he managed to keep his tone even, his feet planted steadily on the stable floor. "Come, now. What is there to apologize for in all of that?"

Her brows lifted. "Anything else?"

"That's all. For now."

The line of her mouth softened, curved. "I am

sorry, truly. I've felt awkward. I wasn't sure what to do after…we…ah. Then I missed you, and I was afraid."

I was afraid too. I missed you. I have always been sure of you. He waited, words bated at the tip of his tongue.

Kate twisted her gloves in her grasp. "I've never trusted anyone in the way I trusted—that I *trust*—you. I think I trust you more than I trust myself. You would not hurt me, and I…I cannot say the same for the choices I've made."

It was being wounded and healing at once. Her trust was a balm, but it was searing too. She had placed him in the role of infallible friend, as surely as she had made of herself wife, daughter, mother. And if she felt trapped—how was he to feel? The role of friend was the only one she had told him that gave her room to laugh.

He did not feel like laughing now. He could not fathom how he had laughed this evening at all.

"You have apologized," he said. "Does that mean you won't do it again? The inconsistent sort of toying with my heart?"

There. Heart. He had said it.

She did not miss the word, clearly more intimate than what she had expected, and her mouth fell open. Startled. Considering.

Then she rallied and moved on as though he'd used a word far smaller. One that fit into the role of *friend, exactly as we were.* "I will not do it again. I am grateful for the sort of easy friendship we have discovered, where I make a fool of myself, you show me improper artifacts, and we get to pet a horse."

"So easy." He could not keep the scoff from his tone. "So…friendship…y."

He ought to say more, but what was the point of words? Being in Wales was a tricky balance. It was a rich vein for exploration, and it was a hammer to pound him into the proper shape.

"Now you're making up words," she said. "Does that mean you forgive me?"

Ah, Kate, lantern-lit and sweet. As sincere in her apology as she had been in her passion and her hesitation. This sincerity was a clutch at his heart, though it felt like a shackle too.

"Yes," he said. "It means that I forgive you. But it does not mean that I agree."

Thirteen

THE FOLLOWING MORNING, KATE CROSSED A SEA.

Their journey had begun early, following an old stone bridge from Anglesey to the smaller Holy Island, where the packet awaited. There she and Evan and Susan bade farewell to John Coachman and to Jerome and Hattie. Hattie stamped her hooves, which were still perfectly shod. Jerome looked at Kate with soft, reproachful eyes that made her heart twist. When the chestnuts turned about, Kate felt as though she were saying good-bye to her family all over again.

But there was so much to see that she set aside the hollowness of parting. The packet in Holyhead Port was swift and solid, a good-sized barque laden with freight and mail as well as passengers. When Kate flapped a glove at Lady Alix, the saucy little mare followed her aboard readily enough.

"You're meant to be *my* horse," Evan grumbled as he led Her Ladyship to a stall belowdecks. Susan, too, went to the quarters below.

Kate found a spot at the bow and looked and looked. The sea was different every time she crossed it, and never had she departed from Wales. The coast was crumbled into rough islands of varying sizes. Anglesey led to the smaller Holyhead, and South Stack, home of a lighthouse that beckoned ships toward safe crossing. The rugged low bump of North Stack, the scatter of the Skerries—low islets that caught so many ships unawares, a lighthouse was placed there too. Seabirds filled the air with their buzzing calls, flying up and landing in great waves of pale wings like air-flung rippling cloth.

When someone took up a place at the bow beside her, she knew who it was without looking. She knew the size and shape of Evan, the feel of having him stand next to her.

"How can you leave it?" she asked. "How can you go to Greece?"

How can you leave me, just when we found each other again?

Friends didn't ask that sort of question. Friends weren't that selfish. So she pretended she wondered only about the sea.

"I'm going where I'm needed," he said. "I want to be needed."

"What a blessing for you. I want to be needed less." What was a life like with no burdens? With mischievous horses, and children who always had clothing the right size, and land that either was yours or wasn't, and none of this in-between fear?

She swallowed hard and tipped her face to the breeze. At sea, there was no need for such thoughts. The sea was neither here nor there, and so it was home to no worries.

"Perhaps we ought both to be careful what we wish for," he said drily.

"Perhaps we ought." The dark blue sea grappled with the boat, the waves hungry tongues. "I would never tell you to count your blessings—"

"God forbid."

"—but I ought to count mine. I'll get to see my children again soon." She looked up at him, squinting into the blue wash of the sky. "And you will too."

She had left alone, but she would not return so. Evan stood beside her, a figurehead at the bow, watching the water ruffle past.

The ferry ride took only a few hours, but Kate wished it had been far longer. As soon as Evan could rent a carriage and team in Dublin, he saddled Lady Alix and rode postilion beside the women. Another ninety miles lay between them and their destination, and it would take five days, at least, to cover.

Susan had become nauseated during the ferry crossing, and a jouncing carriage ride over rough roads turned her positively green. When they stopped at an inn that night, Kate saw Susan to their chamber with warm broth and a compress for her head.

"You shouldn't, my lady," the maid said in feeble protest.

"You can pay me wages for this hour," said Kate. "If that makes you feel better. Now, drink the broth."

Susan had grown up as part of the Whelan House staff. Kate was ten years her senior and remembered her as a child of no more than seven, kicking her legs on a tall kitchen chair as she peeled fruits. Later she'd been a housemaid. For the past five years, she'd been Kate's lady's maid. Sometimes Kate's only companion—not that Kate confided in her.

She didn't confide in anyone. Except Evan.

Maybe.

She pulled back the coverlet for Susan, unpinned the young woman's fine hair, and bathed her face with a cool cloth. It was like taking care of Nora, should Nora, at the great age of twelve, let Kate tend to her.

Of a sudden, she missed her children so much that she had to sit, heavily, and let the bed creak beneath the weight of her wish to be with them.

"Sometimes it's nice," Kate realized, "to have someone need me." But Susan was asleep before she spoke the words.

Now Kate was awake alone, with no one to help her undress and nowhere to sleep unless she could shove Susan over. She ought to have thought of this first, rather than getting caught up being the rogue housekeeper.

Maybe she could ask Evan to…

Evan could… *No.* She arrested the thought as soon as it came into her mind. It would be unkind to ask him for such help.

Even though he had already seen her bare. Even though she thought he would like to see her so again. Even though part of her craved that closeness, that intimate, trusting touch again.

A larger part was terrified of further change. Now that she had got her friend back, how could she lose him again? She couldn't ask him to be a lover, then a friend, then a maid, and not send him—and herself—screaming across Ireland.

No. She would find the innkeeper's wife and get help from that quarter.

And so she did, creeping from her chamber quietly so as not to wake Susan. When she found the innkeeper's wife, a stout and sonsy woman with wide hips, bosom, and smile, Kate inquired as to the possibility of getting a different room for herself.

"I can't," said that lady with apology. "My man's just after giving the last chamber to another couple. If you'd need some extra blankets, that I can give you. You'd make a lovely pallet on the floor."

Kate agreed to this, then submitted to being unlaced by the innkeeper's wife in the inn's private parlor. Best to stay out of her chamber; Susan needed to sleep off her illness. Kate depended on her help when they traveled—and maybe, a bit on her chaperonage.

Thanking her hostess with a silver coin, Kate wrapped one of the blankets about her shoulders to cover the sagging back of her gown. Then she gathered the rest of the blankets and made for the back stairs so she could creep back to her chamber unseen by other guests.

The stairs used by servants and family, narrow and steep, were of rude boards and whitewashed walls. Kate slid along the wall, feeling her way up in the near dark. A window cut high into the stairwell provided a touch of moonlight, enough to limn the edges of the stairs.

A spark was struck a few steps above, and a glow came into being. It moved in a sinuous line, and Kate realized someone in the stairwell had lit a smoke.

"I beg your pardon," she said. "I must get by."

The glow paused in midair. "Kate?"

She tilted her head. "Evan?"

"Yes." By the light of the moon and the tiny ember, she saw him shift to one side. Making room for her to pass? Or maybe to sit beside him. "Nice outfit you've adopted. I'm not saying the cut of it will set a wild new fashion, but it does look comfortable."

"It serves the purpose." She hitched her extra blankets to one hip. "Why are you smoking in here, not outside or in the taproom? You are behaving like a naughty stableboy."

"Not a bad description, though I'm a few decades too old to be called a stableboy without my dignity being wounded. I didn't feel like having company. And it was raining like the devil outside."

She could hear drops still pattering the window above them. "I'll leave you to it, then."

"No, no. Stay with me. You're a sight different than the company of strangers." He waved the cheroot at her. "Want to share my smoke?"

She hesitated, aware of her gown and stays gaping open, shielded only by a rough blanket. Oughtn't she return to her chamber at once?

No, this was a chance to bridge the persistent distance between them. To return to the way things had been, when they drank whisky and shot targets and smoked and talked until all hours of the night.

She mounted the steps to sit at his side, settling the extra blankets on the stair above them. "I can't recall the last time I smoked."

There was hardly room for them to sit side by side

on the stair. Her hip bumped his, cushioned by the bunched skirts and blankets wrapped about her. Still, she felt the closeness as a bolt that prickled—electric, from scalp to toes. It left her warm and tingling, her hands uncertain but eager.

She took the cheroot from him. It was thin, long as her hand from middle finger to wrist, and sharply scented of clove and ash. She held it between trembling fingers.

Evan bumped her shoulder with his own. "How do you manage to look like a lady while wrapped in a blanket, smoking a cheroot, sitting on servants' stairs? Such a talent ought to be taught in every finishing school."

"How do you know that's not where I practiced it? Along with all my other charming, delicate qualities." She snorted, then brought the cheroot to her lips. Inhaling lightly, no more than a sip, she took in the hot, fragrant smoke. It seemed to scour her lungs, a feeling both bracing and disagreeable. "I've no idea. What do you mean by *lady*?"

"Am I going to get in trouble?"

"Not if you give a good answer."

"No pressure, eh? A lady, then, is someone worthy of respect."

This, she had to think about. "I'd hope you knew, Mr. Antiquarian, that appearance has nothing to do with worth."

"Indeed I do know it."

She tried to blow a smoke ring, but only breathed a cloud of fog. "Look, I'm a dragon." She handed him back the cheroot.

"You make a fine gray smoke," he said. "May I ask why you're wearing a blanket?"

"You may. Though you ought to know I'm wearing a lot of other things too." She explained about Susan's illness and exhausted slumber, and the assistance of the innkeeper's wife.

"I find myself enlightened," he said. "Nothing could make more sense than you sneaking about dressed in blankets."

"I thought you'd come to see it my way."

"Without doubt. I would say I could have helped you, but I think that would be a bad idea."

"It is the sort of thing friends might do." She hesitated. "But not when they are male and female."

"And that matters, does it?" He passed her the cheroot.

"Yes. I think it does." She drew on the thin cigar again, aware that her lips were where his had been. The smoke was hot in her lungs, not pleasant. But she wanted it all the more for it being unpleasant. "Do you remember the first time you smoked?"

"Oh, yes." Her eyes were dazzled by the glow at the end of the cheroot, and she could hardly make out his form. But somehow she could tell he was smiling as he explained, "I was about eight years old. I took a cigar from one of the grooms. Coughed till I thought I'd never get my breath again."

"And then?"

"I did get my breath back, and I took another smoke. I couldn't have a groom laughing at me, could I?"

When she returned the cheroot, he held it at arm's length. "Nasty habit. I never got accustomed to it. But it's a way to end the day, like having a drink."

"Or talking to a friend."

"That too. When did you first smoke? Were you a stubborn child like I was?"

"I was, yes. I think grooms must be the tempter for us all. Jonah and I told our father's head groom, Lombard, we wanted to try it. Actually, we wanted a plug of tobacco to chew, because that's what Lombard did. Still does. He is always chewing at something and spitting.

"He had some sort of cigar he said he wasn't going to smoke, so he gave it to us. Told us to take a great big breath." Not the most delightful of her childhood memories. "I coughed. Jonah vomited. I was proud of holding my own better than him."

"Both of us sickened by it, yet here we sit with a cheroot." He blew a smoke ring, then another.

"Here we do," she said. "It's a kind of mastery, isn't it? I won't let a scrap of dried-up leaf tell me it's stronger than I am."

Again, he handed it to her. She burned her fingers taking it, and she hissed. He licked his fingers and pinched it out.

They went into moonlit darkness again. "So many firsts," she said. "I don't often think of them. But as there was a first cheroot, there was a first time you and I met. A first time I saw you. A first time I beat you at target shooting."

"That last one never happened," he said. "I don't remember it."

"Oh, please. I beat everyone at target shooting."

Did she remember the first time she'd met Evan? It might have been as soon as she reached the Whelan lands as Con's bride. "Were you staying at Whelan House when Con came back with me? Is that when we met?"

"It was. He'd gone to England to buy horses, and back he came not only with three mares, but also with a bride."

"The human sort of broodmare," she mused. "What did you think of me?"

He hesitated. "I don't remember."

"Yes, you do. Why won't you say? Is it horrid?" The notion was lowering. She could remember only dimly a time she had not known Evan, and the whole time of knowing him was wrapped in thinking him one of the people nearest her heart.

"Does it matter at this distance in time?" His voice was quiet.

"In a way, no, because it was so long ago. But I'm curious. Our first meeting was the foundation for what we've become since." Whatever that was. Had been. Would be.

"Well, then." He shifted on the step, the wood creaking beneath him. "I thought you were far too young to be anyone's wife. You were pretty and bright and your hair was all of a curl, as though you'd just been tumbled."

"I probably had been," she murmured. Con had had his own idea of how best to pass a lengthy journey. It was a notion with which she had enthusiastically agreed, and which had resulted in Nora being born scarcely ten months after their wedding day.

"I assumed at first that you were some decorative

little English miss. My mistake. For then you marched forward with strides like a racehorse—"

"That is hardly flattering."

"—and shook my hand, hard, as though we were already friends of long standing. You told me you were glad to meet me, and I felt you meant it. After that, I knew you were capable of infinite surprises, and I wanted nothing more than to be your friend in return."

As though his words had unlocked a hidden part of her mind, the memory spilled forth. It had been a day of mixed rain and sun, a day of pleasures on the road and worry about the destination.

"I remember that day," she said. "I was so afraid of you. I knew you were a part of Con's family, and if you did not like me, he would be sorry he had wed me."

Thump. Evan had leaned his head against the wall of the stairwell. "He was never sorry he had wed you."

"I did my best to be a good wife." A thankless task at times, a delightful one at others. "I think I was."

"And a good friend?"

"That was often easier." She clutched at the edges of the blanket. The wool was coarse, itching at the back of her neck where it wrapped about her. "I'm glad I didn't come between you and Con. I'd never have wanted that."

He was silent for several breaths before speaking. "I know you wouldn't have. You always meant well. You still do."

The words were so matter-of-fact that they seemed to well from some heartfelt belief in their truth. She blinked hard, but her eyes filled against sweet pain. "Evan, damn you. Why are you always so kind?"

"I'm not kind, really. But I mean well too, blanket queen." He took her arm and helped her to her feet. "Are you set for the night now?"

She gathered the spare blankets. "Yes, I've everything I need to make a—oh."

"What is it?" As they mounted the stairs, he leaned to open the narrow window and tossed the cheroot end out.

"It's my hair. I need someone to comb it."

"Can't you do it yourself?"

"I can, but it's so long, and it gets tangled after a day in pins. I'll probably shriek when I reach a tangle, and then I'll wake Susan. She's only just got to sleep after a day of vomiting."

"Ah, a day of vomiting. You make the ferry sound like a pleasure cruise. Let's go back across the Irish Sea tomorrow."

"Poor Susan. She'd leave my service."

He opened the door at the top of the back stairs, letting her pass through before him. "All right, countess. I'll comb out your hair. We can't have anyone shrieking or vomiting or waking."

Kate gave an affronted laugh. "You make me sound like an infant."

He smiled, booting the door shut. "My chamber's here. Come inside. Only as a friend, now," he warned. "Don't get any notion that I'm going to follow you to your bedchamber and try to seduce you before a sick maid."

"You're not even going to *try*? You're giving up too easily."

This was the wrong thing to say. "Sorry."

"It's fine," he said, shutting his chamber door behind them and taking up a horn-handled comb from the washstand. "I shouldn't have said what I did either. Stand here, and keep the blanket around you."

The line between teasing and truth was fine, yet the gulf between what they'd been and what they'd become was wide. Was one side, one way, better than the other? She did not know. She only knew she'd rather have him around than not.

And not because he did a damned fine job combing out her hair.

His chamber was a twin to hers: clean and spare, with a fireplace at one side. Furnished simply with a bed, a privacy screen, a table, and a washstand. Evan had seated himself on the end of the bed, which was high enough for her to stand before him, back to him, and let him pluck the pins from her hair. It fell in a heavy spill, tugging at her scalp.

"I've been told," she said for the sake of saying something, "that my hair is like a tangle of wire."

"Your hair is what it is, the way it grows from your head, and that makes it perfectly fine." He drew the comb through from the end, separating tangles into curls, before starting up higher. "As a matter of fact, I have seen tangled wire. It did not in the slightest remind me of your hair."

His touch was gentle and sure. For long moments he worked at her hair, using the fine teeth of the comb and sometimes his fingers when a knot proved recalcitrant.

Never had her hair seemed so weighty. Never had a simple everyday act seemed so intimate. It was completely innocent, one friend helping another through an awkward moment. Yet her slipping bodice and stays abraded her nipples, reminding her of his touch, of how easy it would be for him to touch her again. The comb on her scalp was a wake of sensation, a spot seldom touched that would now belong in memory to him.

By the time he finished, her lips were dry, and all she could think of was turning toward him and into his arms.

"There. It's done without a single shriek." Before she could turn, he was up and off the bed. First stowing the comb within a shaving kit, then returning to her with a fistful of her discarded hairpins.

She swallowed, striving for a normal tone. "How do you know how to comb out curly hair?"

"I suppose…I thought about it a great deal, and did what seemed right."

He wasn't looking at her, and she took the chance to trace him with eager eyes. His dark wavy hair, his expressive brows. The mouth that had kissed her, had spoken such lovely words of comfort. Had joked and laughed over the years, had sworn he forgave her for the wrongs she had done him.

"You are a fine man," she said.

"Glad I've fooled you." He shifted a few items on the small table. "Off with you now, before you ruin my reputation. We'll be on the road early tomorrow. Got your pins? Here, and don't forget your blankets."

For a moment, she thought of asking if she could stay in his room. Just to stay. Just for company and comfort.

But she wanted more than that, and the realization was a precipice over which she did not dare to peer.

She gathered the blankets. "Thank you."

He bade her good night and saw her into the corridor. Then he closed the door without making sure she reached her room.

The corridor was cold, even with a blanket of thick wool about her shoulders, and she ran back to her chamber quickly, knowing she would not sleep for all the questions in her mind.

Fourteen

For the following days in the carriage, Kate was not sure whether, dropped onto a globe without orientation, she would know her surroundings from the land of England or Wales.

Neither country so recently visited had felt like home. Would she know a home when she reached it? After the past few weeks in Evan's company, she was scrambled, disoriented, tipped askew.

Her hair, however, had been combed well, and lay in marvelous neat curls.

When the carriage reached the heart of Ireland, the air seemed to settle about her. Gone were the bracing breeze and drumming of raindrops from the eastern coast. Here the air was milder with frost in the dawn that vanished in sunlight. Every other day or so, a scatter of rain fell, as if the sky were full of mischief that must spill out.

By the time the travelers reached Thurles, this familiar sort of light rain was falling, tapping the carriage windows in greeting as they trundled along the main street. Thurles was a small market town east of a hunt racecourse abutting the Suir River, with all the usual shops.

A medieval tower house, Bridge Castle, crouched on one bank of the river. No longer used to defend the waterway from foes, its crumbling top was peacefully fringed with green, and moss speckled the solid stone walls. At every season, even in drizzle and damp, anglers could be spotted at the river's edge, though whether they'd a hope of catching trout or whether they only enjoyed the chance to jaw with friends, Kate didn't know.

She realized, as the carriage rolled on and the neat storefronts fell behind, that there wasn't a single friend on whom she needed to call now that she'd returned. She'd become so wrapped up in her obligations, especially since Con died. Why, even her closest friend—she shot a glance at Evan, who was looking out the opposite window—was an inheritance from her late husband. Who were *her* people? Who would ever choose to be with her for her own sake?

The questions shifted her into action. Almost without thinking, she knocked at the carriage roof. The driver halted, and Kate opened the door and hopped down. She tipped her face up, collecting chilly raindrops on her eyelids and cheeks, then looked around for someone to greet.

The rain had cleared the street, but—ah! She was right by the apothecary's shop, where the mail was delivered and posted. That was reason enough to enter.

She passed through the door with its jingling bell overhead. The shop was small and close, with myriad shelves behind the counter and a sharp smell of liniment and wintergreen. "Mr. Petty?" she called.

As the door jingled again, the elderly shopkeeper popped out from the back of the shop. A wizened bald man with large ears, Petty's homely face beamed as soon as he saw Evan. "Why, Mr. Rhys! We haven't seen you in such a time, but I would know you in an instant. And how is it you've been, sir?"

Sure enough, Evan—and Susan too—had entered the shop behind Kate.

"Quite well, Mr. Petty. And yourself?" When the apothecary made his own polite answer, Evan added, "Lady Whelan and I met by chance while traveling, and I realized it had been far too long since I visited this fair town."

"Lady Whelan! Sure enough, there you are. Didn't expect we'd be seeing you until the autumn was all done." The apothecary seemed equally delighted to see Kate, though somehow he had overlooked her presence before his counter until that moment. "It's right good to see you, my lady. Out and about in your state."

"Ah—what state is that?"

"Why, your widowhood." He blinked saucer-round eyes. "Got some letters for you, I have, that come earlier today, if you'd like them? Or someone'll come from the house tomorrow."

"I'll take them. Thank you."

"If you're sure? Don't want to trouble you in your time of grief."

Kate looked at him oddly. "It's perfectly fine. I am not in mourning anymore, Mr. Petty, and even if I were, I would be willing to accept mail."

Petty returned her odd gaze. "Not in mourning anymore, my lady?"

"It's been two years since the late earl passed." She tried on a smile. "The time has, perhaps, passed quickly for a busy man such as yourself. And Thurles is thick with dowager countesses." Good Old Gwyn would never let anyone forget the crushing burden of her loss; Kate wanted only to set it aside.

When Petty relinquished the mail to Kate, Evan gave Petty a letter of his own to be posted.

The smaller man regarded it with sharp blue eyes. "Writing to England, eh? And you just come from there?"

Petty did not number among his faults a lack of curiosity. His question awoke Kate's own, and she craned her neck to see the direction on the folded paper. What she saw made her head snap back with surprise. "You're writing to my father?"

"I should have written to him from the road," Evan said. "Your father wants to find himself an Anne Jones, and my parents might know the right one."

Ah. That made sense. "I wouldn't venture to promise that for all the tea in China or all the Anne Joneses in Wales," she replied lightly. "But why does—"

Her question was cut off by another jingle of the bell. "Ah, it's a good afternoon for business despite the rain!" Petty hurried around the counter on bandy legs.

This time it was Janet Ahearn, a middle-aged spinster of pinched features and heavy lilting accent. "Mr. Petty, the last packet of pastilles you made for me fell into powder within a day. I must have more!"

"Of course, of course. And what size of a packet will you be needing, then?"

"A large one, I think," she sniffed. "Larger than the last. Say—make it six, I think. I shall distribute them to the ill as needed. And I'll need the same in a week's time."

"Week's…time…" repeated Petty, scribbling notes on a slip of paper with a stub of pencil. "Very good, very good."

When he finished writing, he stuffed the paper and pencil into his waistcoat pocket. "Look who we've here, Miss Ahearn."

"Oh, heavens! Mr. Rhys." The spinster's sour, narrow features relaxed. "Why, isn't that a fair sight! And how are you, sir?"

"I might as well start opening the mail," Kate murmured to Susan. "It'll give me something to do while Mr. Rhys finishes making his greetings."

And, in fact, she did so—or at least flipped through the bundle of letters. Estate business. Estate business. Estate business. A bill. Another bill. All while Petty's errand boy ran into the street and shouted for all and sundry to come greet Mr. Rhys.

Honestly. It was as though they thought Evan were back from the dead.

A prickle of guilt darted through her. Surely their delight could be understood. He was Con's friend, and everyone had loved Con. Seeing Evan again—half of the pair of handsome rogues—was like getting Con back as well.

Or so they must be thinking. Kate had never found the two to be much alike, and with the distance of years in which she and Evan had grown past Con, she could not equate the longtime friends. It did a service to neither to compare them, and Evan deserved every cheerful greeting on his own merits.

Kate held up her post before her face, pretending to study the directions while she instead listened.

"If your pastilles fall to powder again," Evan told Miss Ahearn confidentially, "you could mix the powder with mulled wine."

That lady's brows and voice lowered, interested. "Will that increase the medicinal effect?"

"I've no idea," said Evan, "but then you'll have a glass of mulled wine."

Sour Miss Ahearn actually *chuckled* at this. "Such warmth is a comfort on a rainy autumn day."

"Dr. Rhys's prescription, then." Evan laughed. When the errand boy returned, Evan gave him a few pennies to buy sweet rolls for himself and his young friends at the baker's.

At Ardent House, Kate had worked so hard to get Evan to laugh. Now the laughter came easily, bubbling out as though Thurles had tapped into a spring of delight.

She had never experienced such a feeling. As Lady Whelan, she was near but not of the town, which was full of Irish. Catholics. People who had known each other for generations. People who worked for a living and played with equal fervor. They took pride in their racecourse, in the rich history of the chase. Evan shared their easeful fondness, and Con had too.

Kate had supported her husband by caring for the children and minding the estate—but in so doing, she realized, she'd not made a place of her own in the town. Instead she perceived a tautness between herself and the people of her late husband's estate. She might be Lady Whelan, but she was also English-born. Her name betrayed her. Her accent betrayed her. She was a foreigner in Ireland, bound here by the children she had created.

As word circulated about the return of the travelers—no doubt sped along by the sight of an unknown carriage before Petty's store—the small shop began to crowd. The people of Thurles greeted Kate with deference and condolence—a condolence that unsettled her with its scrupulous politeness.

The people of Thurles were accustomed still to treating Kate as though she were glass-fragile. Their voices dropped, their eyes went somber, and their mouths solemn.

The widowed countess. *Widow widow widow.*

Once a man died, all his flaws were forgotten. *Poor Lady Whelan. How could she ever recover?*

It had been two years. She *was* recovered, if only she could bring the town to see it. She was Kate, not merely Con's widow.

She made polite chat, but it was Evan whom the villagers wanted to see. Words spilled forth, as if people had been holding questions from him at the tips of their tongues. *Mr. Rhys! My man found the quaintest little old statue while digging in the garden. Can you give it a look?*

Mr. Rhys, are you to ride in the chase?

Mr. Rhys, we did see a handbill for your lecture. Is it true there's smuggling hereabouts?

This last question drew a protest from Miss Ahearn. "This far up the river from the sea? Nonsense.

Smugglers wouldn't bother. Besides, Thurles is a proper sort of town."

"I'm here to find that out," Evan replied. "Not that I doubt Thurles is proper. Or I didn't until I returned to it."

Petty gave a scratchy chuckle. "Mr. Rhys, you've a tongue made for blarney. Sure you're not Irish?"

Evan laughed. "Only in my dreams. Lady Whelan! Come out from behind those letters, won't you? Poor Lady Whelan, she has been suffering from my glib tongue since Newmarket."

Kate recognized this as an invitation to enter the conversation. "Only since Newmarket?" She handed off her letters to Susan, feigning surprise. "Why, I should have said since Cambridge. You've been entertaining me with your saucy tongue since your even saucier lecture."

"You heard him lecture, Lady Whelan?" This was asked by a serving girl from the Prancing Pony, a pretty village woman of no more than twenty. "What was it like?"

"I'm right here," Evan said, "so mind you say nice things."

"What other sort of thing could there be to say?" Kate waved a careless hand. "Mr. Rhys's lecture was so fascinating that my brother vowed he would begin collecting flint."

"He *did*?" This from the wide-eyed serving girl.

"No, he didn't." Evan frowned. "He said he had to see a man about a horse."

Kate felt like teasing him. "True, but as you know, in Newmarket cant, 'man' means 'excavation site' and 'horse' means 'flint.' Well, 'any sort of ancient artifact,' but Jonah meant flint in particular."

Evan arched a brow at her. "Did he, now?"

"Oh, yes." Kate tapped her temple. "We have the twin connection."

"You have a *twin*?" breathed the serving girl. Somehow every question involved her pressing against Evan, surely more than the movement of the people in the shop required.

Kate could hardly fault the young woman, for Evan was a treat to look at—thick dark unruly hair, and the careless, useful cut of his clothing. Stubble that had grown out during the day's travel, splashes of mud on his boots from the road. And those hands…

Those hands, those hands. He had touched her and tickled her on every bit of her body. For that time, she felt beautiful.

Now she felt lumpy again.

Enough of that. She must try harder, that was all. The next person who entered, Kate would speak to without the smallest hesitation.

She soon regretted this vow, for the next person to enter was Finnian Driscoll. Resident magistrate and holder of the bulk of Con's debts, he was a well-fed, well-pleased man of late middle age. His great belly, biscuit-colored coat, and red waistcoat made him look, from the side, as though he were carrying a drum before him.

He had served as resident magistrate since the role was established four years before. As a native of Ireland who had served as an officer in the British Army, he'd done well reconciling the English rulers with the Irish villagers. Privately, Kate thought it was because he went to every church service—making himself both Catholic and Church of Ireland, yet neither. All he needed now to establish himself at the pinnacle of Thurles society was land.

Whelan land. And without a miracle, he would get it at year's end.

"How do you do, Mr. Driscoll?" There was hardly room for the magistrate and his capacious belly to slide up to the apothecary's counter.

"Why, Lady Whelan! What a treat." Driscoll made his bow, curtailed by the close quarters. "We didn't expect you back so soon, with the second week of races in Newmarket only just complete." He looked over her shoulder. "And I heard Mr. Rhys, didn't I? There's a treat too. Didn't expect him to be traveling with you."

"I am full of surprises," Kate said. "A woman of various and startling gifts."

Driscoll ignored this reply, holding out hands against the press of the crowd. "Now, now, everyone, don't be bothering the countess. Leave her be. She must be tired after all her travel."

"Mr. Rhys traveled as long as I did," she pointed out.

He lifted graying brows. "But you're fragile."

"I most certainly am not."

"Ah, you're that brave to say so." He shook his head. "If you're not careful, you'll wear yourself to a sliver."

"I could not become a sliver if I tried my damnedest," she muttered, but Driscoll was already turning to greet Evan.

Thus it always went. Had gone, ever since Con's

death. For her own good, Driscoll looked out for her. Ignored her protests. He talked of her as though she were enfeebled—and who might hear and believe him?

Was this why the townspeople treated her as a widow of glass?

She wasn't in the mood for conversation after all.

"I need some air," she said to Susan. "Come or stay as you wish. I'm neither fragile nor a sliver, and I'm all right on my own."

It was not difficult to slip between jostling townsfolk. They took little notice of a small, roundish woman as they gloried in cheerful conversation. The bell at the shop door jingled to free Kate, and she stepped out into the drizzle to take great gulps of fresh, damp air.

Returning to Thurles was not the homecoming she'd expected. She was back to being a countess, her idyll in England over.

Yet had it been an idyll? How could it have been, when she had never understood whom to be?

Except for one night, came the treacherous memory.

Not that it mattered now. Evan had so many friends here he didn't need another. A petulant thought, and one she tried at once to quash. She returned to the carriage, settling into the enclosed space that now seemed less small than the spaces around it.

When Evan and Susan joined her, beaming at having encountered so many familiar faces, Kate knocked at the roof for the driver to take them to their destination.

"Amazing, Mr. Rhys, the number of people who remember you after two years," burbled the maid.

"It goes to show," Evan said, "that I should not have stayed away so long."

"If you had not," Kate replied, "everything would have been different." She did not know whether this would have been good or bad.

West of the town center lay the looping racecourse. "You have utterly confounded that poor serving girl," said Evan to Kate. "She's now convinced that I led the race meetings at Newmarket, which were in truth coordinated excavations of ancient dwellings."

"Yet you didn't stay for the second week of races? For shame, Mr. Rhys," said Kate. "How will they get along without you?"

"You would be amazed," he said drily, "how well people get along without me."

He was looking out the window when he said this. By now, she recalled his mannerisms well enough to suspect he was hiding some starkness on his mobile features.

"Just because they can," she answered, "doesn't mean it's what they prefer."

Anne Jones—or Janet Ahearn, as they knew her here—saw the letter directed to Sir William Chandler. Petty had laid it on the counter, a careful carelessness of the sort they had worked out years before.

Sir William Chandler. The name was a threat and a promise, a memory and a hope. What had Rhys learned, and what would Rhys tell him? Not who Janet Ahearn truly was, she was sure. After years of slipping beneath notice, she could tell when someone's view of her had changed.

Once she had been a soldier's wife, and then, after being widowed in Spain, a courtesan. Sir William had known her as such thirteen years before. He had not known, until a few months ago, that she had borne his child.

He had left Spain in 1805 as little more than a corpse, stricken by a virulent palsy that stripped the strength from his hale limbs. She understood, then, that he would have concern for no other body but his own.

Once in England again, with all his wealth at his disposal, he recovered. He did not regain the use of his legs, but his health and vigor—by all accounts—were restored.

Anne remained behind in Spain, impoverished and forgotten. Anne did not have the luxury of caring only for herself, as Sir William's babe grew within her. That was when she decided she would do anything, be anything, never to be left powerless again.

Her time in Thurles had a double advantage. It was near Sir William's legitimate daughter. And it was near Loughmoe Castle, from where the wild geese had flown. The geese—rich Catholics who fled Ireland when the Jacobite movement failed—were hated by all those who remained. Their riches were stripped, even the stones of their castles unseated.

It had been Anne's idea to turn those stones to advantage. Anne's, to set the Whelan tenants to carving instead of farming. Smuggling was steadier income than tending the land. With her network of willing recipients on the shores of Wales and France, she saw to that. Thurles was far enough inland to evade notice, but it had a fine river that trailed to the sea, and a watchtower from which she could post notice at all times. Why, she had even pulled the apothecary into the matter. *Packets of pastilles* were nothing of the sort. That old fool Petty enjoyed the adventure of it.

For years she had traveled Great Britain, taking frequent absences from Thurles under the guise of visiting family. She had watched and waited. She'd had her failures—Rosalind Agate had slipped from her power and wed Sir William's younger son—but no matter. Sir William's heart had many ties. None were to Anne.

One was to this eldest daughter of his, this Kate. Already she had become a widow, but there was so much more she could lose.

Fifteen

To Kate, being on the Whelan lands again was the drawing near of a purpose. But as soon as the carriage entered those lands, it felt like the beginning of good-bye.

Good-bye to the land that had so long cradled the earldom.

Good-bye, in a few months, to Evan, who would cross not one sea but two, and would be forever beyond reach.

Kate pressed her face to the window and tried not to think of that.

Stubble dotted the fields, which would soon be burned and drilled for winter barley and wheat planting. All through the coldest months, seeds would slumber, then awaken in spring and stretch toward the sun.

Then came the pastures, where even in autumn, Ireland clasped its green to heart. The grass was nourished and bright from crisp mornings and impish midland rains, and here short, stocky black cows roamed and lowed.

As the carriage rolled along the road, they reached the drive and gardens of Whelan House—which was *not* maintained by the cows, as Kate had told Evan's family. The over-spreading trees were turning to copper and gilt, carpeting the paths and roads with their fallen leaves.

Then the trees opened to sky, and the stately home came into view. It was an ancient H with gabled wings, gray stone walls, a roof of deeper slate, and fat stone chimneys exhaling the ash-brown of peat smoke. The face of the house was covered with clinging vines, their summer-green leaves tinted scarlet or drying to brown.

Whelan House. An unimaginative name, wasn't it? Like Chandler Hall. Before traveling to Ireland, Kate had believed it a land of music and fable, where the names tripped off the tongue like brook water over pebbles. Tipperary. Ballyclare. Tullamore.

Ah, well. After an education at Harrow and Oxford, Con was more English than Irish. So had it gone for generations with the Whelans. Already, Good Old Gwyn was wondering when Declan would be sent away to school.

Evan had gone silent some time before, but he spoke as the laden carriage reached the front steps. "I've never been to this house without the sure knowledge of Con's return." His tone was wondering, tight with loss.

"I have done so," Kate said. "Many times. Many days on end."

She couldn't add *one gets used to it*, because a missing life was not something one ever got used to. "It gets… more familiar."

The structure of Whelan House was ancient, built as though people of the past cared for neither air nor light. There was nothing so snug as the walls, especially in winter, but Kate always felt she were shut up in a box.

This was the shape of the role of the Countess of Whelan. And this was the closest place she had to a home.

In the drawing room that evening, Evan whispered into Kate's ear. "Does Good Old Gwyn come over *every* evening, or is this a welcome home treat for us?"

He had entertained a fantasy of one of those warm, unspooling evenings before a slow fire of turves, with or without a tumbler of whisky. But the arrival of the dowager had just been announced, and Kate had ordered tea to be served in the drawing room.

She sighed. "I did not overlook the emphasis you laid on the word *treat*," Kate said. "But I must admit her visit is no compliment to you. Since Con's death, she has been here for dinner, tea, or supper nearly every day. I've no idea what she ate while I was in England."

Evan closed his eyes in pity. "The dower house is at far too easy a distance."

"I have had the same thought before. Though to be fair, she has to bring back the children today."

Before Gwyn could creak her way into the drawing room, two small figures whipped through the doorway.

"Nora! Declan!" Kate hopped to her feet, holding

out her arms. "I'm so glad to see you! And I've brought you both surprises."

"Not toys, I hope," said a boyish voice. "I'm too old for—Uncle Evan!"

Evan, too, was standing in greeting. "Too old for Uncle Evan? I hope not. You'll have me weeping, and I only have one handkerchief left."

He looked at Kate quickly. Excellent. She had colored, as if recalling how they had used one of his handkerchiefs. He'd had to discard it. Fortunate handkerchief. Would that they could all be used so happily.

He returned his attention to the children. "Good Lord, you've both sprouted."

Nine-year-old Declan had shot up tall, his height inherited from Conall. He had Con's coloring, too: hair of medium brown, dark eyes, and skin ready to tan. In his chin, though, was a dimple like Kate's.

At twelve, Nora was more like her mother, with fine features and a pale complexion. Her hair was dark like Declan's, and she wore it in a long plait.

"Come give us hugs," he said. "But your mother first, or she'll catch fire from her eagerness to see you."

"The flames are starting to prickle all over me," Kate quavered. "Come beat them out with your arms!"

Giggling, Nora slammed into her mother's arms. "The fire is out!"

"It's out, yes." With a smacking kiss on the cheek, Kate hugged the girl.

"You were gone too long! I almost forgot what you looked like!"

"Dear me." Kate met Evan's eyes over Nora's dark head, smiling. "I should have drawn you a picture."

"I remembered," said Declan, taking his turn for a hug. "You look like Nora. I had to look at her the whole time you were gone."

"Lucky you," replied the girl, waltzing past her brother with her tongue out.

Evan laughed. He was shocked by how good it was to see them—and a little sad to see the changes time had wrought. They had grown, and he had not seen it happen. They had found new books to love, new things to laugh at, and much to cry over, and he had not been there to share in their feelings.

If he'd been here, it could only have been because he was a different person with no care for how he and Con had parted. It could only have been if Con were different too.

But...damn. He wished things had been different.

He gave a quick scrub to Declan's shock of dark hair, then tweaked the end of Nora's plait. "Look at you. You are a young lady now."

She scuffed a shoe against the carpet. "I am not. I run too much and freckle too much and shout too much."

"Too much for whom?"

"Too much to be a lady. Nan says so."

"A lady," Evan whispered into Nora's ear, "is someone worthy of respect. That's all. Ask your mother, and see if she doesn't agree."

"I can't ask her that!" Nora's eyes went wide with shock. "That's too embarrassing."

Declan raced to the doorway, then peered into the corridor. "Nan's coming. She must have used the necessary before she walked over here."

"Declan, you shouldn't talk about that," said Nora with the importance of an older sibling.

"Why not? Everyone uses it," said the boy. "That's why it's called the necessary."

Kate sidled to Evan's side. "They're on their best behavior for you. Aren't you pleased?"

"Extremely. If no one talked about excretion, I would think I was in the wrong house. And what ought I to expect from Good Old Gwyn?"

"Good Old Gwyn," Kate whispered, "is just as she always was, only more so. I plan to try something I learned from your sister-in-law."

"From Elena? What is that?"

"Complete and total agreement." Her eyes narrowed with sly humor.

Evan entered into the spirit of the exchange. "That might be entertaining. What should I do? Shall I agree with her too?"

"I don't think you need to. In fact, it might be more fun if you didn't."

The elder countess, frail and drooping in appearance, walked in supported by the arms of two footmen. "Kate! You've no idea what I've been through."

"I don't, that's true," Kate said cheerfully. "Children, would you like to stay, or would you rather visit the kitchen?"

"Kitchen! Kitchen!" Declan whooped. "I'm so starving, I could eat a cow."

"I'll go with him," Nora said. "To make sure he *doesn't* eat a cow." They made their bows to the room, then raced to the doorway. In the corridor, their hard-heeled shoes clacked on the floor, the sound fading with distance.

"My nerves," moaned Gwyn. "My poor nerves." She had by now settled onto a long sofa covered in heavy dark damask, a furniture piece Evan recalled from his last visit to Whelan House.

The slipper chairs into which he and Kate settled were the same, as were the red draperies and the deep-piled carpet, now worn before the hearth. Little had changed in the room or in the house since Con had died. If spendthrift Con had lived, he would have had the rooms redone twice over.

Gwyn put her feet up on the sofa, leaning against a pyramid of cushions bolstered against one arm. "It is good to see you at last, Evan." Her voice quavered.

Her face was heavily lined and powdered. To some, these might seem signs of great age. But Gwyn, dowager Countess Whelan, had looked and behaved this way for as long as Evan could remember. In her own way, Gwyn was as skilled at firing tiny darts as were his parents.

"I am always hearing that sort of thing," he replied. "The people of Thurles were most welcoming too."

"Common people." She lifted a fluttery hand to her brow.

"They are common," Kate agreed. "In the sense that there are many of them. Or do you think people of good sense should *not* be glad to see Evan?"

The older woman blinked at Kate with utter incomprehension.

"They probably shouldn't," Evan agreed cheerfully. "I'm the devil of a guest."

The dowager rallied. "And what has brought you back here? Loyalty, no doubt. Missing those who were once as your family."

If Kate would be shockingly agreeable, he'd be the opposite. "Not a bit of it. I need to confirm some stone samples. Maybe explore the ruined castles hereabouts."

"Work! Always work! I know men haven't the hearts that women do. But you were the closest thing I had to a son since Con died."

"Only since then?"

Kate cleared her throat. "What can I get you, Gwyn?"

The effect was instant and delightful: the dowager shot upright, scattering cushions to the floor. "You dare call me by my Christian name?"

"Yes, indeed." Kate blinked as placidly as one of the little black cows she pastured. "You have always called me by mine, and therefore you clearly wish for greater familiarity. Which makes sense, as I am your nearest living relative and the mother of your grandchildren. I must apologize that it took me so long to grasp your preference."

"I need a headache powder." Gwyn swung her feet to the floor, half-rising. "It's no use to ask for one—"

"Of course it is!" Kate sprang from her chair. "I'll ring for a maid, and you can go with her to the still-room and show her exactly how you want it prepared. You know best about your own health."

With a sniffle, Gwyn plumped back onto the sofa seat. "I haven't the energy to rise right now."

Good Lord. Kate put up with this every day? Gwyn's demands were no kind of a replacement for a friendly evening of chat. Even the fire, with its rounded bricks of peat, flickered in seeming exasperation.

Before Evan could protest, Kate was speaking in a soothing tone. "I understand, Gwyn. You must be exhausted after taking such tender care of the children. We'll cover you with a blanket and leave you to rest."

"I'll manage." One of Gwyn's feet came down right onto a fallen cushion. "Is there anything left from dinner? A little something to soothe my nerves…"

Kate sat again, then looked at Evan, questioning. "Oyster patties, I think?"

"Maybe a few," said Evan. "I ate them as though I were a shark. And Nora and Declan have probably finished the remaining ones."

"Oysters? Such a common food!" Gwyn's mouth pursed. "Con would never have allowed oysters on the table."

"That's true," Kate said. "He preferred much costlier food."

"And now you eat oysters in his absence!" God. The dowager could make eating oysters sound like a moral trespass worthy of an eternity of fire and brimstone.

Kate's eyes were hard, but her tone was honeyed. "We do. We must retrench."

Of all her agreements with Gwyn's nonsense, this was the first one that rang completely true. He took her side with the most ridiculous comment he could think of. "If the vicar hasn't forbidden the eating of oysters, surely it's permissible."

Gwyn sniffed. "Just because he has not forbidden it does not mean it's not *wrong*."

With weary docility, Kate replied, "I agree. There must be many things that are wrong that the vicar has not yet addressed."

Evan pushed back. "What about hoisting a sheep through a window? Con and I did that once at school."

A smile touched Kate's lips. "Quite wrong, surely."

"Or riding a horse into church? We did that too. Well, I rode and Con led the horse."

"I should have to ask the vicar," said Kate. "Likely you were both wrong, but one of you was more wrong than the other. I shall ask him about that when I ask if I may eat oysters anymore."

"You may not," said Evan, "for the oyster season is over. Today's patties were the last available."

"This is true. I shall ask ahead for next year."

Gwyn tracked this exchange with watery eyes, doubtless wondering where she could stick out a verbal foot. "You shall make me sob with all your talk of Con!" she burst out.

"I could remind you of him by putting a sheep through your bedchamber window," Evan said.

"Oh! You make mock of me."

Evan shrugged. "Not really. The sheep was Con's idea."

At that moment, the children thundered back into the drawing room. "We ate all the oyster patties," announced Nora. "Cook said she was saving them for you, Uncle Evan, but—"

"We told her we were starving!" Declan sounded proud. "And she gave them to us with extra melted butter."

"Oysters," groaned Gwyn. "Starving! After all I've done..."

"How about a game?" Kate said brightly. "Let's play *who's-the-saddest*, and see which of us can be the most morose."

"Ah—no, thank you," Evan broke in with hurried

words. God. That was the sort of invitation Gwyn did *not* need. "That's not the sort of game that has a winner. Who would like to see my magic lantern?"

"I would!" said Declan. "Do you have any horrid slides?"

"That depends on what you think of my artistic abilities."

"Uncle Evan's slides are not horrid," said Kate. "They're clever."

He knew she was being "agreeable" Kate, yet the compliment was like a warm touch. "Thank you."

"Awww." Declan kicked the side of his grandmother's sofa. "I wanted to see something disgusting."

"Forgery of historical artifacts for the purposes of smuggling *is* disgusting," Evan said in his serious-lecturer voice. Declan laughed.

"I cannot bear the sight of a magic lantern." Gwyn sighed. "That bright lamp! The glass slides! An abomination against human eyesight. No, no, you must excuse me."

"Very well," said Kate, almost too quickly for politeness. "You may certainly be excused."

"I'll fetch my lantern case," Evan said.

Kate followed him to the doorway of the drawing room. "Now you have the full experience of residents of Whelan House," she whispered. "How did this compare to dinner with your family? Which was the more torturous ordeal?"

She was flushed and pretty, curious and indignant, and he wanted nothing more than to collect her in a crushing embrace. "The dinner with my family was far more torturous," he replied. "Except for the bits with you. I do love watching you play the delightful brat."

"You could try to sound a little less triumphant," she said, but she sounded mollified.

"I could, but I don't want to. It's nice being Gwyn's golden boy for a few minutes. Did you hear how pleased she was to see me?"

"You almost sound serious."

"Do I? I shouldn't have let that happen. Terrible habit to get into." His heart beat more quickly as she looked at him. Close enough to see within him—close enough to kiss.

"So you say," she said. "But I know better. One of us must change."

From her glance backward toward the sofa, from which her mother-in-law was rising, Evan understood that by *us*, she meant herself and Gwyn.

"Why only one?" he asked, and he included himself too.

Kate could not remember the last time she had enjoyed one of her mother-in-law's visits more—or at all. But the enjoyment came only from testing the strangling bond between them.

She had not needed to let Good Old Gwyn take over the manor house for all these years, had she? And she had not needed to be alone.

Had she done the best she could?

Was she doing her best, even now? She'd played the—what had Evan called it? The delightful brat again, and she felt shaky.

Con had been Gwyn's only child, and Kate had allowed her mother-in-law the refuge of deep grief. But it was not a feeling on which she wished to dwell. Not after the first shock of Con's loss, and certainly not now. Gwyn was as mired in loss as the people of Thurles expected Kate to be.

If she were not lost, how ought she to feel instead?

As Evan lit a lamp and set up his magic lantern, Kate exited the drawing room and closed the door on everything she wanted. Peace. Warmth. The smiles of her children.

Instead, she retrieved a pistol and powder from the locked gun case in the study. Exiting through the front door into the sunset coolness of evening, she tacked a slip of paper to a tree and shot a tidy hole through all her questions.

Sixteen

THE FOLLOWING MORNING, EVAN DESCENDED FROM his customary guest bedchamber—another spot in Whelan House that had changed not at all—to find the servants in a bustle.

Declan and Nora, it seemed, had been absent from the nursery since their governess rose, and they had not returned in time for the morning's lessons. The house had been searched from attic to cellar—but quietly, so as not to disturb Lady Whelan. The countess had been in the study since dawn, sorting through the accumulated papers of her absence, and doubtless would not take kindly to the news that her children had been misplaced the day after her return.

"The rogue housekeeper has returned," Evan murmured. In a normal tone, he asked the *actual* housekeeper, "Do the children run away from their lessons often?"

"They didn't used to." Mrs. Teagan, plump and black-clad like every housekeeper Evan had ever seen, clasped her hands in worry. "But these last few months they have, and it's a fuss every time."

Maybe the fuss is what they like. But Evan kept this thought to himself, only asking, "Have any of the grounds been searched? Or have the servants combed only the house?"

"Only the house as yet, Mr. Rhys. Why—have you an idea?"

"I have," he said.

Where else would the children of a Chandler and an Irish earl go when distressed, but the stables?

He left the house, crossing the grounds, and soon reached his destination. The stables of Whelan House were of solid old stone construction, like the manor house. Also like the house, they had been maintained well, and much had been done to make them comfortable. The windows were large, the floors slightly sloping for drainage. The walls were thick, hushing the space within, and the earthy scents of horse and manure and grass-sweet straw were as comforting as a fire on a cold night.

In short, it was a good place to hide from one's lessons. A good place to come even if one had nothing to hide from. Although what that might be like, Evan couldn't say.

He walked from stall to stall, peering in, catching grooms at work, noting a few empty stalls where animals had been sold. But horses kept for everyday work or for the steeplechase were less expensive and finicky than Thoroughbreds, and Evan was relieved to note that most of the empty stalls were being mucked out—indicating that their inhabitants were at pasture or being exercised.

And then he spotted them: two dark-haired

children, not even trying to hide as they curried Lady Alix. They had put her on a lead and taken her from her stall. Declan had shrugged off his jacket, and Nora had strewn her shoes and stockings on the floor.

Lady Alix turned her head toward Evan and fixed him with a tolerant gaze. *Children. What can one do?*

When Declan and Nora didn't look up, he knocked on the swinging door of the cob's vacated stall. "Oy, you two. Have you become stable hands?"

"Hullo, Uncle Evan." Nora passed a currycomb over the mare's barrel in a gentle, practiced pattern. "When I took off my shoes, she tried to eat them. Can you believe it?"

"I can, actually."

"I want to be a stable hand." Declan was combing out the mare's long tail, standing in just the right place to avoid a kick.

"And what are you two doing out here?"

"We had to meet the new horse," Nora said innocently. "Watch this." She picked up a fallen stocking and draped it over the cob's head. Lady Alix rolled her eyes upward, curious, then shook her head until the stocking fell to the ground again. "She didn't try to eat it that time, but sometimes she does."

"She likes tossing things to the floor," Evan said. "You've found her favorite game. Congratulations." He swung open the stall door. "But it's not the right time to play destroy-the-stockings with my horse, you know."

Declan frowned. "You're here because we ran away from lessons."

"Smart lad, not to pose that as a question," Evan

said. "Yes. To be specific, I'm here because the servants were worried that they couldn't find you."

"I'm glad they couldn't find us," Nora replied. "We didn't want to be found."

Evan stepped onto the bottom of the z-shaped frame at the stall door's back. He kicked off from the floor, riding the arc of the door as it swung fully open, then began to shut. "You know," he said idly, "your governess might lose her post if you don't learn."

"I don't want a governess," said Nora.

"I don't want to learn," Declan replied.

"Fair enough. I was the same way at your ages."

Declan waved at him with the comb. "And you grew up right enough."

Lady Alix tossed her head. Smart girl.

"Did I?" For the most part, he supposed he had. He had not lacked for comforts, and he had been safe and content. But the broad arc of his life—hopeless love from the age of twenty-one, life lived under a cloud of grayness—he would not wish on anyone.

"I didn't say I was allowed to have what I wanted, you might note. Only that I wanted it." The hinges of the stable door creaked, and Evan stepped to the floor, easing the door back into its open position. "You've got to decide for yourselves what sort of people you want to be. But I can tell you, I've never been sorry to learn something. Only *not* to learn something. And *I* never had to administer an earldom or entice a gentleman into falling at my feet."

"Disgusting," said Declan.

Nora giggled. "It sounds awful."

Maybe, just maybe, they had listened to him—so

before he could be tempted to use the serious-lecturer voice again, he turned the subject. "How did you like your gifts from England?"

"I liked Nan's." Nora curried a spot she had surely curried twice already, while Lady Alix bent her head to nibble loose straw on the stable floor. "Mama gave her a prayer book, did you know? I liked the face Nan made when she opened it."

"It looked like she ate moldy cheese!" Declan crowed.

"*I* got *ribbons*. And *cloth*." Nora spoke these words with such scorn she might as well have been talking of moldy cheese herself. "She wants me to *grow up* and be a *lady*."

"Oh, the horror of it." Evan leaned against a latched stall door. "Are you sure that's what she meant, Nora?"

"I'm *twelve*. I'll have to leave the schoolroom soon and wear long dresses and never take off my stockings to put them on a horse's head."

Well, shite. He hadn't a clue what to say to this sort of youthful feminine distress. "I think," he ventured, "your mother wants you to have what she hasn't. New things, made the way you like them. And remember what I said about being a lady? You already are one, because you have worth."

Nora opened her mouth to protest.

"No, sorry," Evan said. "No protests. I'm right. You're a lady, and your mother loves you and wants good things for you. It's a heavy burden, but it's yours."

Nora closed her mouth and tried not to smile.

"What about me?" Declan asked. "Why did Mama bring me toy soldiers?"

This, Evan had to think about. "Maybe because she's good at shooting."

"That's for damn sure," said Declan.

"You'll have to excuse him," Nora said. "He says *that word* all the time."

"I'll try to bear up." Evan folded his arms. "How was it staying with your Nan?"

"Fine," Nora said. "I'd rather be home."

Declan pulled a face. "We still had to have lessons."

"To be expected," Evan said. "If the ten plagues of Egypt cover the land, lessons will still remain."

"Is that in Nan's prayer book?" Declan asked.

Nora cuffed her brother with the currycomb. "She didn't see us much. Mostly, she was in her chamber. When I saw her through the open door."

"You opened the door! Spy!" the boy hooted.

"It swung open," Nora said hotly. "I bumped it by accident."

"On the *handle*."

Evan held up a quelling hand, and Nora continued. "She was looking out the window a lot. I think she's sad."

"Why, was she looking at Whelan House?" Evan could not recall the arrangement of the dower house.

"No, the other way. North, toward the woods."

"Maybe she was watching the riders," Declan suggested. "People are always riding through the woods to practice for the chase."

"I wish *I* could ride in the chase," Nora said. "Mama rode in it every year except for the years Declan and I were born."

"I remember that. I saw her ride, time and again."

Evan was delighted by the memory that came to mind. Kate, flushed and whooping, guiding her cob over jumps and hedges with grace and glee.

"Da did too, every year. And now chase season is beginning, and everyone in Thurles will be utterly boring about it." Declan said this with the desperate scorn of a boy who wanted very much to take part in the forbidden activity.

From past years, Evan remembered this season. *The chase* was a point-to-point race, held every November when the ground was soft and spongy. Formal chases for purses were held on the Thurles racecourse, but a steeplechase could be any good pounding race across terrain, held for any wager at any time.

"Maybe someday you'll be a part of it," Evan said. "Now, tell me what you think of Lady Alix. You've buffed her till she's gleaming."

"She's funny." Nora set aside the currycomb. "But she *did* ruin my stockings."

"I think her name should be Spider." Declan regarded the neat tail with pride, then tossed the comb to Nora for her to place alongside the currycomb.

"Why is that?" Evan had to ask.

"Because Declan always wants to name the horses something horrible," Nora grumbled.

Evan covered a laugh. "Spiders make fine webs. Lady Alix can step a beautiful pattern, so the name wouldn't fit her ill. But she'd miss her honorific, I think. Would you like to ride her sometime?"

"We don't ride." Nora walked to the nearest stall, tested the latch, then walked to the next and did the same. And on and on. "We used to. But we don't ride anymore."

A deep vein of capped emotion ran through those words: worried, discouraged, resigned. *We don't ride anymore.* The children of Con and Kate, who had been seated on horses practically the moment they could walk.

Well. Damnation.

"Ah," Evan said. "I—all right, look. I've always been frank with you two, haven't I?"

Declan unfastened Lady Alix's lead. "Except for the time I asked you what would happen if I rode a horse indoors, and you said it wasn't possible."

"I *think* I said horses don't like it," Evan said. "Though what I meant was that mothers don't like it."

"That's for damn sure." Declan walked alongside Lady Alix's head, guiding the cob back into her stall. The mare knocked Nora's discarded shoes with her hooves as she walked by, snorting her satisfaction.

"They also don't like it when you say *damn*," said Nora.

"You said it," Declan pointed out.

"Only when Mama didn't hear it."

"She didn't hear me either!"

Evan rolled his eyes. "We could go on like this all day, and it would be a great joy to me." Both children blew him raspberries. "But here is something I want to know. Why do you not ride anymore?"

Nora shook another stall door, testing the latch. "You're going to tell us we ought to, aren't you?"

"God, no." Evan helped Declan close the stall door on Lady Alix, then reached over it to remove the pony's halter. "I'd tell you that you ought to be respectful and polite, and not say *damn* around your mother. And I'd tell you that you ought to give her a cracking great hug when you return to the house this morning. But I'd never tell you that you ought to ride."

When he turned around, halter in hand, two suspicious faces peered at him. "Why not?"

Because I hate it when people say "ought to" to me. "What business is it of mine?"

"But you just asked us," Nora pointed out.

"You are remarkably intelligent. You take after your godfather. As a matter of fact, I did ask why you do not ride, but only because I want to help you and your mother if I can. Mothers love their children, you see, and they want the best for their children."

This was sincere, though in his experience *best* meant *what I think you ought to be*.

"If you are worried," Evan concluded, "and it is something that she can help with, then she would want to."

Declan kicked at a scatter of straw. "What if she can't?"

"Then she'd probably like to know that. So she'd know she was doing everything she could."

"I don't want her to do anything else." Nora gave a stall door a fierce rattle, making Lady Alix snort her dismay. "I want her to stay with us and not go away again, and I don't want anything to change."

"I've heard that before," Evan mumbled.

"We don't ride anymore," said Declan, "because she doesn't. It makes her worried."

Evan nodded, slowly. "So you want your mother to be with you more. And you don't want her to be worried."

"Yes, and not have to pretend like *we're* not worried. Da died in a fall, and that was horrid." Declan took the halter from Evan, then found a cleaning cloth. "But we also don't want to have to *be* worried, because sometimes we just want to…to be."

"That's for damn sure," Evan muttered.

This was an instantly popular thing to say. "You said damn again. You shouldn't say damn. Mama wouldn't like it if she heard you say damn."

"Declan. Stop."

"I like being with the horses," said Nora, "and I think I would like to ride again. But the tack room is all locked up, and Mama sold the carriages, all except two."

"She sold all the best ones," complained the boy. "The shiny fast ones."

"Who was going to drive them? You?" Nora marched back down the row of stalls, then hung up the lead line.

"Mama could," said Declan. "She's a ripping driver. And I could learn someday. So could you."

Nora wheeled, all excitement. "Maybe you could teach us, Uncle Evan. Now that you're here, we could learn how to drive four-in-hand."

Wouldn't Kate love that? "Ah—no, I don't think that would be a good idea. And that's not why I came back."

"Why did you come back right now?" asked Nora.

"And how long are you staying?" Declan's tone had gone wary.

"I don't know," Evan said. "That's in answer to you, Declan. Nora, it was time."

"It was time a long time ago," said the girl.

"I wish you'd never left," said the boy.

"Yes, I know." Their honesty shamed him. How clear it seemed, the right thing to do. "I wanted to be here." He had never wanted to leave, but in the face of Con's betrayal, he had not been able to stay.

He forced brightness into his tone. "As a matter of fact, I am here to complete a task, and I could use your help."

Declan looked up from the halter he was cleaning. "Is it driving?"

"It is definitely not driving. It is related to antiquities."

"Like the flint Mama sent to Uncle Jonah?" he asked.

"Like the slides you showed us in your magic lantern?" asked Nora.

"Exactly. Someone is making new carvings to look like old, and using them to smuggle. And because of the stone many of the pieces are made of, I think they must be made near here."

"So you have to search every stone. That sounds rotten." Declan tossed the cleaning cloth to Nora, who put it away with a persecuted sigh.

"That would be rotten indeed, not to mention tedious," Evan agreed. "But the situation isn't that dire. Some of the false pieces I saw in England had real wear on them, as though the stone were truly ancient. So I think the fake pieces are made from real pieces." Ugh. Every fiber of his researcher's mind rebelled at the idea.

"Oh, so we only have to search for *ancient* stone." With a hop and a reach, Declan hung the halter in its place. "That still sounds rotten. All stone is ancient."

"He doesn't mean stone dug out of the *ground*," Nora explained. "He means stone that was already dug up and carved a long time ago. Like for an old wall or a ruined castle. Like Loughmoe or Killahara."

"Exactly," Evan said. "Like the—huh. Right. Exactly like Loughmoe or Killahara."

How could he not have thought of those places at once? The ancient castles, long crumbling, would provide a plentiful source of stone for carvings—if it were the right sort. Evan couldn't recall the last time he'd visited a ruined castle. To the Irish, such a structure was rather like the Parliament building to Londoners. Yes, it was old, and yes, they were proud of it. And no, no one else had better offer any criticism, but they didn't want to *go* there. What would one *do*?

"We're not allowed to go to ruined castles," said Declan. "Just like we're not allowed to say damn."

"Why not?" Evan asked.

"Mama is convinced a rock will fall on us and our heads will be crushed like Da's."

"His head wasn't crushed," Nora pointed out. "It was kicked in. That's what old Driscoll said at the inquest." Her tone was dry. Wrung with scorn for the magistrate, maybe, or for the whole notion of an inquest.

God. Evan could imagine this conversation beginning like this, many times before—then being lopped off by Kate's shadowed eyes or Good Old Gwyn's crocodile tears.

"Sit here." In a row—Declan, Evan, Nora—they

sat on the stable floor and leaned against the door of Lady Alix's stall. The mare gave a welcoming whicker, then pulled at her measure of hay. "I didn't know there was an inquest. There was really an inquest?"

"Sure there was," Declan said. "We didn't go. But Mama did. And we overheard her talking about it with the vicar."

"He said it was God's will that Da fell from his horse and died." Nora folded her legs, wrapping her arms around them tightly. "Mama doesn't go to church anymore, even though there's a new vicar now."

The gorge rose in Evan's throat. Con, falling. Kate, left alone, finding no succor at home or at church. "It doesn't make sense." He shook his head. "Your father was an excellent rider. He knew how to take a fall and get right back up." All Evan had known—fourth-hand, third-hand at best—was that Con had died in a riding accident.

"He took a hoof to the head." Declan set his small jaw, testing himself. "That's what the inquest found. It was a bad kick in a bad place."

God's will, the vicar had said to a shocked young widow. A comment no more helpful than: *You have nothing to be sad about.*

"That's awful," Evan said.

That was all there was to say.

"It was," said Nora. "One of the servants said at the inquest that Da was upset, so a groom saddled the horse for the chase. That was awful too, because old Driscoll tried to blame the groom."

"Mama said it was no one's fault," Declan added. "She said that in the inquest."

Numbness crept over Evan, more ice than grayness. "But it was someone's fault. It was mine. We had argued—that's why he was upset."

Not that he had caused the fall or dealt the deathblow. But it was fresh and new, the awareness of how deeply Con had been affected by their argument. Maybe enough to forgive Evan for confronting him? Maybe even enough to change his ways?

If he'd had the chance...if he'd lived.

Nora released her knees, shooting her legs out straight with a *thunk* on the stone floor. "What did you argue about?"

Her tone was curious. Not angry, not even hurt.

"It was about something to do with—a lot of things."

Time and again, Evan had cursed Con's infidelities to Kate. Con laughed it off, always. *You worry too much. It's just a bit of fun.* But the money troubles? Those were no joke. When Con asked Evan for a loan to cover a debt to a moneylender so Kate wouldn't find out about it—well, then matters had come to a head.

You have so much, but you're throwing it away. I'd give anything to have what you regard so lightly.

You worry too much, Con said again.

No, Con. It's not worry. It's anger. And it's not too much.

On a series of elegant nothings and meaningless affairs, Con was beggaring his estate and ruining his marriage. Only Evan's accusation of the former had injured Con's sense of honor. For the only time in their years of friendship, he had seen the blithe earl angry. Furious. The sort of *furious* from which goodwill never returned.

"What were the things you fought about?" Nora asked now.

Ugh. How to explain debauchery and ruin to a child? "I wanted everything to be fine." He hesitated. "Are you sure—he fell because he was upset?"

"No. He fell because he was riding in the chase." Nora looked at Evan oddly. "His cinch split."

"And he died because he was kicked," said Declan, "and that's why Mama is worried and why we don't ride anymore." He reached up, but could not touch the muzzle of the mare from his seated position. Instead, he folded his arms behind his head and looked at Evan expectantly. "Are you well? You look strange."

"I am strange." Evan managed a flippant reply. "All the best people are."

With those few words, he managed to collect himself, and some of the icy feeling melted away.

The kick had killed Con. Not his distraction from his argument with Evan. Not even his fall during the race. It was horrible, but it wasn't—hadn't been—anyone's fault.

In the freshness of new grief, that might have seemed worse than if there were a villain to blame. But after two years of missing his friend, two years of vague, unsettled guilt…it was a relief. And dwelling on *maybe* was a sure way to mire oneself.

Footsteps on the stone floor announced the presence of another, even before black skirts came into view. As a trio, Evan and the children looked up. "Kate."

"I'm so glad I found you all." Without hesitation, she crouched before them.

Wariness dropped over Nora like a veil. "Are you here to make us go to our lessons?"

Kate looked taken aback. "I don't give a damn about lessons. I heard you'd gone missing, and I wanted to find you."

"She said damn," Declan whispered loudly.

"That doesn't mean you ought to say it," Kate replied. "Forget that. Pretend I was a lady."

"How many times do I have to explain what a lady is?" Evan grumbled.

"Where did you look for us?" Nora wiggled her bare toes.

"I came here first," Kate said. "When my mother died, I always went to the stables."

They looked surprised—as surprised as Evan felt—to hear her say this so openly. "How old were you?" Nora asked.

"I was fourteen."

"Did she fall?" The question was faint.

"No, she didn't fall." Kate held out her hands, drawing her daughter, then her son, to their feet. "She was ill. Very ill for a long time."

She gathered her children into an embrace. As Evan watched, the trio settled: a heave, like a sigh, and then they knit into one another. Mother and daughter and son, brother and sister, all interlaced their arms and crushed one another as though they'd been separated far too long.

"I wish nothing would ever change," Nora cried.

"I know," Kate said. "I know. I have often wished that too."

Which would mean she had never taken him to her bed, and they had never traveled together—that he'd never met her family, nor she his, like a courting couple.

"I missed you." Kate's voice was muffled in their hair. She was not much taller than her children. "I missed you so much."

"While you were gone?"

"And this morning, and every time I don't see you for a while. Sometimes when you are only across a room."

And there sat Evan like a lump on the floor of the stable. Seeing them need each other, *wanting* them to need each other. He wished he'd been embraced in that way as a child.

Hell—he wished he were part of that embrace now. What was there to want in life more than someone who said *I miss you when you're across a room*?

The sentiment was sharp and sweet, a candy stick licked to a spearpoint. It made him smile, even as he felt he had become part of the stone floor, heavy and unmovable.

"I missed you too." Nora was the first to break away, folding her arms with trembling dignity. "I think—I am not ready to go back to lessons yet."

"Damn lessons," Declan tried.

"I shouldn't have said that. And you need to stop saying it." Kate gave him a final squeeze, then turned him loose. "Lessons are wonderful. We love lessons. Hurrah, lessons!"

"I hate lessons." Declan looked at Evan—the first to do so almost since Kate had turned down this row of stalls. "But I'm an earl now, and I ought to…learn things?"

"I think that sounds wise," Kate said. She turned to Nora. "What's wrong, my dear?"

Nora cut dark eyes toward Evan.

Unmistakable cue. "I'll see that the earl gets back to the house. Declan, grab your jacket."

~

When Evan and Declan had passed from sight, Kate sank to the floor and patted the stone at her side. "Sit, sit. What's troubling you?"

Before sitting, Nora kicked at her shoes with bare toes. Expensive shoes, sturdy but pretty. Kate had a similar pair herself.

With a great sigh, Nora puddled to the floor at Kate's side. "You gave me all these grown-up gifts from England."

"Yes." Kate waited for the rest of the thought.

"But I'm twelve."

"Yes."

"I'm a child."

"Yes." Kate tipped her head. "And?"

"It's too soon, Mama." She leaned her head on Kate's shoulder, long plait swinging behind them. "I don't want to grow up. Being grown up looks awful. You are so worried all the time, and so sad. You miss Da."

Not exactly, Kate was about to say. But a child's admiration for her departed father must not be tampered with. "I miss the hope of a happy life with your father," she settled for saying.

More than Con, she grieved the loss of what she had hoped her marriage would be. With him gone, there was no chance they could ever repair matters. There was no time to beg him to make everything right.

"I miss him." Nora sniffled. "He was happy all the time."

"He was carefree," Kate ventured. "Always confident." She slid an arm around Nora's narrow shoulders. Squeezed, a half-hug that held a whole measure of feeling. "Nora, I'm glad you told me what was bothering you. But you must know that being a woman isn't always like being me. There are as many ways to be a woman as there are women in the world."

"Really?"

"Really."

The girl lifted her head from Kate's shoulder. Mother to daughter, they faced each other. Kate could tell the precise moment Nora set aside anxiety for an idea.

"Mama. Will you teach me to shoot like you?"

Seventeen

Evan returned to the stable just as Nora exited. "I'm going to lessons now," she said.

"Good for you. By the way, your stockings look terrible."

"Talk to Lady Alix about that," she tossed over her shoulder as she strode off.

Smiling, Evan wound through the stable until he found Kate—much where he had left her. She greeted him with gratifying warmth. "Thank you for walking with Declan. And for staying with them so they wouldn't run off again. I owe you a great debt."

"No such thing. I could help you, and I did."

"I don't want to need help."

He laughed. "I know you don't. So proud and stubborn."

She slid to the floor before one of the stalls. "You're supposed to argue with me and tell me nice things."

Evan sat beside her, stretching out his legs. "Why? Because you don't want honesty along with help?" He split a piece of straw down its length, then tossed it aside. "You are proud, Kate. And you are stubborn. And thank God you're both, because only someone proud and stubborn—not to mention clever and resourceful—would have a prayer of saving the Whelan lands."

"It'll take prayer to save them." She sighed. "I am almost resigned to it. The fact is, Driscoll can demand what he likes. Either he claims the land, or he claims the money, and I must sell the land to raise it." She shook her head. "I can save the house, but that'll be all. Declan will have the responsibilities of an earldom with none of the resources."

Evan eased a hand into one of hers. "When you're not having to save something, maybe I could take a turn with the saving. Not forever. But for a little while."

"No, no. If I don't do everything... Evan, whenever Con said he'd help, he didn't. I can't let go of responsibility, or everything I've scrambled to save will be ruined."

He rolled his eyes. "I'm not Con. The fact that I never loosed a sheep in your house should be proof enough of that."

"I know." Her fingers tightened within his. "I'm not good at...at letting someone else save the world."

"Not the world," he said. "I know I can't save that. But I can help you save this moment. Or another. Whichever you need."

She sat back against the stall door, hitching her knees up beneath her long black skirts. "I had a good moment with Nora. Just now. I don't have so many of those that I take them for granted."

"Good moments are precious," he agreed.

"I held her, and I listened, and I—I cannot believe it. I did the right thing."

Evan knew the feeling that trembled in her voice. Mingled shock and awe—and more than a dollop of *for once.*

"Your children love and trust you," he said.

He was relieved that she did not look at him as he spoke, for his expression would have told her far more than his words.

Instead, she stood. Paced to the only other stall in the row currently occupied and studied the horse within. "They don't have any friends, do they?" she asked. "Like me—they don't fit with the people in the village—the tenants—the servants." Her shoulders hunched. "I got in the habit of listening to Gwyn, or staying home to solve Con's problems."

"You are wearing black again," Evan noted as he rose to his feet. "You looked lovely in color."

"Did I?" She reached out, stroking the fine lines of the horse's head and neck. "I don't know myself in color anymore. I wore it on the journey. Now it seems I ought to go back to the way I was. The Countess of Whelan is a widow."

"You are more than a widow. And more than a countess." He crossed to join her before the other horse, then laid a gentle hand on her shoulder. "Biggie."

She let the nickname pass. "Do you remember this mare? Lucy?" At the sound of her name, the horse's ears pricked. "She was my father's. Con came to Newmarket to buy mares for breeding, and he left with a wife as well." She shook her head, rueful. "I don't know that it's the most flattering pairing."

"You were all Thoroughbreds, so why not?" Evan held out his hand to the mare. "I remember old Luce."

He laughed. "Your father names his mare Lucy. Mine names his Lady Alix." An apt summary of the differences between their families.

"She's the last of those Chandler mares. I had to sell the others." Kate trailed her fingers down the horse's long nose. The mare leaned into the caress, closing her eyes like a kitten being petted. "Lucy isn't all Thoroughbred, so she wouldn't go for much. But I like her all the better for it. She's eighteen years old and as strong and quick as ever. I think she's got a touch of something steady in her, like Cleveland Bay. She's got the black stockings for it."

Kate had presented Evan with the perfect opening. "Your children don't ride anymore."

There was no mistaking what *anymore* meant. For a widow, for a friend close as a brother, there was only one *anymore*. "They didn't want to ride at first," Kate said. "I think they were shaken by Con's accident. Then when I asked if they were ready, they said they weren't." Lucy shoved her fine head into Kate's palm, winning herself a scratch behind the ears. "I think they were humoring me."

"Because you don't ride either?"

The look she cast at Evan was almost despairing. "If I fell like Con, they'd be orphaned."

Time for a taste of her own medicine: the agreement game she'd played with Gwyn. "That's true," he said. "They would be. They could also be orphaned if you were riding in a carriage and it overturned, or if you were climbing around a ruined castle and a stone fell on your head. Or if you grew ill like your mother, or had another baby and died in childbed, or if you were stabbed by an elephant tusk, or—"

"Should I be alarmed you so quickly thought of so many ways to end my existence?"

"It's not what I think, but what I fear," he admitted. "Though I know ticking off fearful possibilities is no way to live."

"I know it too, but I don't change. I wish for nothing to change, and I wish for everything to be different." She turned from Lucy with a sigh—which meant that she was facing Evan, almost close enough to fall into his arms. "Who was Con, Evan? Who the devil was he? Sometimes I think he loved me. Sometimes he seemed nothing but a collection of flaws knit together by charm."

How could they ever know what had lain in Con's heart? Evan knew only his own. "The truth lies somewhere between, I am sure."

"Or maybe they are both true. He gave me a home when I didn't have one, but..."

"*Is* this your home? I wasn't sure, the way you spoke of it in Newmarket."

When she looked at him, her eyes were deep blue-green. A color she would not wear, glossed with tears she would not shed. "I wasn't sure either. But if it is not—where is? Certainly not England anymore. And I cannot split myself. I am not suited for the road."

"By default, then, this is home." He wondered, so hard and so deeply, that the words almost fell from his lips: *Does it help if I am here with you?*

But to ask such a question would be to supplant Con directly, far too directly.

So instead, he kissed her. A quick kiss, a kiss of impulse. A press of lips, heat against heat—but before it could go to his head, he drew back.

"That was a friendly kiss," he said. "That's all. Just…friendly."

"Right." Her brows were knit, one hand lifted to touch her lips. "That—that is the sort of thing friends do."

"Do they do it again?"

"They ought to." She looked at him with such deep wanting, for so many things lost and longed for, that he felt he was seeing into himself.

"Then…as a friend…"

In a tangle of lips and hands, they found their way into an empty stall. Whether they were lying to each other more, or to themselves, he neither knew nor cared as he pulled the door shut, and they sank into clean straw.

A tangle of mouths and hands ensued, frantic shoving of fabric and unbuttoning. His coat came off as her pelisse was cast aside. He rolled to his back, letting the straw poke and prickle through his waistcoat and shirt. Each stab of sensation was an anchor to the now, to Kate climbing atop him, to bare flesh meeting bare flesh. The familiar scent of straw mixed with her perfume, faintly flowery, and with the gasp and play of growing desire.

She reached between them, finding his cock, and pumped it to stone-stiffness in an eager fist. Evan groaned, his hips arching up. "I'm yours," he panted. "God. You are killing me."

"Never." She leaned forward, belly to belly atop

him, and kissed him slow and sweet and tender. Then she straightened, rose to her knees, and bunched her skirts into an enticing tangle that revealed flashes of thigh, the shadow of dark hair. Taking his cock in hand again, she guided it within her. Sleek and hot, the glide of her body onto his was such ecstasy that he gritted his teeth, trying not to spend at once.

Slowly at first, she worked him, a movement as sweet and slow as her kiss had been. Evan lifted his hands to palm her breasts, to slide gown and stays against her nipples, to abrade the tender skin until she flushed and moaned. Her thrusts grew erratic, hips jerking with the build of pleasure.

"Evan!" she called, breath coming in pants now, cheeks a beautiful flush, and all that curling hair falling in spirals about her face. He took her hips in hand now, guiding her ever more quickly, deepening the thrust. Finding the angle that made her quake, that made her clench about him and shudder and say his name again.

When she gasped with the aftershock of climax, he pulled free and rolled to the side. He jetted immediately, hard, over and over into the straw. *God.*

"I haven't spent like that in…I don't know how long," he groaned, rolling to his back again.

"I haven't since the last time we were together." Kate hitched herself onto one elbow and gazed down at him. "Evan, I…"

I'm yours too. His mind filled in the missing words, willing her to speak them. But she didn't. She only looked at him, her gaze honest and steady as a heartbeat.

"Well," he said. "We'd best put ourselves to rights."

"Oh. Yes." She sat upright, tugging at her bodice. He refastened his breeches, righted his garments, and eased back into his coat.

Evan had enjoyed combing out Kate's tangled hair, but picking straw from it was even better.

"A robust greeting," he said. "I like it. I shall visit you in the stables all the time."

"You put me to the blush. But surely you say that to all the women."

"Nonsense. Only to the beautiful widows with riotous hair." He plucked another bit of straw from her curls, teasing her nose with it.

She batted the straw away, wrinkling her nose, then sat up. "I know it's not the done thing at a moment like this, but I want to..." She shoved at her skirts, looking hesitant.

For a pair who could never be intimate again—supposedly—they'd made a good job of it. Shut inside a stall, groping like two virgins. So eager for each other they had hardly stripped off any clothing before they joined.

It could hardly have been more different than the elaborate, tentative seduction Kate had first arranged for Evan. And...he liked that.

If only she would stop making his heart stutter and sink by shoving at her clothes and abandoning her sentences at crucial midpoints. "*I*," he prodded, "want very much to hear the end of that sentence. But considering what you just did to me, I cannot imagine what you might want that I would not agree with, most eagerly."

There, that was a good cover. He straightened the knot of his neckcloth.

And still she sat, worrying at her lip. "Since you're with me," she said, "I should like to open the tack room...and think about riding again."

He had not expected anything like this, and relief was a cool breeze over his apprehension. "Think about it? Only think?"

She tried a smile, though it hung crooked. "It's better than trying not to think about it."

"True, and that's well said. Not to think about it does not bear thinking about." He rolled to his feet, then held out a hand and helped Kate up. "I should be honored to promenade with you to the tack room."

As they unlatched the stall and left its intimate confines, Evan could have sworn both mares—Lucy and Lady Alix—looked at them knowingly.

"What of it, lasses?" he said. "You've enjoyed the company of a stallion before, I'd wager."

"You are defending our behavior to the horses," Kate said as she preceded him toward the back of the stable. "Now I know all is right with the world."

In Evan's opinion, the fact that she had made love to him again—and that she was thinking about riding again—and that she was taking him to the tack room—were far better signs that all was right with the world. But to each their own.

Eighteen

Once Kate retrieved a key, she unlocked the door to a small room with which Evan had once been familiar. As a guest at Whelan House, he'd ridden almost every day, and the tack room had been as bustling as the kitchens.

Now it was silent, a room as restricted as a wine cellar. But it was still a bright and pleasant space, paneled in honey-brown wood and floored in squares of native stone. High windows allowed daylight to filter in, but wall-mounted lamps would be lit if needed at night.

The walls were studded with hooks and gridded with shelves, the floor dotted with saddle horses and storage chests. The space smelled pleasantly of leather and the light oil used to keep it in trim, the scent wafting from sidesaddles, bridles, halters and leads, saddles for men, carriage harnesses. All were hung, mounted, stored, and maintained with admirable care.

Except for a small wooden saddle horse in the corner, its burden covered over with an oilcloth. Kate moved toward it, her hand hovering above the cloth.

Before she spoke, Evan guessed what lay under the cover.

"That was Con's favorite saddle," Kate said quietly, as if they were in a Catholic church observing a saintly relic. "Light and strong. Good for hunting or racing. He was using it that day."

"May I see it?"

"If you like. But it won't be sound any longer. It was shut up that day. It hasn't been oiled for two years."

That day. That day had been endless for Evan, and he hadn't even known until weeks later that it had marked the end of his friend's existence. "I saw him in that saddle many a time."

"I did too." Kate grasped the oilcloth. "But in the end, it is nothing more than a saddle. It was silly to shut it away, wasn't it?"

"It wasn't silly." Grief takes many different forms. So he'd told her, and so he believed. If one needed to grieve by hiding a saddle, so be it.

When she whisked the oilcloth off, she sighed. "The cinch was split. That's why he fell. The leather is quite spoiled." She stretched the cloth between her hands, ready to toss it over the saddle again. "I shouldn't even keep it. It's doing no good here."

"Wait." Evan caught the edge of the cloth, kneeling before the saddle. He took the cinch in his hands. Indeed, the leather had gone dry, its surface hard and dark and brittle. But there was something wrong about its appearance. "This didn't split by accident, Kate. This cinch was cut."

"Cut?" With a billow, the cloth fell to the floor.

Kate was at his side in an instant. "How do you know? How *can* you know?"

"The same way I can tell a sculpture was carved recently, with modern tools, then splashed with mud. It doesn't look *right*. Leather wouldn't split like this, no matter how brittle it got. Look, when I tug it in a different place, it doesn't split again."

Her fingertips reached for the saddle, tentative. "Did someone cut the cinch where it had split? So the saddle couldn't be used again?"

Grimness settled over Evan. Oh, how he wanted to say yes. "I can't be sure. Maybe if someone cut it right away, because the damage is old. But I think—look, there is a clean slice through this bit, and then the rest is distorted." As though its fragile width had been snapped by the strain of a galloping horse, its rider taking a leap over the first jump in a chase.

"What are you saying?" Kate huddled, crouching before the saddle. "That someone cut—no, everyone loved Con. No one—that can't be. There was an inquest, Evan. It was an accident."

Her voice held more than a hint of a plea.

The cut and snapped leather was no larger than a pair of braces, but it was weightier than stone. The evidence was real, there in his fingers, but he still could hardly believe it.

"Con didn't saddle his horse that day," Evan said. "Who did?"

"One of the grooms. Adam—something. Jones, maybe."

"God. Not another Jones." Evan sat back on his heels, dropping the cinch.

"He isn't here anymore. He packed his bags and left, maybe a month later. But he gave notice. He was going east to live and work with family. I never thought—do you think there was something wrong? Did he..."

"Maybe he...did." What other word could they bear to put to it? "This Jones couldn't be certain you'd believe Con's fall was an accident. Nor could he take the chance of destroying the saddle and raising questions. So he had to leave."

Kate sprang to her feet, skirts tangling with the fallen oilcloth. "You have developed this theory with mighty speed. You want to murder Con off, when he's been peacefully dead for two years."

Evan rose , facing her down. "Of course I don't want that! But wouldn't it be better to know the truth?"

"What good would the truth do if it wouldn't *change* anything?"

Evan snapped up the cloth from the floor and tossed it back over the saddle. "You're right. God forbid anything *change*. God forbid we face an uncomfortable truth, Kate. Best to cover it up and go on as you were. Isn't that always your solution?"

The words bled, unstoppable. He did not want to stop them, even though Kate went white as if she were the one bleeding. "Have you spoken your piece?"

"No!" Evan slapped a hand against the honey-pale paneling. "I could say it a thousand times, and I'd still not even touch the half of what I want to tell you."

Kate accepted this, silent. Her gaze was fixed on the heavy brown cloth. She trailed her fingers over it, gently as she had once touched Evan's face for a kiss.

"You're right, Evan," she said. "You're right. If he was—if this saddle was tampered with, then covering it won't help him. I was shocked at first, that's all. But I want to understand what happened."

"And will it help anything, to understand?"

"Yes." She looked up at him, head held as high and proudly as a racehorse. "Because it's *right*. It's the right thing to do."

"Yes," Evan said. "I agree. I think so too."

That was why he lectured, why he painted fraud onto glass slides. It was right that the truth be understood, the false spotted for what it was.

With a final pat, Kate turned away from the covered saddle. "I want to speak to Driscoll. This didn't come up in the inquest, and he was the one who examined the saddle."

"You remember the inquest so well?" Evan asked.

"Every word. Propriety, bless it, kept me from Con's funeral, but it couldn't keep me from the inquest. I was shocked, yes, but I was also *angry*."

"At whom?"

She nudged a bridle, setting it to swinging on its peg. "At Con, mainly, for leaving me alone. I'd never thought to be a widow at twenty-eight. I thought we'd have another fifty years together."

"Did you want those fifty years?" He shouldn't have asked this, but it helped, sometimes, to understand.

"What a question. How could I be so cruel as to say no?" She took another step, set another bridle to dancing. "But now, he's been gone for two years, and I cannot imagine those two years any differently. Time has a way of making the impossible seem inevitable."

Inevitable that Con had died? Inevitable that they should all have grown older and beyond him?

It did seem inevitable, now that she put the word to it. Con was the sort of spirit who could never be old. Con had boosted the sheep through the window. Con had led the horse into church. Evan helped, Evan rode along, and Evan followed.

Con wed on impulse, taking on lifelong vows as easily as he changed his clothing. And Evan made the vow no one had asked him to make or keep. The vow no one had wanted at all.

I will love you forever.

There was hardly time to hide the feeling, naked and deep, before Kate turned to look at him with eyes that had seen far too much. "If his death wasn't an accident, Evan, do I have to come to terms with it all over again?"

"I don't know." He closed the distance between them, then plucked a final piece of straw from her hair. "No one knows that but you."

Nineteen

Kate wanted to make the journey into Thurles almost at once.

Plans for riding were abandoned anew after finding the troublesome cinch. *The murderous cinch?* Kate didn't know how to think of it. Evan took it from the saddle and tucked it into his pocket.

But it was there, and they couldn't forget it.

Instead, they walked. Kate wrapped herself in a gray cloak, a shapeless garment that fell over her like a blanket. How long ago it seemed since she'd worn a blanket and shared a cheroot with Evan on a set of narrow stairs.

Just when she thought she was ready for something new, she was blasted by something that rocked every bit of the familiar.

Coming to terms with the randomness of Con's fall, only to realize it had probably not been an accident.

Taking Evan as a lover, only to realize how much she dreaded losing him. Then taking him again, with all the vigorous clandestine groping of people who yearn for each other yet fear discovery.

So had they been brave, or were they afraid?

Judging by the harsh line of Evan's jaw and brow beneath the brim of his hat, the answer was different for each of them.

And now, with the space between her legs still tender, she didn't know a damned thing except the path beneath her feet.

It was a path that led through pasture and field. Two years ago, when winter settled its weight so heavily, the land had been seared with frost and made barren. Potatoes rotted in the ground, while barley was nipped before it could go to seed.

Now the land was coming back. If Con had not left such debt, good harvests and careful spending would bring healing to the estate coffers. Time was the cure for much.

The path led them through the heart of Thurles, past familiar shops and faces. The medieval lines of Bridge Castle peered down at them, a single fortified tower with blank-eyed windows.

Kate remembered her vow to ingratiate herself with the people of town. To be more than the mournful figure who barked orders from Whelan House.

So many of the English dismissed the Irish as poor and careless. But *she* was English—or had been? And she knew the people of Thurles to be much like those of Newmarket. Some were wealthy, some lived in poverty, some were skilled with their hands, and some relied on the strength of their backs. Some had large families, and some were childless. Some were happily so.

Some were not.

She had wanted more children herself. When one's father was always absent, one needed company. Kate had found it in the wrong place. She should have leaned on her siblings instead of seeking a husband. She should have made more friends. Real friends, like Evan, who understood her better than she understood herself.

Which, right now, was not saying the devil of a lot.

She recognized a slight figure with scraped-back black hair, exiting the bakery with a basket over one arm. "Good day, Miss Ahearn," she greeted the spinster.

The woman peered over pince-nez. "Lady Whelan, good day. And you too, Mr. Rhys." She paused in her walk. "I must thank you for your suggestion of the mulled wine. Most effective, it is, at chasing away the pains of the day."

"I'm glad you found it useful," Evan replied. "As the weather grows colder, you might take a dram of whisky as well."

Janet Ahearn was newer to Thurles than Kate herself, and gone often to her family in Dublin. Yet she fit better into the town than Kate did, accepted without question despite her pinched features and pinched purse.

Miss Ahearn and Evan continued in this light vein, exchanging comments and gossip—something about pastilles and packets. Their speech fell into a similar cadence, lulling Kate until her name was mentioned.

"I beg your pardon?" Kate asked.

"I said, Lady Whelan," commented the dry little woman, "that it is good to see you in proper mourning again."

"Oh." Kate clutched at the edges of her cape. "I didn't—"

"And I," said Evan, "thought the opposite. Good day to you, Miss Ahearn. Enjoy those cakes."

Kate elbowed him as soon as they had passed out of earshot. "That was our game for Good Old Gwyn. You don't have to be disagreeable now. I think you gave poor Miss Ahearn the vapors."

"Disagreeable I might be, but I was also being honest. Miss Ahearn can go take a headache powder if she needs to. You looked fine in color, Kate. There's already enough gray in the world."

Gray slate roofs, gray stone pavement, a gray wool cloak. He was right, and yet: "I have few colorful gowns that suit me," she said. "Everything else was dyed black, or it was from before."

"Before, before. And what is wrong with before?" Evan gestured expansively as they walked. "Mountains grew and crumbled *before*. Winter came and went *before*. Driscoll let his waistcoats out *before*. In the grand scheme of the world, surely wearing a gown made *before* is not so much to dare."

"A fine speech, and one with which I'd agree if fashion were a matter of logic. But it isn't. It's about feeling. And I feel different now."

"Oh? How different?" When she looked at him, his eyes were dark as drinking chocolate, and as warm and bracing.

"I dressed for Con then. Now I want to dress for myself."

His brows, so readily arched, lowered—and his mouth went soft, curling at one side. "My dear Biggie, how do you do it? I cover you in a blizzard of ridiculous words, and in a few syllables you cut to the heart of what matters."

She had to look away before she stumbled. "It's just a gown. A few gowns. Gowns that don't exist yet." She shivered inside her cape, as though his quiet compliment were a hand trailed over her bare skin. "And I did notice that you called me Biggie."

"I hoped it would make you smile."

"You don't have to call me by a silly name to make me smile."

"You're doing it again." Evan sighed. "Being all delightful and profound."

"You're doing it again," she said. "Teasing me so I am not crushed beneath worry."

"Hold to that realization, and that amazing teasing skill of mine, as long as you can." Evan halted, looking around him. "We must find Driscoll. Where do you think he'd be?"

"It's nearly noon?" When Evan nodded, Kate said, "He'll be in the Prancing Pony."

The town's inn and public house, it crouched like a fist between the finger-slim shops that abutted it. Not that this was a bad thing, for fists were sturdy and solid. Other than its bowed front window, the Prancing Pony had little of prance about it. It was a great brick slab with a gabled roof that poked above neighboring buildings, boasting a public ground floor and two stories above for travelers and guests.

Evan and Kate entered its hushed depths. Within the taproom, every bit seemed made of wood. Darker than a forest, there was a wood ceiling with smoky wood beams, wood-paneled walls with scraped bits of a lighter brown and time-rubbed darker areas. The tables, the serving bar, were all wood. Behind the bar, lamps lit a brilliant array: bottles of every shape, filled with every drinkable color, and casks hooped in gleaming metal. Besides offering drink, the Prancing Pony was a fine place to get a meal—or so Con had said. When would Kate have had occasion to eat here?

The serving girl, Aileen, came by to greet them—stumbling against Evan, Kate noticed. She decided to change matters. "We'll sit with Mr. Driscoll," she said. "And we'll have the fried potatoes."

"I like a woman who takes charge," Evan murmured in her ear after Aileen walked off with the order, cheerful as ever. "And fortunately, I also like potatoes."

"Who doesn't? Breathe in that scent." It blanketed the room: frying oil and salt, something heavy that promised warmth. "When we sit with Driscoll, by the way, you'd best do the talking about the cinch. He has this way of speaking to me, like a kindly old hound who can't be bothered to obey."

"And you want me to bring him to heel, do you?"

"Don't belabor the figure of speech. It was a fine one, but it will only be pushed so far."

"Fair enough. I shall stop myself while you're admiring my wit. Ah—your children told me all about the inquest." Kate gasped. "So I'll do a not-terrible job of picking through the questions for the magistrate. Look, he's seen us. By the window."

All her wondering about *how the devil did Declan and Nora know what happened at the inquest* had to be halted.

Though she could guess. She had listened at a door or two—or a hundred—when she was a child.

Driscoll, clad as ever in a red flannel waistcoat and a great coat of pale biscuit, struggled to his feet from behind a table laden with dishes. "Mr. Rhys, Lady Whelan! Do join me."

"Are you certain?" Kate simpered. "We wouldn't want to intrude."

"Not at all, not at all." The magistrate eased back into his chair, looking doleful. "I was about to take my leave, but—with such good company, I might indulge a little." He motioned for the serving girl, who had just reappeared in the public room. "Aileen! Another platter of potatoes. And some for my friends."

"We've already ordered," Evan said. "Fried potatoes, as a matter of fact."

"You'll be a happy man. Ah! Here it comes. They had only to dish them up, I suppose." He beamed with the sort of pride one felt when introducing a friend to something one liked very much. "Simple fare, but sometimes that's the best."

Kate didn't answer. She was too busy inhaling. The potatoes were chopped into wedges, fried until crisp. The scent collared her, making her stomach roar.

"Go on, go on, Mr. Rhys! Eat them with your fingers, if the lady can forgive it."

"Being a lady," Kate said, "has nothing to do with being a potato invigilator. But you must both eat your luncheon as you see fit." And she picked up a wedge, puffing air onto her hot fingertips, and bit off a piece. The crispy exterior yielded to her teeth, shocking her with salt and heat, then a smooth mealy inside.

For a few minutes, there was no sound but that of plates being tugged back and forth, of the occasional *hiss* as fingers touched hot oil or tongues were lightly burned.

When Kate had managed to stuff herself with an amount of potatoes that made Driscoll lift his heavy brows, she gave Evan's foot a little kick beneath the table. *Get on with the questions.*

There was no graceful way to bridge the gap between potatoes and criminality, but Evan did a creditable job. "I thank you for allowing us to join you, Mr. Driscoll. For it's you we were in search of."

"Oh? What's happened?" He turned the disobedient-hound look upon Kate. "Is your boy making false fox tracks outside the tenants' chicken houses again?"

"What? No—I—wait, again? No, that's not it." Kate shook her head, making a note to ask Declan what he knew about fox tracks. "No, it's because of—well, you remember Lord Whelan's death, I'm sure."

The hound grew more mournful, all pouchy eyes. "Oh, yes, yes. I remember." Driscoll leaned back in his chair, folding his hands over his great belly. "He was after falling in the chase. Got a kick to him. Terrible, it was."

"And why did he fall?" Evan leaned forward, closing the distance Driscoll had opened.

"Why…? He just did." Driscoll blinked. "Saddle slipped. People fall on the chase course all the time. Horse clips a jump, misses a stride. It puts a dreadful strain on the tack, and—"

"Did anyone look for a reason? Was the jump off?"

"It wasn't that I know. Other riders took it in

stride—before the race was halted, which it was as soon as the cry could be let out."

"Did you encourage anyone to check the condition of the tack?" Kate broke in. How odd it was to fill one's mouth with crisp potato, to delight in the taste, and hate the words one must speak.

"Checked it myself, Lady Whelan, but I knew what I'd find." Driscoll patted his belly, then leaned forward again. "Tragic. So tragic, it was. But it was years ago. Nothing you need to be worried about now. You've suffered enough, surely."

Evan picked up the thread of inquiry again. "But at the inquest, Mr. Driscoll, you implied the groom was at fault."

Driscoll looked up, seeming to search for answers on the deep wooden ceiling. When he met Evan's eye, his lined face held great sorrow—even as he busied his fork again in his pile of potatoes. "I did, at that. A regrettable impulse born of my own distress, it was."

"Or a deduction based on your own skill?" Kate ventured.

Driscoll stopped, mouth open, a potato wedge halfway to it. "What do you mean?"

"What," said Evan, "if the groom *was* to blame? And what if the fall wasn't an accident?"

The older man dropped the potato. "You can't think you've found out something new now, Mr. Rhys."

"I'm a suspicious sort—it's why I'm here. My lectures, you know. Fraudulent antiquities. Smuggling."

"You can't think the late earl was involved in such matters." Driscoll laughed again, but his eyes had gone…odd. Rather than a patient old hound, he looked cornered. If his ears could have gone flat, they would have.

You can't think: twice, Driscoll had used this phrase. It sounded like a warning, and the last bite of potato stuck in Kate's throat. "I hadn't thought so at all," she said. "Why would you suggest such a thing?"

"I didn't. Mr. Rhys did." Driscoll moistened his lips, then picked up his tankard and tipped it high to drain the last drops.

"I really didn't," Evan said, "but it's something to think about."

"Oh, I wouldn't say that." Driscoll was all mournful cheer again.

Kate replied with chill courtesy. "No, I'm aware you've been careful to say nothing at all."

"Let's leave the path," Evan said on their way back to Whelan House. "We can cut from the north and walk through the woods instead."

Had the errand gone well? He wasn't sure. He'd never even pulled the cut cinch from his pocket to show Driscoll.

Maybe that was for the best. Something had been odd about that conversation. He could feel it in the pit of his stomach—and that wasn't the feeling of having gobbled fried potatoes.

No, it might be that Con had secrets not even Evan knew. Fraudulent antiquities…it seemed so unlikely. But why had Driscoll jumped to that conclusion? Had it already been bridged for him?

Evan's feet hushed over drying fallen leaves. "Your children talked about some of the ruined castles nearby. Loughmoe, is that right?"

"That's one of them, yes. No one's lived there for decades." Kate stumbled over a root, catching herself on Evan's arm. "Sorry. You think—the sculpted stones?"

"Who would notice if a few went missing?"

"Not my children," Kate murmured. "They aren't allowed to go to such places." Then she added in her normal tone, "But you aren't thinking of going there now, are you? Loughmoe Castle must be five miles from here, at least."

"Let's walk until we get tired of walking."

"A fine plan, but for one flaw. How will we get back again, if we're tired of walking?"

He touched the dimple in her chin. Like a kiss, it had always looked to him. "Then we'll run."

Trees arched over the path where it continued through the wood, making a sun-dappled tunnel of branch and leaf. Their booted footfalls sounded soft on the path, carpeted with fallen leaves in all shades of yellow and brown.

When the path broke into a small clearing, Evan tipped back his head. Through the dapple of gold leaves and the first bare branches, the sky was like cobalt glaze, translucent and blue, wisped with clouds like thrown cotton.

"Sit with me," he said.

"Here?" Kate looked around, her hands working at the edge of her cloak.

"Right here." Evan whisked aside some damp leaves, then stretched out on the ground. He tossed his hat aside, folded his arms behind his head, and looked up.

After a moment, Kate joined him, settling onto the ground in the soft folds of her cloak.

It was easier to think about what was right in a place like this, and have it seem simple. There were no slides, no crowds to convince. There was land to cross, and his hands and eyes to use, and if something seemed gray, then he could look up toward the blue.

"That cloud looks like a wedge of fried potato," he said.

Kate choked. "Does it? Well, *that* cloud looks like the expression of shock on your face when I…steal your hat." With a quick snap, she caught it up and flung it back over her head.

"Minx." Evan didn't even budge. "You can have my hat. I'll only look more handsome if I get a bit of sun on my manly features."

She laughed, but the tone was a little out of tune. "Are you never serious? How can I know what you feel?"

Listen to me. Look at me.

But there were only so many times a man could be frank, then be left behind. Kate, the one to leave during the night. Kate, the one to take his kisses, then get up from the bed of straw.

"I'm a man," he said. "You're not meant to know what I'm feeling. I have this stoic exterior, and within me, muscles and virility."

"How tempting." She settled at his side again. Trailed a hand down his chest. "I like the muscles and virility, Evan."

"Oh, I could tell."

Her hand rested over his heart. "But in truth I like it all."

The gray cloak covered her arm, stretching across his body like a fog. And suddenly, he couldn't bear that there was something so important about himself that she didn't know.

"You want to know what I'm feeling," he said. "The truth is, I can't always put a name to it." And he told her about the grayness: how it came in a wave, how it sometimes ebbed. But it was like an ocean and a tide. It was always there, and it would always come back. It had always been with him, and it had never been understood, because it was beyond the scope of understanding.

While he spoke, she looked at him—at first. Then she settled into a copy of his pose, her arms folded in a pillow behind her head as she stared up at clouds that shifted.

When he finished, she was still looking into the sky. "It is like grief."

"It is like some grief." He traced her profile with a gentle fingertip. "Everyone grieves differently. This is leadenness of spirit."

Although now that he had told her, he felt nothing but the blue above, reflected within.

"I have not felt what you describe, so I do not understand it," she said slowly. "But I want to. Does it last?"

"It is always there, faint like mist. Sometimes I forget about it. Sometimes it creeps over everything."

What is the purpose of it all, Evan? What does it matter?

So asked his mother, once, about his excavation of a midden. About his efforts to learn about the past: one of the only things that mattered to him.

And so what did a question matter? What did it matter what food one ate? What drink passed one's lips? What did any of the God-damned bits of every-day existence *matter*?

He didn't have an answer. But for the moment, he had Kate at his side, and a cloud above that truly did look like a wedge of potato.

Or a smile.

"What brings the color back, when you feel so gray?" Kate asked.

"Sometimes, nothing but time. When I am more fortunate, I can bring myself out of it with an effort of will. Thinking of others. Trying to do something worthwhile in the world." He raised himself onto one elbow, then dropped a kiss on her nose. "Being with you."

"Then you'd better be with me." She crooked her finger into the edge of his waistcoat. "Do your best, Evan, to show me something worthwhile."

"What's this, insatiable woman?" He feigned shock, covering the real thump of his eager heart. "Are you asking me to tickle your loveliest bits while you call them terrible names like lumpy?"

"No. I'm asking you to be with me, as I am." Her eyes were sea-deep and warm, and her lips held a tremulous curve. "I'm not perfect, Evan, but...I think I might be just right."

"I know you are," he said. "I have always known that."

And beneath the blue sky, they banished the gray.

Twenty

While Kate was occupied with estate business that afternoon, Evan—and the sliced-off cinch from Con's saddle—prepared to pay a call of his own.

He rode this time. Since Lady Alix was likely to be footsore from the long journey across Ireland, he took a smart chestnut with a white snip on his nose that made the gelding look as if he'd been nosing about in cream. Their destination: a cottage on the edge of the village.

Evan looped around Thurles, not expecting or particularly wishing to see anyone—but as he guided the sure-footed chestnut across a field, he overtook a small, wizened figure he soon recognized as the old apothecary, Petty.

"Good afternoon to you, Mr. Rhys." Petty squinted at Evan, his face a wreath of kindly wrinkles. "Out for a constitutional, I am. And yourself?"

"Paying a call," Evan said. To someone who might be more forthcoming than the magistrate. Driscoll had much to protect, including the safety of the town and his own reputation.

Since Petty had come his way, Evan paused to question the old man as well. With him, Evan took a different tack. Relaxing his hold on the reins so the gelding could lower his head to crop grass, Evan said, "I did think I'd explore some of the sights while I'm here. I missed the old places, you know. Nothing gets in your heart like Ireland."

"Sure and certain," agreed Petty. "Where would you be wanting to look? There's the chase course, before the crowds start their flocking in another week."

"Always a fine sight." Evan clucked at the gelding, halting the horse before it took too many steps away from Petty. "I've an interest in antiquities too, as you know. I thought of learning more about Irish history."

"I knew you were after being a smart man. And how would you like to learn? Thurles hasn't much of an archive, though Whelan House might—"

"Oh, I'm no scholar," Evan interrupted cheerfully. "I'd rather get my hands dirty in a field than my nose dusty in a book. Which is the nearest castle I might explore?"

The old man pushed back his hat, scratching at his head. "Killahara, I expect. But I don't know if you could look around there. It's Trant land, and the baron keeps his tenants in the castle."

"No, that wouldn't do. An inhabited castle will have people making modern changes. I want to see history as it was." He snapped his fingers in feigned realization—causing the chestnut to lift his head and eye Evan with doubt. "Loughmoe Castle is also near, isn't it?"

"It is, it is. If you're on the back of a horse," the

apothecary agreed. "But I don't know what sort of condition it might be in." He slapped his thighs. "Old legs couldn't make that distance in a constitutional."

"Do people commonly visit there?"

Again, Petty scratched his head. "Can't say, really. The crops haven't been good since the terrible cold year. People of Thurles, we keep busy enough getting by."

Ah, 1816—it had been a difficult year all over, for many reasons besides Con's death. During a bad harvest, an apothecary might be shielded from immediate want, but if hungry tenant farmers hadn't the money to buy his goods, he'd be feeling the pinch in his purse too.

"Does anyone live in Loughmoe?" Evan asked. "I wouldn't want to intrude."

"Not for years and years." Petty spat on the ground. "Family were wild geese."

Evan racked his brain for an explanation. "I do apologize, but you'll have to help me. I'm sure the castle was not owned by waterfowl."

"Not that sort of geese, no. The wild geese were Jacobites, those who fled."

"Ah." This, Evan understood. Jacobites were those who disputed the line of succession to the English throne—broken during the Stuart years, when it seemed the world would be torn and made bloody between Catholic and Protestant. "So they were Catholic."

And when their safety was endangered, they picked up their wealth and fled—leaving behind the tenants who had been their foot soldiers, plus a castle to fall into ruin.

For the first time, Petty looked wary. "And which church do you be going to, Mr. Rhys?"

"One in Wales, and that not for years," Evan said. "I've no goose in this fight."

But he wondered. Loughmoe would bear further examination after he paid his call.

"I'll let you get on with your walk," he told the older man. "Not that you need it, Mr. Petty. You're looking fit as a fiddle."

"More of your blarney." The old apothecary looked pleased. "Off with you now. Off with you."

And with a tip of the hat on both sides, they parted ways. Evan clicked to the chestnut, nudging the horse back into stride, and continued his journey.

He came to his destination from the west, where Thurles trailed out to farmland, and before the manicured racecourse grounds began. Here was a single cottage that backed onto the drifting River Suir. The building was small, a plain rectangle of whitewashed coarse stone. A stout chimney poked from each end, and a roof of thatch overlaid it like combed hair.

All around the cottage, in a riot of warm autumn color, were woody shrubs and flowering plants. It took a skillful hand to coax so many varieties to life, to keep them looking wild but neatly in their places.

"Mary, Mary, quite contrary." Evan dismounted the gelding, tying him to a post beside the cottage door. "How does your garden grow?"

Before he could lift his hand to knock, the door opened. "You were speaking that old rhyme again," said a pleasant lilting voice. "I saw you through the window."

"I can't help it. Your garden always brings it to mind." When his hostess stepped back, allowing him over her threshold, he swept off his hat and made a bow of greeting. "How do you go on, Mary?"

Mary O'Dowd was a woman of about thirty years, with hair of vibrant red and a pale face as mottled as the moon. She hadn't always looked thus. When Evan, little more than a youth, first met her—then a kitchen maid at Whelan House—she'd been as smooth-skinned as a peach. Con couldn't resist her, and he made her his mistress.

That was before Con met Kate. But it was also after. The smallpox had almost taken Mary's life three years before, and...well, there was something about almost losing a person who had been very dear. The threat of loss had made Con discard the *had been* and remember the *very dear*, and he nursed Mary back to health in this quiet cottage. Evan had never seen his friend display such tenderness.

In a strange sort of way, it was almost honorable.

"I'm all right," said Mary. "Had a tough while going on these past years, since..."

Since. There was only, ever, one *since*. "I know. You've made a fine home for yourself and the child." A boy or a girl? He didn't know. Mary's baby hadn't yet been born when he left Ireland—intending to stay away for good.

"I've a fine son," said Mary, "and he deserves no less than a home that suits him."

A boy. Con had another son.

Evan was glad to see that Mary was getting on comfortably. The interior of the cottage was similar to the outside: whitewashed and crisp, chilly but cheerful. The rectangular space was divided into two rooms, one much larger that encompassed a cooking area, a small table, and a few chairs. The smaller space must be the bedchamber. Bright curtains trimmed the windows, and on the mantel above the cooking fire, a few precious ornaments had been arranged.

A little black-haired boy ran from behind the single door. "Da? Da come?"

He wobbled, the uncertain run of a chubby young child moving with more speed than steadiness.

Mary darted to scoop him up, giving the boy a smacking kiss on one cheek. "He didn't, love. Da can't come. You know that. But this is one of Da's friends, Mr. Rhys."

"Mitter Ree," said the boy, and then buried his face in the curve of his mother's shoulder.

"Hello, lad," said Evan. There was no mistaking his parentage, with the jet hair and the wicked dark eyes. "This one will be a handful for you, Mary."

"His name is Conall." Mary looked at Evan over the shoulder of the boy. "Do you—I thought the earl might have liked it."

"It's a fine name," Evan replied. "Yes, I think the earl would have liked that."

As far as Evan knew, this was true. Con wanted what he wanted, and he never shied from notice. When Con wed Kate, he had paid Mary off with a stipend. Well-intentioned, doubtless, but good intentions didn't last long. Evan knew his friend to be guilty of infidelity, the casual, emotionless sort. Con tumbled a pretty maid or visiting widow with as little care and as much delight as one would crack the crust of a fancy-topped crème brulée.

Evan had never liked crème brulée, and he didn't like the elasticity with which Con regarded his marriage vows. Somehow Con had never got a bastard on any of his paramours—until Mary.

He'd been proud, excited. For Evan, that had been the beginning of the end, watching Con squander money, knowing he had not one family to take care of, but two.

I'll make sure Mary's child is cared for, he'd insisted. Laughing.

A bastard? What kind of life can a bastard hope to have?

My child—Con refused to use the word *bastard*—*will have a good one. I'll see to it.*

See to it, then, said Evan. *But I won't watch it happen. I can't watch what you're doing to your family.*

You can watch Kate well enough, retorted Con—and Evan knew then, he *knew*, that Con had long understood Evan's hopeless love for Kate. Maybe he thought Evan would love her enough for them both, while Con ran around with other women.

Or maybe he didn't care—not for his wife's heart, and not for his friend's.

Everything Evan held dear, Con valued little. And so Evan left, swearing never to return. Remaining would be like watching someone shoot horse after healthy horse. It would be like a museum director watching every precious item in his holdings burned and crushed.

But he had returned after all. And here was Mary, delivered of a healthy son, whom Con had not been able to care for.

The cut-off cinch was heavy in Evan's pocket. Driscoll's odd, clumsy dodge about Con and false antiquities lay heavily on his mind.

And he noticed something he hadn't before.

"Mary," he said. "Where did you get that statue on your mantel?"

Mary jogged the little boy on her hip. "The dolphin, you mean? Con gave that to me. He said it was a Roman one."

"So it seems." Evan crossed the room to look at it more closely. The stone sculpture was the size of the O his fingers could make curving together, the dolphin's nose almost touching its tail.

"Is it worth something?"

Evan picked up the statue, hefted it—too light for solid stone—and squinted at it. Somewhere, if it were of the type he'd seen so often, there would be a join. *Aha.* With a wring of the dolphin's neck and a squeak of tight-fitting stone, Evan yanked the sculpture apart. It was hollow within, and empty—like the false antiquities Evan had lectured on. And it had come to Mary from Con.

What did this mean? That Con was connected to the forged antiquities somehow? As Driscoll had carefully *not* suggested?

Evan looked into the little space, feeling just as hollow. "No," he said. "It's not worth any money. But if it's worth something to you, you should keep it." He pressed the pieces back together, unable to help admiring the skill of their join.

"It is," Mary said from behind him. "Besides my boy, it's all I have of Con."

"You went to his funeral, didn't you?"

"I did, and I go to his grave all the time. Sometimes we see the countess."

"The countess?" Evan set the dolphin back on the mantel with unsteady fingers, then turned. "The—the young countess?"

"The young one, Con's wife," Mary agreed. "She's a real lady."

With a gentle hand, she covered her son's ear. "She didn't deserve to be run around on, but—Con was going to run around anyway, see? And I wanted it to be with me. I couldn't be quit of him." Her mouth trembled. "I took a few weeds from the churchyard wall. We'll bring them back, and Conall can lay them for his da."

"Fowers," said young Conall.

"That's right," Mary said. "Flowers for your da. I want you to know him as much as you can."

What do you want your boy to know? Evan almost asked. *Con was my closest friend for years. I don't think anyone knew him better.*

Even so, there was much about him I never guessed.

From the mantel, the dolphin seemed to smile.

So Evan asked a different question instead, hand in his coat pocket to brush the sliced-off cinch. "Mary, did you know a groom named Adam Jones? He worked at Whelan House around the time Con died."

Mary tickled her son's side, her brow creased with the effort of recollection. "The Welsh fellow, you mean?"

"He was Welsh?"

"Sure he was. Welsh as you and Miss Ahearn."

"Miss Ahearn is Welsh?" Evan realized he was repeating himself. "That cannot be. She's from Thurles."

"She sounds like she's been in Ireland awhile, but that's no County Tipperary accent. If you could hear speech with Irish ears, you'd know her voice for a Welsh one, like yours."

This was both interesting and odd, but not precisely to the point. "Was Mr. Jones angry with Con? Maybe an issue of pay, or… What do grooms get angry about? A wager gone wrong?" Who would know, at this point in time? It had been two years. Evan could almost feel straws slipping from his grasp.

Mary opened her mouth—then closed it, shaking her head. She set her child down with an instruction to play with his blocks in the bedchamber. When Conall had scooted off, Mary spoke—quietly, so quietly Evan had to draw near. "I'm a good Catholic, though I've done my share of sinning. And there's something wrong in this town."

This, Evan had not expected. "With whom? Where?"

Mary jerked her head toward the back of the house. "It goes down the river. Ever so many boxes, but of what?"

"Boxes?" Evan struggled to follow.

"Wooden ones, great big ones floating by at night. I asked Mr. Driscoll about all the boxes once, and he said he had the matter in hand. Gave me a shilling for my trouble, treating me like a housemaid peeking on naughty guests."

"And these boxes come from upriver?" Evan asked. When Mary nodded, he said, "Then I need to search upriver."

Loughmoe Castle was upriver on the Suir, wasn't it? Loughmoe, and its wild geese so long flown.

"Don't search alone," Mary said. "The young countess would go with you, I'd wager. She's a crack shot."

"Thank you, Mary," Evan said. "I don't think I'll go to the castle yet. By the by, how are you getting along? Have you means enough?"

Mary winked, the sauciness that must have drawn Con's eye so many years ago. "I get a shilling for my trouble every time a box goes by, so I do all right."

With that, Evan took his leave from Mary. Instead of returning to Whelan House or cutting north to Loughmoe, he rode further west. He crossed the Suir on a stone bridge, the chestnut's hooves making a pleasant ringing clop.

West they rode, past fields, until farmland became manicured and rough stone walls became tidy white-painted posts.

Here they were at the racecourse, a gravesite of its own. An uneven oval, smooth green turf chopped by hedges, outlined by white fences, split by a ditch. It was the tidy version of life. Problems for those who never otherwise encountered them.

This wasn't fair, Evan knew. Anyone who owned or could borrow a horse could ride the course. For many, the race was a wind-whipped escape from the grind of everyday life. When soaring through the air on the back of a horse, unwashed nappies and burned meals and that sprained finger one had got at work didn't matter so much.

He urged the chestnut onto the silent course. The gelding's ears were pricked, and he tugged at the bit. He recognized the track and was ready to set off at a gallop. "No races today, boy," Evan soothed. "I just want to have a look."

He rode the chestnut to the first jump, then swung down. Holding the reins, he walked around it, hedge and fence, and then examined it from either side.

The chestnut snorted, shaking his fine head.

"You're right," Evan said. "I don't know what I thought I'd find." After two years, it wasn't as though a letter of explanation would be tucked into the neatly trimmed jump.

Here on this site, the fifth Earl of Whelan fell. It was due to tack that someone had damaged. Someone Welsh, who fled.

Someone named Jones.

Jones, like Sir William's old friend. The criminal mastermind, Anne Jones.

Who was Welsh, and who had fled from the baronet, taking the secret of a lost daughter with her.

Like the horse, Evan shook his head. Coincidence—all of it. He was weaving connections that weren't there. Nothing was here now but a fence and a hedge, both of the sort Con had jumped hundreds, maybe thousands of times.

"Why did you do it, Con?" Evan murmured. "Why did you take the leap?"

The answer came easily. He'd done it because he loved it, and because he never expected any harm to come to him. This was why he'd raced, too, and why he had betrayed Kate. Why he'd asked Evan to keep his secrets.

And didn't Evan understand? Those were the same reasons Evan had visited Whelan House so often over the years: because he loved being there. It was like his home. He never expected Con to return with a bride who took Evan's heart, unknowing, and never gave it back again.

Even so, he had assumed his friend would always be there. That the cinch would hold. That Con would bounce up from every fall. And that the one who possessed Kate, the greatest treasure imaginable, would value her as she deserved and give her what she wanted. Show her she was enough, just as she was.

But Con had gone silent, and Evan had too. So many years wasted. So many years apart. So much he could have said, should have said—and so much he dared not, lest he frighten Kate from his side. Lest he break his own heart beyond repair.

Anguish ripped through him, a keen of such rage and sorrow that he dropped the chestnut's reins and sank to his knees on the turf. Right after the maiden jump, at which Con had fallen and met the end of his life. Evan crumbled for all the words unspoken to his friend, the letters unwritten to Kate, and all he still could not say to her.

Twenty-one

That night, Kate braced herself for another visit from Good Old Gwyn. But as they waited for the customary quaver at the drawing room door, Evan opened the glass-fronted curio cabinet in the corner and shuffled through items within.

Mysterious of him, yes. But why should he not? He seemed to fit here; he always had. He had been a part of Whelan House before Kate herself.

"How long," he asked, "have you had this bust?" He emerged from the depths of the cabinet with an odd carved statue in his hands.

From her perch on the long sofa, Kate looked at it blankly. "Is that mine?"

"Surely it is. I found it in the cabinet."

"It must have been in there since some time before Con died. He was always switching those items when he ordered new draperies and things like that. I stopped looking at what was in there a long time ago." Kate rose, crossing the room to join Evan and get a better look at the item.

"It's definitely *not* an ancient bust," Evan said. "For

one thing, it's extremely small. I can hold it in my hands. And for another..."

Kate, peering over Evan's shoulder, laughed. "It looks like Lord Liverpool." Indeed, the bust bore a startling likeness to the prime minister of England—but in classical garb, and with a laurel crown. "That's awful. I wish I'd spotted this long ago. I could have used the laugh."

"I think it must have been made as a joke," Evan agreed. "Especially because—wait a moment." With a wrench at the head, it squeaked and turned on the neck—then popped free.

"Good Lord," said Kate. "You've beheaded the prime minister."

"We're in Ireland, so it's permitted. Different country. Hardly even a crime." Evan tipped the little stone head. "Fine joinery, fitting those pieces together so neatly. You see the hollow inside?"

"That's not usual for statuary, is it?"

"For cast bronze, but not for stone."

He handed Kate the head, and she studied the hollow within. It looked chiseled out, the marks rough. "What could it be for?" Her brief spurt of humor had faded, and now she could not think of a question to which she wanted the answer.

Evan's mouth had pressed into a grim line. "I suspect that these statues are used in smuggling."

"Because they appear to be statues," Kate realized, "and nothing more." She didn't want to hold the funny little head anymore, and she handed it back to Evan as though it were a scalding potato.

"Customs agents won't care about statuary. Not

falsified pots, either. They're looking for obvious riches, like silks and coins."

"What does it mean that Con had one?"

Evan looked troubled. "It might mean nothing at all. He might have seen it in a shop, thought it funny, and bought it. It's not a forgery, because it's not meant to pass as anything old."

She swallowed. "What else could it mean?"

Carefully, Evan fitted the head and neck together. They seemed not to want to join, and he had to shove with gritted teeth to squeak the pieces into place. "It could mean that Con was involved in smuggling."

"But why?"

Another question to which she did not want the answer—yet this one came to mind easily.

Because they had always worried about money—always. Or to be more accurate, Kate had worried about money. *Don't buy that, please. We can't afford that. The rents aren't enough.*

Don't, can't, aren't. Hers had become the voice of absence. A challenge. Con always responded with a *don't, can't, aren't* of his own. *I don't need to worry. You can't curtail my pleasures. Things aren't as dire as you say.*

Con wouldn't have minded the adventure of smuggling—and he wouldn't have minded the extra money gained for looking the other way. Money for carriages and curtains and carpets, for gifts far more lavish than a bolt of cloth and a few toy soldiers.

Evan's thoughts seemed to have followed the same line. "With Con, the *why* is not difficult to imagine."

So easy, in fact, that she assumed at once it was true. "I wonder what his pleasure was. Stolen gems?"

"A fine guess. I knew you had the criminal instinct."

"It's the company I keep," Kate said lightly. "I used to be a perfect lady."

"And now you're a just-right lady, is that it?" Evan tossed the tiny prime minister from one hand to the other. "What shall we do with this fellow?"

"Pitch it into the fire."

"Nonsense. It's stone. It won't burn."

"Put it back into the curio cabinet, then," Kate decided. "But I won't keep it." Never before had she felt a possession as a burden, but now she wanted to smash it. A great sweep, a clearing out that would make Whelan House into the home of her shaping. "I haven't changed anything since he died. At first I didn't want to, and then there was no money. But now..."

Evan tossed the bust into the cabinet with more force than care. "What's this? Are you talking of change? So much excitement for one evening! You're going to make me swoon."

"This is only good sense. These old walls are so thick. What do you think would bring more light into the space?"

"A great hole in the roof," he said promptly.

"Take that back at once. A sound roof, I am relieved to say, is one thing this house does possess."

But even as she joked, she wondered. *Who* had her husband been?

~

The following morning, Kate entered the study. As usual. And regarded the pile of work on the desk. As usual.

Ledgers, letters, questions, demands. Blotting paper, ink bottle, quill, sand. All in a pile for the earl, but one earl was gone, and the other was only nine years old. There was no one to sort through the papers but the countess.

She was more than a countess, though. Yesterday her hair had been tumbled, her skin warmed by passion. The awareness was unexpected—unfamiliar. Not unwelcome.

For a countess was also a wife, wasn't she? Or in Kate's case, a widow. And a mother who had been wed, and a lover who had been a friend. A lady who could seethe with anger, a friend who could be aflame with lust.

There were so many ways to be imperfect, but that did not mean they were not right.

"Time enough for these papers later," she decided. There was a walk she needed to take. She collected a fistful of blooms from the hothouse, then set off.

A brief burst of a sun shower had wet the grass, leaving the strands sparkling with drops. Kate had worn her great gray cloak again, and its hem became damp and heavy almost at once.

When she crossed onto the Church of Ireland lands, the new vicar—clipping the hedges before the little church—turned to greet her. A medium-sized, medium-looking man in every way, Reverend Jerrold nonetheless had a manner of great warmth. "Lady Whelan, what a pleasure. It's not often I see you here."

She waved her handful of flowers at him. "I'm on my way to the churchyard."

"Ah." He bowed. "I think it's empty at present. Take all the time you wish."

Kate turned the corner of the church, a wee stone building of great anciency. The churchyard at its side was neatly tended and just as old, with some markers worn illegible by time and rain.

One was new, comparatively, its trimmed edges still sharp. The name and dates were writ large, but Kate would know them by heart if the stone were blank.

Conall Ritchie Durham, Fifth Earl of Whelan. The courtesy titles, the dates. Beloved son, father, husband. A life in a few short lines, ending at the age of thirty-two years.

Good Old Gwyn had wanted a large marker. Something to collapse before and sob over, Kate had thought uncharitably. It was a flat tall slab, curved at the top. Simple, yet grand and looming.

In the darkest pit of shock after Con's sudden death, Kate had stayed away from the churchyard. She felt too conspicuous, her every feeling scrutinized. Was she grieving enough? Was she mourning properly?

But on this fine autumn day, it was pleasant to be there. The churchyard was green space in which, overhead, sounded the fluty call of a thrush. To birds, the trees in a churchyard were like any others: good for perching, for making homes, for finding seeds.

She set down her flowers, then gathered her long skirts to one side and sat beside the tall grave marker. "Conall Ritchie Durham. Here you are. It seems strange that you should be still when there's a chase coming up. You always did like the chase."

Every kind of chase. How well she remembered their first meeting.

"What is your Christian name, Miss Chandler?" he had asked.

Young and sheltered as she was, Abigail Chandler recognized the glow in his eyes as admiration, and she could not bear to see it snuffed. Which it surely would be if she told him her name, wouldn't it? *Abigail.* Abigail was provincial. Abigail was agog and easily impressed. Abigail was a nickname for a maid. Abigail would make do.

Abigail was not who she wanted to be for this young man of fashion. Instead, she told him her second name. "I am called Catherine." A queen's name.

"Are you?" He winked. "May I call you Kitty?" His voice was a purr that seemed to make this name, too, into a small one.

She drew herself up. "I prefer Kate." A name of decision. Quick on the lips, quick with a quip.

Thus she was ever after. But after they were married, she found that even Kates had to make do. Even as Kate, she had to make the best of something that had once seemed lovely and full of promise, but became quite the opposite.

"I loved you once, you know." She pressed her hand against the cold stone, stroking the smooth line of it. "You did know, didn't you? You used that to your advantage." Talking her into a quick, passionate interlude in the stillroom, surrounded by spices and dried herbs. Persuading her not to wait up for him, when he went God only knew where. Coaxing her for a ride in another new carriage…and another.

Con had been like a wood fire, bright and warm and snapping. Kate was the low flicker of peat. They had complemented each other, sometimes. Sometimes they had not understood each other at all. But they had done well, as well as they could. And once upon a time, he had loved her too.

A creak at the gate made Kate look up. There stood a woman outside the churchyard, with the simple clothing of a servant. Beneath her cap, she was veiled, her arms full of wriggling child.

She seemed not to want company, for as soon as she saw Kate sitting in the churchyard, she stepped back. After plucking a few weeds from the top of the low wall, she passed on down the road.

Kate watched them walk away. The little boy, barely out of leading strings, was a solid bundle who resisted his mother's embrace. Likely he wanted to get down and walk at the creeping pace of a toddler. Nora and Declan had been the same once. Every rock in the path had been fascinating, every crackling leaf on the ground a wonder to touch and—if Mama wasn't watching—to taste.

The memory made her smile. "Our children are beautiful, Con," she said. "I think they'll be good people. Evan…" Her voice broke, and she lifted her hand from the polished marble. "Evan knows how to make them happy, even better than I."

Her throat closed on the remaining words, and she patted the marble. "I wonder who we'd have become if you had lived, Con. Would we have been happy again?"

If…would…maybe…

She felt too shy to speak of Evan anymore. Taking a lover was too new, and the friendship between the two men was too old.

Not that she thought Con could hear her. She was talking to herself as much as to him. But there was a comfort in saying the words; speaking them gave them the weight they needed to become truth.

"This is a beautiful place to lie," she said. "I know you'd rather be striding around, and part of me will always have difficulty imagining you otherwise. But the turn of the seasons is gentle here, and something is always green. There's no snow, no hail, rarely even a storm." This was not Newmarket, not Holyhead. There was no mistaking Thurles for anything but itself.

The sun was steady now, and she let her bonnet fall back. Gathering up the flowers, she arranged them before the headstone. They were showy, as Con would have liked. Roses of dark crimson, tender cyclamen of white-tipped pink, and pink carnations. The smell was heavy, making her stomach roll with queasiness, but they looked lovely together.

Flowers had meaning, and she had chosen these carefully. *Mourning*, they stood for. *Good-bye. I will remember you always.*

"Thank you for bringing me to this beautiful place, Con," she murmured. "I think...it finally feels like my home."

And then she leaned against the marble monument to Conall Ritchie Durham, the fifth Earl of Whelan, and let the sunshine warm her all over.

Twenty-two

KATE FELT THE TICK OF THE CLOCK ON THE DRAWING room mantel in time with her heartbeat.

Dinner was completed, and the lamps had been lit against the early-setting sun. Another day was nearly gone, but this one had been far from ordinary. It had included a visit to the churchyard, for Con. Embraces for her children, who were now finishing the lessons they'd begun so late that morning. Business for the estate. Much to think about—for what Con had made of the past, and what she might like to make of the future.

From the open doorway, Kate overheard carriage wheels, then a rapping at the front door. The cultured low rumble of a servant's voice, then the familiar answering quaver of her mother-in-law.

No. Absolutely not. Kate was *not* up for a game of *who's-the-saddest* right now. "Do you want to go shoot?" she blurted.

Evan looked pointedly at the window. "Ah, no. It's almost dark outside."

"That adds to the challenge."

"No, I do not want to go shoot."

"Good Old Gwyn will be in the drawing room in less than one minute."

Evan grabbed Kate's arm. "I would love nothing in the world more than to fire hot bits of lead at a defenseless target. Lead on, my lady."

They slipped through the second door to the drawing room, making their way to the study with *shhhhing* and barely contained laughter. Kate unlocked the gun case and removed two pistols and a horn of powder, along with a bag of lead balls. "I can load for you if you like," she said.

"My manly dignity won't allow it. But I won't offer to load for you, because even my manly dignity allows me to admit that you're much quicker at it than I."

"I've practiced more than you." She relocked the case. "A countess has few proper ways to spend her leisure hours. For some reason, blowing the devil out of bits of paper is one of them." Which reminded her to grab a bit of foolscap from the desk, and a tack.

Evan held the study door for her. "Isn't it dull to shoot, knowing the result ahead of time?"

"I never know the result ahead of time. I only try not to miss."

He rolled his eyes. "You never miss."

This was true. "Even so, it's not dull to succeed at something. Small successes are often the only ones women have."

They made their way through the fading daylight to the edge of the wood, a safe distance from the house and stables. Kate tacked up the bit of paper, then returned to Evan's side. "This is twenty paces. A nice easy distance."

"Says you." He took the powder horn and a lead ball and loaded his pistol. "Your children said Gwyn was watching the forest the whole time you were gone. Why do you think that might be?"

"I can't imagine." Kate squinted as she shoved the ball into place. "Maybe she was watching for someone?"

"Yes, I think so too."

Kate fumbled the bag of shot. "I was teasing. For *whom* would she be watching?"

"I would dearly like to know." He took the bag of shot from her and tucked it into his coat pocket. "Never mind. We've pistols to shoot. Trees to injure. But you've only hung one target. You're going to shoot that to ash in an instant, and then what will I aim at?"

"The ash," she said. "Oh, here. I'll give you a target of your own. I have a handkerchief we can tack up for you."

"I am flattered that you think I could hit something smaller than a stable door."

"For someone who's not me, you're not a bad shot at all. Go ahead, take the first shot."

He aimed, sighting the bit of paper, and fired. When his hand lifted from the straight line and they both looked at the target, it was…

"Damn. It's far too dark. I can't even tell if I hit or not."

"I think you did," said Kate. "The white bit looks smaller." Carefully, she crouched and set down her pistol. "Though we don't have to keep shooting at all. Safety first, all hands on deck, keep together, advice, advice, et cetera, et cetera."

As she spoke, she straightened and permitted her hands to explore. There was something about dim light that was freeing, something attractive about hanging a scrap of paper and watching Evan Rhys notch a piece from it.

He was good at so many things. Right now, he was good at drawing her from the worried past into the sunset, rose-gold present, and she wanted all of him.

"My dear lady, what's this? Hungry for me again? I knew I was irresistible, but madam, there ought only to be one loaded gun during our intimate interludes."

"Your pistol is spent. It's perfectly safe." What she felt at the moment was not, however, a spent pistol.

"That would be a fine figure of speech, if it were not patently untrue. Manly dignity and all that. My pistol is never spent."

"I saw it spent yesterday. More than once."

"Yes, well, those were unusual circumstances. A pistol can only be fired so many times before it needs to cool. Anyway, it's not spent now."

She could have listened to him all day. She could have wrapped her arms in an endless embrace about his narrow waist, his solid chest. "You are perfect. This is exactly what I need."

"What is?" His voice sounded warm, and she leaned her head against him in a cradle.

"You, joking. Here. With me. Like this." She took a deep breath, letting him fill her lungs like shared smoke. He smelled like grass and black powder, like all of outdoors. "Evan, I have changed my mind."

Within her grasp, he went stiff. "Oh? What about?"

"Almost everything. I went to the churchyard

earlier, and I realized…I want to wear color, and I want to take you to bed again."

He let his pistol fall to the earth. "Not to straw? Not to a forest floor?"

"Well. There was nothing wrong with those. But—I'm thinking of a bed, as we shared in Newmarket. I was too afraid then. But here, with my familiar life about me—I feel braver. I'm ready for pleasure."

He shook free of her embrace, stepping back. "I see. And I'm to provide it? You've decided on that?"

How strange. She had half-expected—well, more than half—he would cheer. Instead, he looked coolly at her, like a man asked for a favor he did not want to grant.

Twenty paces to the target was an easy distance. Suddenly, two paces between her and Evan seemed a great many. "Well—only…if you want to, yes. I thought you wanted to. In Newmarket, you seemed upset that I left the bedchamber. When I said we couldn't do it again, and I didn't want anything to change. But now, I am ready for a change."

He stepped back again, treading on the unloaded pistol he'd dropped, and cursed. "So change is all right if it takes place on your terms, and you expect me to wait for it?"

Heat flooded Kate's cheeks. Shame? Embarrassment? Anger? All of them at once, in a startled roil. What the devil was he *on* about? "Evan, I thought this sort of affair was what you wanted."

"Did you think so? I knew it wasn't. It never was."

Her jaw dropped.

It was dark now, almost, and he was only a shadow

backed by the bleed of the setting sun. When he spoke, the harsh edge had melted from his voice. "I don't mean that in the way you've undoubtedly assumed. I mean that I've wanted far more. Kate, yes, I wanted to give you pleasure, but that was never all I wanted. I wanted to be with you in every way. Talking before a fire. Showing you the most grotesque of artifacts. Stuffing ourselves with potatoes."

"I didn't stuff myself."

"Possibly the most unimportant bit of my beautiful speech you could have seized upon, but I will let it pass. It's just—the everyday things are the things I want. Losing to you at target shooting. Talking to your children, who are part of you, and very much their own wonderful selves."

The slapped feeling was ebbing from her cheeks. She had misunderstood, maybe. This sounded like agreement. "We can do all of that," she blurted. "We have been. I'm saying I like all of that."

"I like it too," he said. "But you went to the churchyard today, and yesterday I went to the racecourse, and—what shook a few realizations loose for you did the same for me. And I want more than a half measure of you."

She spread her hands behind her, but there was nothing to lean against. "What do you mean?"

"I don't want to keep waiting. I don't want to be the man who gets doting flowers on his grave. I want to have the right to give you flowers, every day."

"You could! I would be happy to get flowers from you."

"Because?"

"Because you said you wanted to give them to me?" It was the wrong answer, she knew it as she spoke it, but she could not imagine the right one. Her mind seemed stuck in a mire of unexpected words.

He sighed, a sound as low and soft as if it were the breath of his soul. "Because I want to be yours, and I want you for my own."

It was a sentence simple and clear as a perfect crystal, and as blade-sharp at the edge. It seemed to cut her off at the knees, so she had to sit down, hard, on the ground.

Evan loomed above her, a perfectly cut silhouette. "You don't like hearing that? You don't like me having wants other than yours?"

"No, that's not it at all." Kate reached up with one hand. "I do like that. If you only wanted the same things as me, you wouldn't be you. And I wouldn't want you to be anyone else."

"Well. That's something." He took a step closer to her, letting the movement brush their fingertips together. "I've spent the last two years learning the difference between real and false in history. But we've falseness in our history too. Do you see it?"

She scrabbled for his fingertips, and he drew back again. "I don't see it, no. You're my closest friend. You *know* that."

"I do. But I won't be a false statue anymore. I'm not hollow, and for God's sake, I'm not a sculpted cock for your enjoyment. You're hot and cold as a spring day, and you want there to be no change at all between us once we're outside the bedchamber." He crouched to pick up his discarded pistol. "Or the stable. Or the forest."

Her throat caught. "But so much has changed already. I've reached for you, and I want to be with you again. I'll change more, too. I'll wear color. And we only just found the cut in the cinch, and—"

"Excuses, Kate. Will you always have an excuse to hold back?" He slapped his palm with the pistol, a dull pained sound. "I don't give a damn what gown you wear, as long as you like it. And I definitely don't want you using anything we've been through as an excuse not to go through more."

This stung, and she scrambled to her feet, fired by indignation. "What *we've* been through? Tell me, Evan, what did *we* go through together in the past two years? Where were you when my husband died? When did you ever lose someone you once loved?"

Her words startled even her with their force. She felt jarred, shaken, broken open. She strained to see him in the purpling dusk, to know how his face had changed at what she'd said.

For a moment, he let the words ring into silence. "I've lost much," he said. "You don't know how much. But you're right. I wasn't there for you. I wasn't there for either of us."

Amazing, the soothing effect of *you're right* on jangled nerves. "I didn't mean to make any excuse," she said. "Why—I went to Con's grave today, as you know. I told him—well, it sounds silly. I didn't tell him anything, because he's gone. But I said, for me—I said, you make the children happy."

"A remarkably fragmented anecdote. And did I figure in relation to you at any point?"

I didn't dare say. "One can't speak to the grave of

one's dead husband about another man." The attempt at lightness came out ghoulish.

"So many rules of propriety," Evan mused. "I will never learn them all. And I'd wager right now, you're thinking of being a countess or a mother and wondering whether you ought to have changed out of your black clothes. We're alone, and you're still not thinking of us."

"Not only of *us*, whatever you mean by that, because all those things are part of me! That doesn't mean they aren't valid reasons to keep things as they are."

"Excuses." He took something from his pocket. A lead ball, she could tell from the way it moved. It was small and rolling within his hand.

"Reasons, Evan."

"If we're arguing over the semantics of why you won't be with me, then that's all the answer I need." He dropped the lead ball, cursing. It bounced in the grass, becoming invisible. Of instinct Kate caught it under the heel of her boot.

"That's not what I'm saying at all, Evan. I do want to be with you. But...the way we've been." She gritted her teeth, hoping he'd understand the meaning behind the tangled words. "You're *leaving*. You're going to live in Greece in a few months. I can't go there with you. Declan is the earl. We can't...anything you and I have together could be only temporary."

"You have never asked me not to go to Greece."

Her mouth fell open.

"But maybe you realized that already. Maybe you suspected that if you asked, I'd say yes."

"I couldn't ask you to change your life for me," she whispered.

"You could if you wanted to share it." His fist clenched. "I can't do this anymore, Kate. God help me, I can't do it. If you want me, you need to court me good and proper, like the fine gentleman I am. And if you don't want me, I'd prefer to know that now."

The ball was sharp under her heel. It felt much larger than one bullet, one shot, or one chance to wound. "Why can't we go on like this? Enjoying each other for the time we have?"

"As I said, because I want more than a half measure of you. And I deserve someone who wants more than a half measure of me."

"So you're leaving again? You're giving me up?" The world had changed from autumn to winter in an instant.

"I don't know that I can. I don't know that there's anyone else for me. But I can't have this halfway sort of love with you anymore."

Love.

Dimly, she remembered that she had a loaded pistol at her feet somewhere. "Love," she echoed.

"I shouldn't have said that," he muttered. "It's no good, is it?"

"No, no. You should have. It's—it is good. It's good." She couldn't get warm, couldn't get enough air. "I love you too. You know that."

"But not in the same way," he said. "And not enough."

Not enough, he said. All the things she tried to be, and it was not enough. Whatever she could give, it was not enough. Divide herself as she might, there was not enough of her, yet she remained divided. Not enough of anything to be *real.*

"I think I know what gray feels like." Her voice was no more than a thread of sound.

"No, you don't," he said. "Gray is not a passing emotion, Lady Whelan. Gray is a way of life. Now, are you going to take your shot?"

Her shot. As though she cared about taking her shot now. As though there were a target she could hit that would make her feel she'd earned a victory.

She kicked away the fallen ball, then crouched to feel about on the ground for her pistol. The sun was nearly gone now, and she could not even see the bit of paper she'd tacked up.

Angling her arm away from them, she fired into the ground. "There. Safely discharged. We can lock it away again."

"Typical," Evan said. "She fires into the ground, and she still comes closer to hitting the target than I did." He bumped her with an outstretched hand, then found hers and pressed the second pistol into it.

"Where are you going?" The question burst forth, more pitiful than she would have wished.

"For now? Indoors. Don't worry, Lady Whelan. I'll stay long enough to sort out this matter of the cinch."

Lady Whelan. When a moment ago, he had called her Kate. A day earlier he had even called her Biggie to make her smile. "The matter of Con's death, you mean." She felt nothing could make her smile now. "And why should you sort it out?"

"Because I loved him. Not as you did, but as

someone who took me just as I was. In that sense, he's the truest friend I ever had. And he deserves the truth in return."

"What do *you* deserve?"

"More than what you want from me."

And he walked away, leaving her in the dark.

Twenty-three

The following morning, Evan left the manor house early. The sooner he searched Loughmoe Castle, pried open a box floating along the river behind Mary O'Dowd's cottage, shook a few answers free from Finnian Driscoll and anyone else who put a block in his path, the sooner he'd be done. He'd have settled every question to do with the Whelans. He'd be done with Ireland, and on to…somewhere.

Where to start? He considered this as he saddled the chestnut gelding again. The sliced-off cinch was heavy in his pocket. So was the pistol beside it—his own, for even a serious lecturer must have a way to defend himself while traveling.

He'd visit Loughmoe Castle first. Why not? All castles hereabouts were gray. The sky was gray too, a dimness that didn't even hint at the color it would become.

Before turning the gelding onto the road northward to the castle, he made the brief jaunt to the churchyard. From over the low wall, he easily picked out Con's stone, large and sharp, drawing the eye. Over its velvety green grass lay a bundle of softening hothouse flowers and a twist of weeds that looked to have been knotted by a small hand.

He removed his hat, putting it to his heart.

"You were always a lucky devil, Con," he said. "Not least because of my friendship."

As he settled his hat back into place, he could almost imagine the inevitable wry humor of his friend's reply. One could never forget a friend of such long-standing—especially a friend like Con, swift and joyful as a wink.

Maybe he'd been good for Con, a little ballast for all the young earl's buoyancy. He knew Con had been good for him. Despite Kate. Because of Kate. Curse Kate, and bless her, and—and enough now. Enough.

He turned the chestnut away, nudging the horse into a trot when they reached the road. Edged by autumn-brown trees, it followed the course of the River Suir, which ran brown-gray and placid and open. No crates drifted down its length this morning. It looked innocent, as if nothing had ever been placed in it that was not right, and it lapped with a soothing intensity at its banks. From somewhere in the trees, a robin gave its delicate peep, a sound almost too high and quiet for the ear to pick out.

The ride to Loughmoe Castle, set outside the village of Loughmore, was not a long one on the back of a smooth-trotting gelding. Soon enough, as the gray sky lightened, the road had taken him within sight of the great ruin.

The castle was set in an open space, around the edge of which trees crowded like eager spectators.

Many were now bare-branched, though a few still held to their leaves and to the memory of green.

Loughmoe Castle was, at the first distant glance, a wrecked and ruined old structure. A square tower house onto which had been added a stretch, and another great tower over time. The castle was shaped like a squashed H. How the pediments had once been shaped, no one could guess, for the high walls looked nibbled at the top. It was difficult to remember that each nibble was the absence of huge blocks of trimmed stone.

But there was something off, and Evan halted the horse at the edge of the wood until he could place a finger on what that something was. "Someone is here." He knew, just as he knew when he saw a new statue made to look old. Now, what was it nagging at him?

The walls were overgrown with climbing plants above and below. Bushy and verdant, as though they'd drained life from the trees around, the leaves spilled over the top of the ragged wall. Amidst the tangle of green, the tower windows blinked like sleepy eyes.

"The windows." Yes. That was it. The windows had been cleared of cover.

This was no abandoned structure. What it was instead, he couldn't be sure—yet.

He tied the chestnut to a tree back from the wooded edge, out of sight of the castle. Then—feeling slightly ridiculous, but wanting to use caution—he crept and crawled and peeked his way from the wood to a crumbling wall about the castle. No more than waist-high, and more gravel and grass than stone, it made a fine barrier behind which to hide. Look about. Move on.

Within the bound, the castle yawned above him.

The older tower was far more crumbled at the top than the other parts of the building, with rounded corners to its slab-like walls. Windows had once peered from stone frames. Now the frames themselves were broken, only pieces of the lattice remaining. It was all open now, roofless, the upper floors fallen. Underbrush grew within, as if the forest had leapt the intervening grass and taken up residence in here.

"I knew a great hole in the roof would brighten a space," Evan murmured. For a flash, he wanted to tell Kate, to make her laugh. Then he remembered there was no purpose to telling Kate anything anymore.

When Evan stepped into the space, careful to set his boots quietly, he caught the unmistakable earthy scent of burning peat. The space was being used, that was clear—and used *right now.* He kept to the brush-shadowed walls, eyes searching for some clue. There the worn old stone had been moved aside, revealing paler, smoother stone beneath. There were the scratch marks of tools that had pried them free.

"Unwise," he said below his breath. The stone walls were vertical mosaics, and undermining them could cause a disastrous fall.

What had he thought he might learn? Now that he was here, poked by dry ivy and surrounded by more gray than he had imagined, he couldn't say. Yes, there were signs that stone had been taken from the castle. Yes, it matched the stone of the false carvings. But there were so many missing links, from the carver to the purpose of the hollows to the boxes floated past Mary's cottage—probably full of crated carvings or the smuggled goods that would be pieced out inside.

What did it matter, if it didn't lead to Con? If Evan couldn't find the answer to the sliced-off cinch that had dumped his friend to the turf, who gave a damn about the rest? He did. He knew he did, in a time that was less gray, because it was right to care about honesty.

So he held fast to that knowledge, threadbare though it now seemed, and pressed onward through the tangle within the castle walls. He followed the scent of peat, wishing for the nose of a hound. Now it seemed stronger, now fainter. When he found the source of the fire, he'd find the people tending it. He'd see what they were doing.

Ah, he must be getting closer—he heard footsteps now, ringing echoes in the hollow stone tower. Voices speaking, a tongue he did not understand. Those sounds, too, echoed and distorted, but the flip and play of the language sounded like Gaelic.

Overhead, a horrid heavy grating sound signaled the shift of a rock. Evan had just time to look up for its source, then fling himself back against the wall, before everything went dark.

Kate was supposed to be reviewing the household accounts. She was supposed to be checking rent rolls. She was supposed to be directing the governess as to what Nora and Declan should be studying. She wasn't. She was sitting at the study desk with all her supposed-to's spread out before her, seeing nothing but a blur.

Evan was gone. He had left that morning before anyone awoke but the servants. Oh, he had left his belongings, and he'd be back—but he'd told Kate his intention to act and leave, and he was already all but departed. Her tea had grown cold. She'd been unable to eat this morning. She couldn't think, couldn't settle.

The frantic knocking at the front door, overwrought even for Good Old Gwyn, was almost a relief. "She probably forgot something here last night," muttered Kate.

When she had returned to the house after their fight, hands full of pistols, Evan was nowhere to be found, the children had hidden themselves upstairs, and Gwyn was prostrate on her favorite drawing room sofa after being *abandoned* by *everyone*. This as two maids fanned her and loosened her slippers.

Good Old Gwyn.

As Kate dutifully stood now, prepared to greet her mother-in-law, the butler opened the door—not to Gwyn's quaver, but to a spill of hurried male voices. Something was wrong. The children were inside—so the horses? It must be the horses.

She took the corridor at a trot, then pulled up sharply at the sight of the knot of rough men and the worried-looking butler. And the blood, a slow drip onto the marble floor of the entry hall. "What has happened? Is someone hurt—oh, my God! Mr. Rhys! What has happened to him?"

The paunchy figure of Finnian Driscoll pushed forward to sweep a bow. "Terrible thing, isn't it? Mr.

Rhys was found like this by the Suir. He was set upon by footpads, looks like. Hit on the head, pockets all turned out. Terrible, terrible thing."

Kate craned her neck, standing on her toes to get a better look at Evan. So much blood! "Is he all right? Will he be all right?"

"He's out right and proper, my lady. I saw the doctor as I hurried over with these gentlemen." The villagers supporting Evan's weight shuffled awkwardly. "He's on his way to have a look."

"Thank you." Kate felt shaky, breathless. "Fibbs, please direct these men to Mr. Rhys's chamber. He must be settled at once." As soon as the butler guided the rest of the men off, Kate sank against the wall.

"There, now, Lady Whelan, you mustn't fret." Driscoll laced his hands over his belly, bouncing on his heels. "You'll be safe enough in your fine house. Getting to be so you wouldn't know who was traveling through your own village. Best to keep your distance from the Suir, or take a companion with you."

Kate was not of a mood to play the agreement game. She summoned all her will, shoved herself upright, and lifted her chin. "This, Mr. Driscoll, is not *fretting*. *Fretting* is what a little girl does if she loses her favorite ribbon. I am a grown woman, and you have brought my houseguest back bloodied and unconscious. I am, shall we say, *displeased*."

"Well, now." The magistrate lifted his hands, supplicating. "I wasn't one of them who found him."

"And who did? The men who carried him upstairs?"

The hound dog eyes reproached her. "I can't say, I'm sure. Now, don't worry your head about what or who. It's my job to worry about that. And don't you worry about Mr. Rhys, for the physician's on his way."

Enough of this nonsense. She needed him out of her house.

She blew out a breath, willing herself to remain calm. "What do you advise I worry about, then?"

Driscoll's brows knit. "Well, there's your debt." He chucked her under the chin, and she recoiled. "But you shouldn't worry about that either, my lady. I'll take care of everything. Say the word. We'll trade land for debt and speak no more about it."

"No. Thank you," Kate said as demurely as one could with a clenched jaw. "I'll continue to worry for a bit longer."

As the villagers filed out, having settled Evan upstairs, she watched them leave, trying to memorize faces. It was no good. They all blended together in homespun and floppy hats and beards, and her eyes threatened to well over at any second.

Once alone in the entrance hall, she looked about for something to throw. "Pier glass. Candlesticks. Table with foolish little gilt legs. I can't afford to break anything in my own house." She settled for kicking the front door.

An answering knock sounded on the outside. "The doctor." She hauled open the door. If the physician were surprised to be greeted by the lady of the house, he did not betray such a feeling. Kate directed him to the patient, then shut the door, tried not to look at the blood on the floor, and followed the man to Evan's room.

His examination was short, consisting primarily

of wrapping the patient's head in a bandage. "The laceration," he pronounced to Kate, "is not severe. Head wounds offer a ghastly appearance, but they heal quickly. Now that pressure has been placed on the length of the wound, the bleeding will stop."

This ought to have been reassuring, but there was a far greater concern. "He is unconscious, Doctor. When will he wake?"

The courtly old man's face looked like crumpled paper. "I am sorry to tell you, Lady Whelan, that I do not know. A blow to the head has unpredictable effects. He might wake in an hour, or a day, and be fine. He might be forever altered in personality. Or he might simply fade away."

"Right," Kate said faintly. She dismissed the physician, who promised to return to check Evan's progress the following day. "Give him water and beef broth," were the final instructions. "If you can get it into him in his current state."

"If it will help him, he will have some. I will make sure of that."

As soon as the man was gone, Kate sank into a chair beside Evan's bed.

"This is unkind of you, Evan." She worked to keep her tone firm. "I am particularly sensitive when it comes to men leaving for a ride with all their possessions still here at the house, then returning with their heads crushed. Oh, that's not funny, is it? But if I don't laugh, I shall cry, and if I cry, then I won't know how to stop."

The laugh was ragged, at the edge of tears. She swallowed it down, adding, "You wouldn't let me into your bedchamber, but you see I got here all the same. Did you not once tell me I would be invincible? And so I am, Evan."

No response, of course, but shallow breathing.

She must be the rogue housekeeper—that was all. She couldn't manage more right now, raw and worried as she was, and more wouldn't help him. Efficiently, she removed his boots, laid a spare sheet over him and tucked it about his chest, then rang for an order of beef broth.

"You're going to wake up. Your countess has ordered it so."

Twenty-four

He didn't wake up that day or that night.

When someone else was in the room with them, Kate bore up with great good cheer. "He must be tired," she told Declan when he was ushered in, curious to view the invalid. "He needed a rest from our talking," she suggested to Nora, who entered next. "He'll wake as soon as he's ready for another fill of words."

"I don't talk nearly as much as Declan," Nora pointed out. "And he looks horrid."

"That's because beef broth spilled all over, when it ought to have gone into his mouth. You looked the same when I fed you broth as a baby."

This was startling and intriguing enough that Nora had several more questions. Instead of leaving, she was persuaded to stay and tend Uncle Evan. "But only with water," she said. "He's already enough of a mess."

"I agree," said Kate, who marveled at how easily Nora took on a grown-up role.

That was something good to come of this time in

the sickroom. And the chestnut horse Evan had ridden out had come back safely to the stable.

When Kate was alone, between the comings and goings of servants and her children, those seemed the only good things. Evan's breathing was still steady and shallow, but nothing else changed. He was there in the bed, looking whole and ready to wake, but he was not really there at all.

Kate realized this in the wee hours of the morning, when night had already been endless, yet hours of it remained. A lamp flickered on a table beside Evan's bed, and the dancing paleness of its light cast ghoulish shadows over Evan's face. Was he moving? Was that a twitch of an eyelid? No—only the movement of the light, leaving behind a hollow shadow. Evan looked already to have receded, his skin drawn tight.

"I'll give you some water," Kate said, for something to say.

When she took the glass in hand, she was shaking, and she set it down before she slopped it all over Evan's face. Her fingers were claws, stiff and tired. The water was no more than the bandage about his head, a means of pretending to treat an injury she could not understand.

She sank back into her chair, folding her arms at the edge of the bed, and looking at Evan, chin in hands. Could one be exasperated with someone whose life flirted with its end? She shouldn't be, probably. But she was. "You went looking about for smugglers, stubborn man. I would have gone with you. But you wouldn't have that, would you? You were the perfect friend to Con. You owed him, you thought."

Shallow breathing, slow and steady.

"Good response. Right. I'll pretend you've said, 'I did owe him, Kate.' And I'll be glad, because he was lucky to have a friend like you, and I'll be angry, because you put yourself in danger for a man beyond help. And I'll be worried, because I never suspected there was any danger at all. I still don't know the shape or source of it."

God, she wished he would move. She would give anything to hear one of his flip replies, teasing her to unexpected laughter, or to see his eyes crinkle with sharing it.

Sitting at his side, keeping this vigil, was like finding the shape of grief.

"I would give anything," she said quietly. "Anything mine to give. But that's easily offered, isn't it? The Almighty will not come down and demand this house in exchange for your recovery."

If she were offered such a trade, she'd take it without hesitation.

"I know what you think you owe Con. And I know what you owe yourself. I do not know what I owe you, though. Or is *owe* the right word? I do not know what I can give, or what I ought. I was the perfect wife to Con, and I tried to be the perfect friend to you. The perfect mother, the perfect countess. But I became all cut up inside, and then you wanted a bigger piece."

Was that right? That didn't seem right. He had never wanted to divide her. Evan had told her she was just right. Evan had nicknamed her the rogue housekeeper, laughing.

Evan hadn't wanted a piece, no matter how large or small. He had wanted her wholeness. He had given her children encouragement to step back into her arms and had not asked a place for himself.

He had wanted her happy and whole, and—and how could she not have understood? When he dropped the word *love* into their argument, it carried a sting. A bitter word, unwilling, with a tired, thin shape. The sort of word one flung at another out of obligation. Love unwanted was a painful thing. That he loved, and that it was unwanted, was what he had felt, and she could have sunk with sorrow at the realization.

She had forgotten that a different sort of love, the bedrock sort, could exist too, and so she had not recognized it for what it was. She had come to think of love as flashing and bright, plummeting and intense. The falling star, not the earth on which it landed.

As grief took many forms, so did love, its happy twin. It came in a disguise, behind the face of a friend. It spoke with a familiar voice. It shared her heart by adding to it, a bounty she had never expected.

"I love you," she said.

In a fairy tale, this—along with a kiss—would have brought the sleeping prince magically awake. Evan reacted not at all.

But what if he could hear her in some way? What if some part of his spirit might respond to her words? She would bother him into staying. She would persuade him to wake, just by wanting it so damned much. Her heart beat for two.

"I've hurt you. I said I didn't want anything to change between us, but I took every intimacy you would give. I was so selfish. I hope—that is not the way I always was. I hope that in itself was a change. And if I would change for the worse, why should I not change for the better? I don't want to be fearful, Evan. I fear losing you, so much right now. I feared losing you the first time I saw you again in Cambridge. That fear is from love—but I'll act on the love now, not the fear. I would lose you by risking nothing, so instead I will risk everything. Only wake, and I will show you."

These words were not persuasive enough to initiate a medical miracle.

"Let's try water again. The doctor thought it would help." She rose on legs made unsteady by fatigue, fumbling for the glass. The flicker of the lamp, or her own bleary eyes, caused her to misjudge the distance, and instead of gripping it, she tipped it. Cool water hit Evan in the face before Kate's wet fingers righted the dripping glass.

"Sorry about that." She felt for a cloth then wiped his face with the edge of the sheet. "We seem to be short on handkerchiefs. Again."

His lids moved. She was not imagining it this time, was she? No, it was not the flickering light. Dark lashes rose, fell again. The shallow breath became deeper, like the catching of breath after a long sleep.

"Kate," he mumbled. "Water."

She all but collapsed into her chair, then drew it closer to the bedside. "Yes. I'm here. Kate. Water. I threw it on you, but—maybe that was good, because you're awake. Are you awake? Do you want water?" She took up the glass again, carefully, and cradled his head so he could take a sip.

"Why...?" His voice was thready and faint, his body still. She set aside the water and leaned close to his lips, listening. "Why do I smell like a butcher shop?"

She snorted. "That, of all questions, is your first? There was an incident with beef broth."

"What happened?"

"Nora and I spilled it when we were trying to get you to take some. I took off your cravat and collar, but you ought to have a bath."

His expression altered—a flicker of *oh, please, you know that's not what I mean.* His hand moved, fingers flexing toward his head.

"You were hit on the head."

A tiny nod. "A stone. Grazed me."

Kate sat up straight. "A footpad threw a stone at you?"

"No, it fell. In the castle."

"If I didn't know you better, I'd think you were delirious. But I do know what you mean. You went looking for evidence of those statues." Kate cursed. "Was there a footpad at all? Were you by the Suir?"

"At Loughmoe."

Kate cursed again. "Driscoll fed me a pack of lies. Or the men who took you to Driscoll fed them to him." Far less palatable than potatoes, these were.

"My coat...the cinch..." His hand made a wave, a grasp.

"Your coat's here. You had the cinch with you? There is nothing in the pockets now. Those footpads have unusual preferences."

"No footpads. Old stone," Evan mumbled. "Good way to be injured. Noble."

The crook of his mouth, more than his fragmented words, told Kate he was making a joke. Relief was like a wave. "Yes, Evan. If one must be hit on the head, it should be by an old stone from a castle." She smoothed back his hair, for a reason to touch him. "Now I know you will recover. And wasn't I the one who was supposed to be hit on the head by a stone? You'd come up with all these ways for me to meet my end."

"Had to test it for you. Seems it wasn't a good idea after all."

"I believe that. It won't kill you, but it'll make you powerfully determined."

He moved a hand, brushing hers, and she caught it. "Mary, Mary, quite contrary," he mumbled. "But Con was contrary."

A random observation, but she took it in stride. "He certainly was. That was part of his charm, wasn't it?"

"Too much." His eyes were closing again, his voice growing fainter. "He said he'd care for her and the boy. He should have cared for all of you."

"What?"she whispered, doubting her own ears. "Cared for whom?"

"Mary, Mary," Evan said again. His eyes closed, his breathing slowing in the fall of sleep.

Kate stretched out beside him on the bed, boneless. Puzzled. And yet...*not*, exactly. Evan's words had the ring of familiarity, something she'd learned but never allowed herself to know.

His longtime mistress had had his baby, and that mistress's name was Mary. This much Kate had long known. Everyone in Ireland, it seemed, knew. Con had built two families for himself, and he had provided for neither.

What could have created a permanent breach between Con and Evan but a matter of honor? Con could not be brought to care for the welfare of others, but he could not bear to be criticized for it. The appearance of honor was the only thing Con held fast to. Everything else was a possession to be admired, then forgotten.

Queasiness seized her, and she rolled from the bed and scrabbled for the chamber pot. She was sick into it, again and again, until she was heaving nothing but sour air.

This was what she had feared: not change she chose, but change in spite of herself. Change that rocked her world and made it unfamiliar. The two men she loved both hid secrets from her: Con to protect himself, Evan to protect his friend.

Oh, God—and they thought they were protecting *her* too, didn't they? *Keep this from Kate. She's better off not knowing the truth.* They could apply this to debt, to smuggling, to anything they wished not to bring into the light.

As if it could ever be better to live a lie that might crumble. Who was helped by hiding the truth? By pretending everything was fine, and they were all content? As long as they pretended, such contentment could never become real.

You are not perfect, but you are just right. If this were true, why hadn't she been enough for Con? If she were just right as a wife, why had her husband strayed? Why hadn't he cared about anyone's well-being but his own?

Or maybe that was what one did, if one were an earl and one's wife was *just right*. She hadn't divided herself into pieces alone. The more she tried to be for Con, the more diminished she became. Yes, he was the one who had strayed, but they had first become unhappy together.

With watering eyes, Kate covered the mess in the chamber pot with a cloth. Her hands were steady now, steady as Evan's breathing. He slept, and he would wake when he was ready. Already the night promised to end, the black outside the windows turning to gray.

"Some grays are good." She watched him sleep, innocent of what he'd shaken within her.

It was for the best: that she knew. Right now, he slept on. His task was to heal. Hers? To stop being such a damned fool and to learn all she could. Con had left more affairs unsettled than even Kate realized. She would put them right—not for his sake, but for everyone else's.

Easing open the door, she looked for a servant who might spell her at Evan's bedside. Instead, she spotted two huddled figures in nightshirts, sitting in the corridor outside the bedchamber.

"Declan. Nora." *You know you have a half-sibling, right? And as much as I worry about money, the baby's mother must. More so.*

She was so surprised to see them that she almost spoke the words uppermost in her mind. They deserved to know, but there was much more she needed to learn first.

She crouched beside them, the lamplight from the room filtering over their pale, tired faces. "You must be worrying over Evan. He's sleeping now, but it's the good sort of sleep."

Nora sagged against Kate. "Will he be all right?"

"He made a joke about being happy to be hit on the head by an ancient stone, so I think he will be absolutely fine."

"We want to see Uncle Evan," Declan said.

She hesitated. "He's not your uncle, you know. And the room smells of sickness and old beef broth."

Nora peered at the doorway, wrinkling her nose. "We can see him after the room is cleaned. And he's better than our uncle, because we don't *have* to call him uncle, but we want to. You and Da picked him as our godfather."

"And he picked us to spend time with," added Declan. "So he wants to be in our family."

Did he?

They were so beautiful, these young people. She'd had a part in creating them, but they were not of her. They were themselves, better than she could ever have imagined.

She smiled, wanting to ruffle their hair, but restraining herself. "How did you two get to be so certain of everything?"

They looked at her blankly. "What is there to be unsure of?" asked Nora.

"A fine question," Kate said. "Right now, it is the one uppermost on my mind—above all the other things."

"It must be horrid being a countess," said Declan.

"Sometimes it is. Sometimes it has its benefits. But being a mother is even better." She dropped kisses on their heads, then stood. "Keep watch on the lamp for a moment, will you? I need to find someone to take my place in there."

And then? She'd find the answers to her questions. Likely she could find out most of them without even leaving her household, for servants knew everything that was going on upstairs and down. A servant raised in Thurles, native to the land and raised among the longtime families, would know even more. Would know where to look for answers that she didn't possess herself.

With quick steps, Kate followed the corridor from Evan's bedchamber to her own suite of rooms. She opened the door and crossed to the nook belonging to her lady's maid, Susan.

"I'm sorry," she whispered, shaking the shoulder of the sleeping maid until she turned over, startled awake. "It's so early, I know. But Susan, you must tell me whatever you can."

Twenty-five

At an hour of the morning respectable for being received as a caller, Kate left Whelan House. She was armored as well as a countess could be: bathed and fed, dressed in a riding habit, her head topped with a hat studded with silk flowers that had once seemed so smart.

She also carried a pistol, because even countesses needed the assistance of a shot sometimes. She would not use it to kill, but to put fear into someone? Yes, indeed. And maybe to maim—if necessary.

Awakened early and peppered with questions, Susan had been abashed and fearful until Kate reassured her and fetched tea from the kitchen. "With your own hands!" Susan accepted the cup from Kate, still huddled in her bedclothes, but was so distressed at being served by the countess that Kate again offered to take every helpful act from Susan's wages.

This unlocked both a laugh and the maid's tongue. She knew Con's mistress well, having been a servant at Whelan House for some of the time Mary O'Dowd had.

"Mary, Mary," Kate murmured.

"You'd know her by sight if you saw her about the village," Susan said, evidently taking Kate's low reply as confusion. "She has hair red as a fox pelt, and she's as pocked as the moon since a few years ago when she took ill with smallpox."

Kate raised her brows. "She's prettier than she sounds," Susan said.

Kate raised her brows still further.

"Not that it matters," Susan hurried to add.

So it all spilled forth, with a smoothness that cemented together the broken pieces Kate had collected over the years. Con had split from Mary at the time he wed Kate. But he went back to the mistress, time and again, even as he slaked his casual lusts with other women too.

It was an odd sort of fidelity. Maybe it was the only sort of which he was capable.

"And how does she live now?" Kate asked. "The late earl cannot have left her well off."

"I don't know about that. I know she gets money and doesn't ask questions. It's always better not to ask questions." Susan clutched at her sheet. "Isn't it?"

"Was that a question?" Kate arched a brow.

"Are you angry with me?" Susan whispered.

"With you? Heavens, no. You were reluctant to tell tales that were none of your affair, and such discretion is admirable. No, I'm not angry at all." Kate answered with perfect honesty, almost surprised to realize it. "I'm not angry at all. Just weary, Susan. Weary and ready for answers."

The first seeds of this bramble knot had been sown

before Kate met Con. More had been added when they married, still more when Con overspent their income year after year. When Mary O'Dowd grew ill, drawing Con back to her side; when the winter grew harsh and crops failed. All this, over years, had ended in a slashed saddle cinch and a dead earl.

All this, over years, had continued even since Con's death. But it would stop now. It would be sorted out. And everyone would get what he or she needed.

Starting with Driscoll. Driscoll, who didn't know who had come upon the injured Evan, but seemed otherwise certain of the circumstances. Driscoll, who—as Susan said—kept Mary O'Dowd supplied with coin, but was not her protector. Driscoll, the first to blunder into a link between Con and a set of odd little statues with pull-apart forms. Driscoll, who had bought up Con's debts after his death. Debts he would never have been able to secure were the earl, charismatic and full of promises, still alive.

To Driscoll she would go—after she retrieved a constable. Even countesses in possession of fashionable hats and pistols needed additional protection sometimes. Dressed in her riding habit, she entered the stables and greeted surprised grooms. "I should like Lucy to be saddled, please."

And for the first time in two years, Kate took to the back of a horse.

When they set out into the morning air, fresh and cool as only autumn can be, Kate felt solid in a way she had not for quite some time. Riding Lucy, rocking with the flowing cadence of the horse's strides, was like being part of a team she had abandoned. It was like rediscovering part of herself. One that looked higher and moved faster.

One that would have a dreadfully sore backside the following day. But that didn't matter now. Kate nudged Lucy into a trot, and together they covered the distance between the Whelan lands and the town of Thurles.

Almost as soon as they fell into a walk on the high street, they encountered a commotion. The landlady who kept the lodging house beside Bridge Castle was out in the street, wailing to an interested crowd. "Gone this morning, and without a word!"

Lucy pricked up her ears.

"I agree," said Kate. "Let's find out what's happened."

A quick word at the edge of the crowd told her what had passed: Mrs. McIlhenny had awoken at her usual hour, gone to collect the weekly rent, and found Miss Ahearn's room vacated. Ever since, there had been much wailing and gnashing of teeth.

"Did Miss Ahearn steal from her landlady when she left?"

The ear Kate had caught belonged to a housemaid of Mrs. McIlhenny, who answered in the negative. "Only her own things, plus a funny little stone sculpture the missus used to keep on the mantel in the parlor. But that were a gift from Miss Ahearn, so I don't think it's stealing, like."

"Right." This was getting more and more curious. "Miss Ahearn paid her rent? Or was she behind on it?"

"She wasn't, at that. Always beforehand, she was, and she left enough to cover the next month."

"Then what is your mistress wailing about?" As

if seconding Kate's question, Lucy shook her head and snorted.

"The missus, she likes to wail. And who am I to stop her?" The housemaid winked. "It's as good as a holiday, hearing her go on like this. Think I'll get a currant bun and enjoy the show."

Kate nudged Lucy onward, letting the bay pick her own footing through the crowd on the high street. "What does it mean, Luce? She had family in Dublin whom she visited often. They must have had some emergency, and she had to go to them at once."

Lucy's ears flicked as Kate spoke. With a little shake of her head, one warm brown eye regarded Kate. *You know better than that.*

"The sculpture, hmm? I agree. That's damning evidence. But of what, I don't know."

It was time to find Driscoll. At Bridge Castle, Kate found a constable on duty. She persuaded him to come with her after swearing on a Bible, on the soul of her dead husband, and on her dear late mother, that Mr. Driscoll had been involved in injuring Evan Rhys, and she needed an officer of the law to confront... well, an officer of the law.

The constable, a ruddy-faced young man with a shock of hair the same shade as his chestnut horse's coat, mounted up and followed Kate and Lucy to the Prancing Pony. "Will he be in there?"

"He's always in there," Kate replied grimly.

But she was wrong, or was after a few seconds. When the constable swung down from his horse and entered the public house, a great crashing of furniture ensued. Then shouts, then another crash—and then the constable jetted forth, shouting, "He's gone out the back!"

Before the young man could remount, Kate wheeled Lucy. Tightening her leg around the pommel of the sidesaddle, Kate bent forward, looking through the churn of the crowd still blocking the high street.

There! Driscoll's rotund figure was unmistakable. He had mounted a white horse and tried to set off at a good clip, but the crowd prevented him from getting away quickly.

"After him, Luce." Kate spurred the mare along, giving her a quick pat on the neck. "The constable will have to catch up when he can."

Progress back up the street was frustratingly slow, as Kate reined Lucy in every other step to avoid treading on someone. She kept the white horse in sight, and even caught up a little when a familiar housemaid, currant bun in hand, dodged back and forth before the white horse and the magistrate.

The maid winked and waved at Kate as they went past.

Free of the crowd, Driscoll urged his horse into a gallop. "Not a bad seat for a big man," Kate murmured. Lucy's ears pricked again, and she stretched out her head, taking the bit. "Quick as you like, girl. Quick as you like."

The mare needed no more encouragement than to be given her head, and they were off. Kate held the reins only to guide, laying her heart against the mare's neck. The horse did best when given her head, allowed to choose her own speed and stride. She hadn't raced for so long, and she loved it.

Lucy wasn't the only one. *God*, Kate had missed this. If they'd been galloping for any other reason, it would have been sheer pleasure. Lucy's gallop devoured the path, scattering leaves already stirred by the strides of the white horse. Driscoll looked over his shoulder, muttered something, then guided his horse off the path and into the surrounding wood.

Did he think they wouldn't follow? The thrill of the chase was in her blood now, and in the mare's too. Kate kept a light hand on the reins, just enough to guide Lucy along. A fallen log blocked them, and Lucy took it with a gather of her haunches, then a leap. They swooped through the air, landing with smooth strides and a whoop from Kate's throat.

Smaller branches they took in stride, curves around trees no obstacle. A puddle? Lucy ran right through it with scarcely a break in stride.

"You'd be queen of the chase," Kate gasped, the wind of the gallop taking her breath. "Better than the chase." It wasn't a loop around a track; it was real, and winning this race would mean something important. If they could catch him.

Driscoll was guiding his horse back toward the road, where the larger animal's longer strides would give him an advantage. "Enough of this." Holding the reins in one hand, Kate worked free her pistol with the other. She had one shot, and she must make it count. Sighting her target between Lucy's ears, she aimed, accounting for the bobbing of the horse's stride.

"Sorry, girl. This will be loud." She squeezed off the shot.

With a panicked whinny, Lucy reared up. Kate

dropped the pistol, clutching the reins with both hands and soothing the horse with quiet words.

Only once she had brought her horse under control did she take a survey of what else had occurred. Driscoll lay on the ground, groaning, his white horse already yards down the road and galloping quickly away. Beside him lay his hat—which, if Kate had aimed as well as she thought, was now adorned by a tidy bullet hole.

She rode toward him, halting Lucy at the fallen man's side. Yes, from here she could see the powder burn and the hole. Driscoll might have been injured by his fall, but Kate's bullet had wounded nothing but a fine beaver-felt hat.

"You shot me!" groaned the magistrate.

"I shot your hat. You're on the ground because you can't keep your seat." She lifted her chin. "Most people who fall are absolutely fine."

Most of them. But not all.

She slid from Lucy's back and was sick in a bush.

When she straightened, she took in her surroundings. The bush was not simply part of the brushy growth alongside the road. It edged a garden, a riotous and bright garden belonging to a whitewashed stone cottage.

From the doorway peeked a woman with red hair and a pocked face. When she met Kate's eye, she hurried forth, a squirming toddler in her arms. At the sight of Driscoll, groaning on the ground, she gasped. "Good gracious! Lady Whelan, is everything all right?"

Kate blinked. "Mary?" She knew the woman by sight, but they had never spoken.

During Con's life, they had existed side by side, each doing the other the courtesy of pretending she was not there. Each thinking hers was the greater claim, maybe. Kate had won Con's hand, but Mary had his heart.

"Yes, my lady. I'm Mary." The woman dropped a curtsy.

The graceful movement was familiar. "You're the woman from the churchyard," Kate said, not quite saying what she meant.

"I am. And this is my son." The woman paused. "His name is Conall."

So. They had all met at last.

It was neither difficult nor dramatic, as Kate might once have feared. What had they to compete for now?

"The earl would be very pleased," Kate replied with perfect truth. "I have been curious about you, Miss O'Dowd. And I am so sorry, but I have just been sick in your garden."

"Sick!" shouted the little boy.

"Think nothing of it," said Mary. "Happens all the time."

"Does it really?"

"Well, no. But here comes a constable, and Mr. Rhys not far behind, and they're both looking a bit green. My! See if they don't get sick as well."

Twenty-six

Evan had awoken with a painful head and vague memories of telling Kate something about Mary, Mary. When he learned that Lady Whelan had ridden out that morning, he knew exactly where she must have gone. "I have to find them. I have to..." What he'd do, he didn't know. Had Kate been devastated to hear of Con's bastard child? Or had she already known?

Was she angry? What was she going to do?

Over the protests of the housekeeper whose turn it was to tend him, he jammed on his boots, caught up his coat, and bolted from the sickroom. Ignoring his aching head as best he could, he ran for the stables. There the chestnut gelding—returned safely after their outing to the castle, thank God—was just being saddled for a groom to take him out for exercise.

And behind him, a stable hand was returning Lady Alix.

"I'll take her," Evan said, and swung up onto the familiar back. A sentimental choice, maybe, to ride her rather than a fresh horse, but he knew this lady would run her heart out. He urged the mare into a gallop, setting his teeth against the jolt of each stride. Wind tickled his collarbone, his chest, and he realized he'd ridden out with the same old shirt, collarless and without cravat.

"What a sight I'll make, old girl," he muttered. "Maybe distract the ladies enough to keep them from killing each other."

But the tableau he came upon when he rounded the turn to Mary's cottage was the last thing he would have expected. There was a constable on horseback ahead, and the great bulk of Finnian Driscoll lying on the ground, and—and there was Kate, reins in hand, dropping a curtsy to her late husband's mistress and bastard child.

He reined in the chestnut, head thumping with agony, and slid from Lady Alix's back. "Did I miss all of the excitement, or is there more to come?"

"Evan." Kate looked at him with some surprise. "You ought not be out of bed!"

"I couldn't stay away." He tried for a sweeping bow, but it made his head pound more.

"How did you know we'd be here?"

"Where else would you be?"

"I'm here by chance." She looked at her horse, which Evan recognized as the mare Lucy, and then at the groaning figure of the magistrate. "I was trying to speak with Driscoll, and he fled. He led us here."

"Likely wanted to hide behind the cottage, by the river," suggested Mary.

Evan accepted this. "I assume there was a horse that dumped him off? Or is he a deceptively quick runner?"

"She shot me!" Driscoll moaned.

"Stop saying that," Kate replied. "I only shot your hat. Yes, Evan. There was a white horse. I regret that he was frightened. I do not regret that he discarded his rider. Mr. Driscoll, you seemed eager not to encounter this constable. And why could that be?"

The man moaned and turned onto his side.

"Hullo, what's this?" Evan handed the reins of the chestnut to the bemused Kate, then crouched beside Driscoll. "A pistol fell out of his pocket."

"Is it loaded?"

"It is not loaded. It is also not his." Evan took it in his hand, slapping it against his palm. Lady Alix nosed him, bumping the pistol. "No, girl. We can't play the dropping-things game right now." He squinted at the small gun. "This is my pistol, which was taken from my coat while I was unconscious. Here, my initials are engraved on the stock."

"Very fancy," noted the constable.

"Thank you," said Evan. "Mr. Driscoll, would you still like to say that I was set upon by footpads, now that you've been found carrying my pistol?"

"Theft, Mr. Driscoll?" The constable whistled. "That's mighty bad."

"It's certain you will lose your post," Kate said. "The question only remains, which crimes would you like your replacement to hear at the assizes?"

Driscoll paled. "Help me up." Still at his side, Evan hoisted the large man to a seated position. The effort left both of them perspiring. "No, there were no footpads. No attack either. You were found at Loughmoe Castle, grazed by a falling stone. It was an accident!"

"And who found me?"

"I don't know exactly who." The magistrate's eyes—Evan could not stop thinking of them as reproachful hound eyes—shifted away. "It could have been anyone."

"Maybe we didn't miss all the excitement after all," Evan said.

From the edge of her garden, Mary spoke. "I'll be taking my boy inside now. If you need me for questioning..."

"That's fine, Miss O'Dowd," said the constable. "Our business is with Mr. Driscoll. Now, then, who was there at the castle ruin? Sir?" He swallowed. A young man, this confrontation with a venerable magistrate was obviously coming difficult for him.

The magistrate sighed. "There are ten families, maybe twelve, who work the stone in their spare moments. They're the families hardest hit by the famine two years ago. I truly don't know who found Evan. There were a half dozen, Lady Whelan, as you saw, who brought him to your house. They were all of a panic, afraid they'd be blamed, so I said I'd cover for them."

"I merely want to be clear about this," Kate said. "You said you would cover for smugglers. Who brought you a man almost dead of a head wound?"

"It wasn't *that* bad," Evan said. "I got out of the way of the stone."

"It *was* that bad. You didn't see yourself." Her mouth scrunched into an odd shape. "You don't see yourself now, either."

Evan cursed, then picked up the hat on the ground beside Driscoll. He stuffed it onto his head. "Ignore the bullet hole in the hat and the bandage on my head. Driscoll, I'm just borrowing this. You're to have it back as soon as the constable is ready to take you away."

Driscoll had gone a most unpleasant color.

"If you need to be sick, there's a suitable bush right over there." Kate pointed.

"It was Miss Ahearn's idea." Driscoll moistened his lips. "See, to the Catholics who stayed after the Jacobite movement failed, there's nothing worse than the wild geese."

"Wild geese?" Kate asked.

"Rich Catholics who fled Ireland," Evan explained. "I learned that...what day is this?"

"Thursday."

"Then I learned it two days ago."

"Right, that is," Driscoll said. "They abandoned the cause, they took their money, and they left their tenants behind. Their castle became a shell. So Miss Ahearn, when she came to Thurles, had the idea of turning the wild geese to advantage. They could give us a living now, when a century ago they failed to."

"In what way?" asked the constable.

"Copying the statues and things the nobs in England like. Carve old bits of stone into new, and leave a space to hide things inside."

"Such as?" Kate asked.

"Whatever someone will pay us to hide. A note between lovers. A stolen necklace." Driscoll shrugged. "It was just a bit of money at first, but enough to see me made resident magistrate once Dublin Castle set up a post."

"Miss Ahearn must be a dedicated Irish patriot," Kate said drily.

Something sparked in Evan's battered memory. "She's not Irish at all. She's Welsh. Mary said so. Said she'd recognized the accent as being like mine."

"But her family is in Dublin," Driscoll said. "She said she wanted to help them."

"You are ready to blame Miss Ahearn," Kate said. "How sad for you that she's left Thurles and cannot corroborate your story."

"Left Thurles?" The magistrate was now the color of a lovely split pea soup. "When?"

"This morning. Surely you could hear her landlady screeching, even from your seat in the Prancing Pony?"

Driscoll shook his head. Setting a broad hand against a tree, he hefted himself to his feet. "I didn't know. She must have taken fright after you were hurt, Mr. Rhys."

"But she didn't hurt him?"

"No! No one was supposed to get hurt." The magistrate-for-now heaved a great sigh then looked at Kate with kicked-dog eyes. "Not the earl either. It was a warning. He was to fall and to know he fell because someone had tampered with his tack. He was to take it as a threat and stop interfering. Stop trying to take a greater cut."

"A greater cut," Kate murmured. She made some movement that set the two horses whose leads she held to shifting and stamping. "He was taking money."

"Had to get the earl to look the other way." Driscoll sounded apologetic. "And if no one was getting hurt, what did it matter? We're not Jacobites ourselves. All we want is full pockets and a safe life."

Full pockets and a safe life. Ha. "You've created nothing of the sort," Evan pointed out.

For emphasis, Lady Alix nipped the hat from his head and let it fall to the ground.

"Full pockets," said Kate. "You still want them. You pulled the earl into a crime, and you bought up his debts. How dare you." Her light eyes were practically shooting sparks. "How. Dare. You."

"That was Miss Ahearn's idea. I swear I wouldn't have done it if he hadn't died. I thought the operation would have to stop when he died."

"Yet it did not. And *you* did not."

Evan swooped up the man's hat from the ground, handed it to him, then took a step back. "You asked what it mattered? It mattered because it was wrong. And how can you say *if no one was getting hurt* and talk about a *safe life* when a man died?"

"An accident!" Driscoll waved his hands. "Accident, accident. Jones was devastated."

"I am so sorry that the groom was distressed by my husband's accidental death." The scorn in Kate's voice was thick enough to bury them all. "You must permit me to send my condolences. To where did he flee in his *devastation*?"

Driscoll, the fool, answered her. "Miss Ahearn found him a place in Wales, I think, somewhere nice and far away. He was Welsh himself, so he liked that."

"You can't keep the Welsh out of Wales," said Evan. "Do tell me. Was Ahearn her real name?" The blow to his head seemed to have jarred loose a memory. Sir William's voice, asking for an Anne Jones. *Forty or forty-five years old. Very pretty. A criminal genius.*

Janet Ahearn—the same initials, flipped—was the right age. Pretty? She tried hard not to look so. A criminal genius? That, he didn't know.

"Ahearn was what she always wanted us to call her." Driscoll looked hopeful. A decrepit old dog being offered a bone. "Her real name, I think, was Jones."

"Well, shit," said Evan. Everyone gaped at him, and he muttered an apology.

Shit, though. He'd found Sir William's Tranc, only to see her slip off again.

"Was she related to the groom?" the constable asked.

"I don't think so," said Driscoll. "They were both Welsh. There are a lot of Joneses in Wales."

"A realization that never ceases to amuse," Evan said.

"If you two are ready," the constable said, "I'll be taking this man off now."

Driscoll blanched. He really was turning ever so many food colors. "Don't let him take me! Mr. Rhys—Lady Whelan—what did I do that was so wrong?"

Evan looked at Kate. "How would you like to answer the man? What do you want to do? You're a countess, and you're guardian to an earl. You've the sway here, my lady."

For a long moment, Kate used her free hand to pet the necks of the horses she held. "We've no real proof of anything," she said at last. "The only crime we can prove is that he stole your pistol. Since it's worth more than ten shillings, he could be kept till the assizes for that, tried, and transported."

"I didn't steal it," Driscoll said. "I...found it."

"It doesn't matter. Evan, I fault Driscoll for taking your possessions, and for not telling the truth about where you were found. I fault Adam Jones for cutting a strap that indirectly took a man's life. I fault Janet Ahearn, or Jones, or whatever her name is, for developing a cock-eyed plan that made a dozen families party to smuggling. If Driscoll is gone, and if it stops, I will be satisfied."

The pounding in his head quieted, soothed by her calm words. And yet... "Why, Kate? It was wrong."

She traced the line of Lucy's mane, setting the mare to blinking her contentment. "Because there are many ways to be wrong. One way was to tuck up within Whelan House like a snail, trying to hold the world together by clutching pieces tightly. And another was Con's, to befriend those who relied on him without ensuring their livelihood."

"You cannot think this was all your fault and Con's."

"No, people made their own choices. But is the world the worse for a few stones being removed from Loughmoe Castle?"

"I don't know. Yes."

Kate's smile was gentle. Sad. "The quality of mercy, Evan."

"How can you feel mercy when you lost a husband?"

"I wouldn't have at first. But time passed, you know. It's a delightful beast. It took my loss, and it brought me you instead."

The constable shifted awkwardly. Evan laughed.

"And," Kate added, "anyone who can carve a likeness of the prime minister so finely, or who can join two pieces of stone with barely a visible seam, has talents that can be turned to use. Legal use."

It could end now—sort of. She was offering them the chance to begin anew, to unravel the scheme and weave their lives into a new pattern.

"Mr. Driscoll," said Evan. "I am prepared not to prosecute you if you resign your post as magistrate. And if you leave Thurles for...where should he go, countess?"

"Ardent House in Wales is remarkably nice," Kate suggested.

"True. And the company regards itself as the best sort. But I'd settle for your departure to another part of Ireland. Somewhere you have to start fresh." Was that relief in the sagging features? Evan hoped it was. "Somewhere you *can* start fresh," he added.

"I'll do it," said Driscoll.

"Should I let him go?" The constable looked from Driscoll to Evan to Kate, then back.

"Stay with him until he sends his letter of resignation to Dublin Castle," said Kate. "Then he can go."

"I'm in debt to you, Lady Whelan," said Driscoll.

"I thought it was the reverse," she said crisply. "Or are you offering to relinquish your claim upon my land?"

"Yes." His unhealthy color was subsiding now. "Yes, all of it."

She shook her head. "I'm not asking you to deny yourself the money you're owed, only not to take my son's birthright. Keep me informed of your address, and I shall send payments on a regular schedule until my late husband's debt has been discharged."

Evan stroked his chin. "You know, Countess, you could claim the excise reward for finding the smugglers."

Driscoll blanched again. Interestingly, the constable

did too. Those keeping watch at Bridge Castle must have had more than one source of employment.

"What smugglers?" Kate asked. "If there were any smugglers, they needed a way to survive when Con wasted their rents and didn't watch over them. Now, I will. And I'll make sure we return to financial health together.

"I don't see any smugglers now. But if they turn up in the future, I will see them then. And if Whelan tenants need help, they may see their countess at any time."

"You're a marvel," Evan said. "If her ladyship's statement is acceptable to everyone—Constable, are you ready?"

Driscoll's horse had not returned, so the constable allowed the older man to mount his horse.

"Did you take the cinch from my coat too?" Evan asked.

Hesitantly, the magistrate drew forth the leather strap from his own pocket.

"Bind his wrists with it," Kate said. "I can think of no better binding."

As if in atonement for all he had taken from her, the soon-to-be former magistrate bowed his head and held forth his wrists.

In the still edge of the forest, Evan and Kate waited until the constable had led Driscoll out of earshot, out of sight.

"And now what, my lady?" Evan asked.

"And now you should be thrown back into the sickroom," she said.

"No throwing, please. My poor head cannot stand it. I don't even want to ride again."

"Then we'll walk," she said. "Unless you'd rather run?"

They walked, each leading a horse. Lady Alix and Lucy put their heads together, like two old friends enjoying a good gossip, and strode through crunching leaves with the energy of much younger horses.

"Did you come to Mary's cottage to rescue me?" Kate asked after a few minutes.

"I wondered if you'd twit me about that. As a matter of fact, I did, and I haven't heard a word of thanks."

She rose to her tiptoes to press a kiss to his cheek, then continued walking with Lucy. "I did tell you I love you."

He stopped walking, stunned all over again. Lady Alix nosed him in the small of his back.

He ignored the horse's prompting, as tentative joy began to spark within his chest. "Did you? I was knocked on the head. Couldn't hear a word of it."

"Are you certain? You revived with great swiftness after I dashed you with water."

"Let's dash you in the face with water and see what that does for you." He reached for her, and she backed away, squealing. "Kate, I didn't hear it. I can guess, but I don't know. I'm already guessing and not knowing about so many things. Won't you tell me what you said?"

"I said…well, not in so many words…or actually in more words, because I was sorting it out—that I am yours—whole. Just as I am wholly a mother, wholly a countess—oh, but when I wed you, I won't be a countess anymore, will I?"

He shook his head. "It'll take me a while to sort

through all that, poor injured fellow that I am. But I think I missed a proposal."

"I am paving the way for your question. Now you know the answer."

The spark of joy became a flame. "It's all the answer I've ever wanted."

"Or maybe I should ask you, after all. You said I ought to court you."

"Skipping straight to the proposal? How forward of you."

"I've already debauched you. Your reputation lies in my hands."

There followed a delightful demonstration of what hands could do when reputation was not a concern. "Behave yourself," Kate hissed, even as she took advantage of his open-collared shirt. "The dower house is within sight, and Good Old Gwyn might be looking out the window. By the way, if you doubted my love for you, the fact that I am groping you while you stink of old beef broth ought to banish such a doubt."

"The fact that you cared enough to slop me with beef broth and water is evidence enough, my love." Chastely, he laced his fingers in hers, and they continued to walk their horses in the direction of the stables.

"Good Old Gwyn, what was she watching for?" Kate wondered.

"Maybe for Driscoll. Maybe they were lovers, and she'd follow him from Thurles."

"You're joking."

"I am, though they wouldn't make a bad pair. His solicitude, her delight in being…"

"Solicited?"

"That cannot be the right word," he said. "Maybe she was watching for someone who would bring her Con's share of the money? If he knew about the statues made for smuggling, surely she did too."

"I don't know about that. One of the countesses—specifically, me—was remarkably thick about the whole matter. And you credit the light criminal element for surprising morality."

"Well, that's my guess. And by the way, if we're to be wed—"

"*If.* Are you being coy with me?"

"I don't wish to take anything for granted."

She caught his free hand. "Evan, don't go to Greece. Please don't go to Greece. I couldn't go with you while Declan is young, and I don't want you to go anywhere I couldn't go."

He could not remember a speech he had ever delighted in more. "Then I'm yours. The Ambassador to the Ottoman Empire will likely cry into his pillow for months on end, but I am yours."

"And I'm yours," she said.

Finally. *At last.*

Evan kissed her—quickly, for the horses were impatient and the walk was long. "So. *When* we are wed, how would you like our relationship with Good Old Gwyn to go on?"

"I don't suppose she really could go to Wales." Kate sighed. "What a pity. Your parents seem the sort to enjoy a good game of *who's-the-saddest.*"

"Doubtless they would, but I couldn't do that to Elena. She has enough to be going on with, living with my parents and my brother."

"True, and she taught me the agreement game. I must send her a lovely gift of thanks."

"Don't let it be flint. I know how you are about giving people flint."

"I won't send flint. *Honestly*." Kate kicked a few fallen leaves at him. "No, I think what we'll do with Good Old Gwyn is hire her a companion. Someone paid to listen and agree—won't that keep her happy?"

"Happy in her unhappiness," mused Evan. "Maybe. It'd have to be a very well-paid companion."

"I wonder if Mary O'Dowd would want the job. Or is that too cruel?"

"It might be," Evan said. "To Mary."

"Yes, that's what I was thinking too. But we ought to offer, at least, for she won't have a steady stream of shillings to rely on anymore. And I think—I'll have regular at-home hours, twice a week, to anyone who wants to call. Good Old Gwyn will be welcome during those times."

"And not during others?"

"Of course, she would be welcome. But if she wants to visit a newlywed couple unawares, she'd best be prepared to see some vigorous…ah, sport."

"Ah, the agreement game. I don't think I've ever heard it being played so pleasurably."

"Just wait until you actually get to play it."

There followed another improper interlude, stopped only when Lucy shoved her head between them and whickered.

"I know, I know. Almost within sight of the stables," Evan said.

One last question came to mind, for the seeming

answer had surprised him so much. "Kate. Did you not mind speaking with Mary O'Dowd? Seeing her with her child?"

"I think not." She flicked a hand. "A countess needs an earl, a wife needs a husband, a child needs a father. A mistress needs nothing but a man. Con fell away from me, and in time, he might have fallen away from her too."

"Do you think so?"

She walked on, one silent step and then another. "No. I don't think he would have. He wasn't without honor, our Con. He wasn't without a heart. I think he was always hers."

"I won't fall away from you," Evan said. Six words, standing in for all the words in his heart. He had always been hers.

"I know you won't. And I won't either."

They had reached the stables now, where grooms waited to take the horses. After handing off the two animals—who seemed to be rolling their eyes at the ridiculous humans as they walked away—Evan took Kate's hand again, and they turned toward Whelan House.

"I think," Kate said, "I will call upon Mary."

"Again, you surprise me. To befriend her?"

"I cannot know that. It depends on so many things, not the least of which is time. But I imagine we would have a lot to talk about, don't you? And I won't be sick in her bushes."

"Oh, I don't know that you need to go that far. It was the start of a fine tradition."

"I think it is the start of more than that."

His head whipped toward her. Eyes downcast, cheeks flushed, she was smiling.

Had he thought the joy within him a spark, a low flame? It was a bonfire, turning the world from gray to gold. "Do you think so?"

"I…more than think." Her hand cradled her belly.

With a whoop, he swept her into his arms.

Twenty-seven

"*How* MANY WEEKS DO THE BANNS HAVE TO BE CALLED?"

Declan was yanking on Kate's sleeve, drawing her down the small hill away from the little stone church.

"Three weeks," she said. "This was the last."

Neither she nor her children were used to attending weekly services, but all were nudged back into the tradition with the promise of a wedding. The Reverend Jerrold had accepted their return with as much quiet grace as he had always accepted Kate's absence, and the balm of his reaction was knitting wounded bits in Kate's soul. Bits that had been grieved for the life she'd never had, and bits she had thought beyond grieving.

Sometimes sad accidents happened, like Con's fall. Sometimes wonderful things happened, like a newfound love. And the world abided, and the stone church remained.

It was a comfort to know that such things remained.

She would keep going to services even once the wedding ceremony was complete. Declan was impatient because Kate had found so many people with whom to chat afterward, which was the beginning—she hoped—of friendships.

And in another seven months, there would be a baby, and a christening.

For the time being, the chase after Driscoll had been her last. Considering when she'd missed her courses, she must have conceived on her first night with Evan.

"So much for my precautions," he had said when she told him. That night, he took her in his arms, kissed her thoroughly, and demonstrated the benefits of *not* having to take precautions.

Declan tugged at Kate's arm. "Come *on*, please, Mama. They're already in the churchyard."

She slid and scooted down the slope, happy to be pulled by her son. When they reached the low wall, she saw that Evan was standing beside the stone, and Nora in front of it. "Declan," Evan said, "we're saying hello to your old da. Do you want to?"

Kate pretended not to notice that Evan's eyes were wet. "Hullo, Con. You'd have loved how Evan rode in the chase."

"Hullo, Da. You wouldn't have loved it at all," said Declan. "Uncle Evan finished sixth."

"Considering I'd never ridden the course before, I think it was not bad," Evan said loftily.

"You didn't win a purse," the boy pointed out.

Evan arched a brow. "Neither did you, so stop twitting me about it."

"Mama would have won," said Nora.

"Your faith in me is delightful. Several years ago, I'd have given it a good try," said Kate. "Maybe next year I will again."

She and Evan had prepared the children for the inevitable announcement by asking them whether they'd like a sister or brother. "Do we get to place an order?" Declan had asked.

"Not…as such, no," Kate said. "I'm just wondering."

"I already have a brother, so I want a sister," Nora said.

"I want a sister too," Declan said. When Nora gaped at him, he threw up his hands. "What? Sisters are good. And I want one that I can be older than."

The memory of this conversation was sweet to Kate.

As Nora walked around her father's headstone, she bent to pick something up. "Look! Someone has left a twist of weeds here."

"There must be someone else who cares about your father very much," Evan said. "Leave it there, Nora."

"But it's *weeds*," she said—though she set the twist down with care.

"It's the thought that counts," Kate said. She knew who had left the little twist there.

She still wasn't sure how to tell her children of the existence of their younger brother, Mary's child. Maybe when her own baby came, and Declan and Nora had another half-sibling, they could be introduced to young Conall.

Maybe. There were a great many changes for their family to grow into. Sometimes her heart felt overstretched by all of them. But it was far better to have it stretched beyond comfort than shrunk beyond the point at which it could be touched.

"Wise words," said Evan. "Children, remember

that when your mother gives you flint for Christmas. It's the thought that counts."

"Come closer so I can elbow you," Kate said.

"I'll do it! I'll do it!" cried the children. As Evan made his way to the churchyard gate, he was surrounded by two fast-moving elbowing dervishes.

When Evan had battled them off, laughing, and shut the gate behind them, Nora asked, "When you marry Mama, are we still to call you Uncle Evan, or should we call you Da?"

Evan's eyes met Kate's, his brows lifted. *What do you want?*

She shrugged. *You can decide.*

"You can call me whatever you like," Evan answered. "And you can change it whenever you're ready."

"Whatever we like? Can I call you Spider?" Declan asked.

"No," said Evan. "But only because you have decided it is a good name for a horse. Otherwise, it would be a perfectly appropriate name for one's stepfather."

Nora bounced on her toes. "Mama, can we ride when we reach home?"

Kate clenched her teeth. "No. Maybe. Yes." It was easier to climb onto a horse herself than to know her children were doing the same. Even though most people who fell were fine.

They had to be allowed the freedom to fall. Otherwise, they'd be bound and divided as she had once been.

"Your mother," Evan said, "is playing a wonderful game where you only listen to every third word she says."

"Is that true, Mama?"

Kate smiled. "No. Maybe. Yes."

Nora looked her up and down. "You seem happy. Did you know, Mama, Uncle Evan has loved you my whole life?"

"Did everyone know this but me?" Kate asked.

"I didn't know it," Declan said. "And I don't think Nora did either."

"I did!"

Declan shot off. "First one to the stable gets the first ride!"

Arms pumping, plaits flying, Nora was quick on his heels.

"Do you want to join the race?" Kate asked. "You might be able to overtake them, and then you could have the first ride."

"They would never forgive me. And since I've permitted them to call me whatever they like, I've got to stay on their good side." He held out an arm. "May I walk you home instead, fair lady?"

She slipped her hand within the crook of his arm. "It would be my honor, sir."

They strolled along the path from the church, framed by the bare-branched trees of early winter. Kate had a new red pelisse, and a sable hat that covered her ears and kept them from getting cold-nipped. It was delightful to choose colors again, to feel ready to bear them.

"I received a reply from your father," Evan said. "The letter came yesterday. I forgot to mention it."

"My father." Kate rolled her eyes. "And which of his secrets are you helping him to research now?"

She had been, to use a word which she had recently employed to great effect, *displeased* recently when Evan told her the mysterious Anne Jones they were to find was, in all probability, the mother of Sir William Chandler's daughter. If so, Kate had a half-sister no more than a year or two older than Nora.

Another one of those changes that had tugged at her heart in unexpected ways. "Con had an illegitimate child. My own *father* has an illegitimate child. Are there any men who can keep their cocks under control?"

Evan feigned offense. "There most certainly are. I myself am a model of calm and control."

She had settled into the curve of his arm, laughing at the ridiculousness of it, crying a bit at the secrets held so long. When she became calm and reached for him, he acted in a way that completely belied his vow of control.

So, a reply had finally come to all of the news of the past month. Kate looked at the sky, letting the paleness fill her vision. "And what did my father have to say to you?"

"We were thinking it couldn't be the same Anne Jones, right? Because of all the myriad Anne Joneses in the world, what would be the chances that the one your father sought would settle right by you?"

She already knew the answer. "He doesn't think it a coincidence, does he?"

"He does not. As Janet Ahearn and as Anne Jones, she traveled all the time. Her excuse was that she visited family in Dublin, but likely, she was in Wales or England. Working with God knows who on God knows what scheme. But she needed a place to settle, and so she picked...here."

"Sir William Chandler's daughter." Kate scuffed her toe against the path. A light mist began to fall, chill but not unpleasant. "She came here because of me. The smuggling took place from here because of me."

A cold drop slapped her in the face. "In a way, Con died because of me." She tipped her head. "I don't mean to blame myself. But—it's odd, isn't it? The threads of the past are attached in so many ways."

Evan stopped walking. He straightened his arm, dropping her hand, only to embrace her shoulders instead. "Con no more died because he married you than he died because he and I argued. His death was a tragedy, the result of many bad choices. I think marrying you, and having a friend who cared enough to argue with him, were *good* choices."

She rested her head against the wall of his chest. "The best ones he ever made." Another drop hit her face. This time she put out her tongue and tried to catch another. "I've been thinking about something new," she added.

"Thus begins another wondrous adventure. And what shall it be?"

"That is exactly what I have been wondering. You liked lecturing so much. If you remain in Ireland, what will you do?"

"A fair question. I don't know that there's a need now for a stuffy old prune to talk about false antiquities. We've cut off the flow at its source."

"This time."

"This time," he allowed. "But do you really think

Tranc would return, now that we know what she looks like?"

"No, not here. But in case she does, the new magistrate will keep watch. Once we have a new magistrate."

Evan regarded her narrowly. "You are wearing a dangerous sort of expression, my love. What are you thinking?"

"Well." She feigned innocence. "The new district magistrate will be appointed by Dublin Castle. I can't imagine who it'll be, but I can put in a good word. The new master of Whelan House might not be a bad choice."

He shook his head. "Me, sitting over petty sessions? Can you imagine it?"

"Making the sort of wry comments you make at your lectures? I think you'd have excellent attendance, and you'd do an admirable job. Now you'll get to lecture on lawbreakers instead of history breakers."

His mobile brows lifted. "It's a thought."

"A thought about which you think...what?"

"I think...I like the idea. I'll put myself forward. I wouldn't do a perfect job, but—"

"You would be just right for Thurles."

"Exactly." He grinned.

"And I'll support you at every step." She matched her actions to her words, grabbing his arm again, and setting them back to walking.

"Every step? Even the steps to—"

"Oh, Lord. Here it comes. A clever remark designed to topple my words over and start me to giggling."

"Is it working?"

"That depends what the next word would be."

"Biggie," he said, and tickled her in the side until she was tottering down the path, tipsy with giggles and rain spattered over her face.

"I was thinking something else too," she said.

"What did I do to deserve you?" Evan kissed her on the head, getting a faceful of sable hat.

"All sorts of dreadful things, probably. But if you miss teaching a group of people, Ireland is surely full of folks who would like to learn about history. Or study a magic lantern and see the images it makes."

"I don't know about all their kings and things—the true Gaelic history of the place. A classical education has little bearing on one's homeland."

"Then maybe you would like to learn. You can join Nora and Declan for lessons."

"Damn lessons," he said with a laugh, then sobered. "You know, I would like that. If this is to be my home—our home—then it ought to feel like such. I wonder who could teach me?"

"Maybe old Petty. Or maybe there's an archive somewhere."

"Then we could paint some new slides. What would you like to show?"

"Something with gray in exactly the right amount." She slipped an arm around his waist. "For you."

"For me," he replied, "gray seems far away right now. And by will and activity, maybe I can keep it at bay."

"If you do not, and if the gray comes over you all the same, then the good things in life will be waiting when it recedes."

"Will they? What are those good things?" The look in his eye was devilish.

"You'll have to catch me to find out," Kate said. And laughing, she ran along the path toward her home, knowing that Evan would be with her all the way.

If you loved *Scandalous Ever After*, don't miss Theresa Romain's sparkling Regency Matchmaker trilogy. Read on for an excerpt from

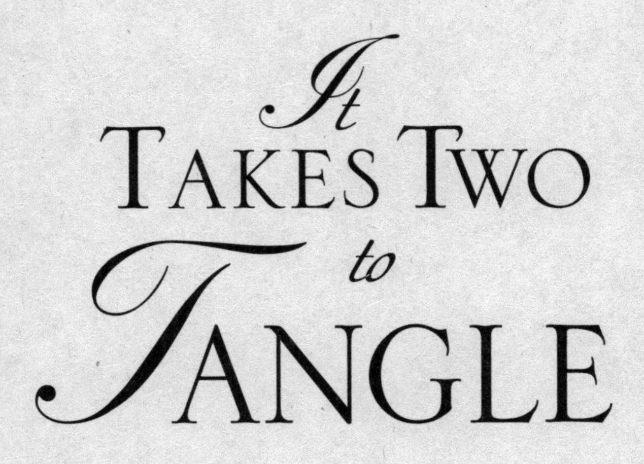

One

July 1815
Tallant House, London

It was no good. The canvas still looked as though a chicken had been killed on it.

Henry Middlebrook grimaced and stepped back, casting his eye over his work. In the cooling light of early evening, his vermilion paint looked ghastly.

He dragged his brush over one corner of the canvas and regarded it again. A slight improvement. Now it looked as if someone had killed a chicken on it, then tried to clean up the evidence.

No matter. He could fix it later somehow. Or hide it in an attic.

As he stepped forward again, ready for another artistic attack, Henry's foot bumped the fussy baroque table on which he'd set his palette. The palette rattled perilously close to the edge of the table, and Henry swooped for it before it tipped. He lost his grip on his paintbrush and could only watch, dismayed, as the wide brush flipped end over end and landed with a faint thump on the carpet.

Well, damn.

"How lovely!" came a cry behind him, and Henry turned.

His sister-in-law Emily, the Countess of Tallant, was standing in the morning room doorway smiling at him. She wore a gown the watery, fragile pink of rose madder, with some part of it pinstriped and some other part of it beaded, and her auburn hair arranged with a quantity of pink-headed pins.

Henry did not understand all the details of women's fashion, having spent the past three years learning the significance of shoulder epaulets, forage caps, and stovepipe shakos. Still, the effect of Emily's ensemble was pleasing to anyone with the slightest eye for color—which Henry had, though no one looking at his canvas would possibly think so.

"Good evening, Emily," he said, shifting his foot to hide the fallen paintbrush. "I might say the same to you. You look very well."

"Nonsense, Hal," she said. "This gown is a full year out of fashion and is suitable for nothing but lolling around the house. I must go change for the ball, as must you. What I meant was that it's lovely to see you painting again."

She craned her neck to look behind him. "And it's even lovelier to see you resting your palette on that dreadful table. Jemmy's Aunt Matilda gave it to us as a wedding gift. I can only conclude she must have hated me."

Emily walked over to Henry and held out her hand

for the paintbrush, which he sheepishly retrieved from the floor. She scrutinized it, then began to daub the gilded table at Henry's side with red curlicues.

"I'm not the expert you are, of course, but the texture of this red seems a bit off."

"Yes, it's too oily. I'm out of practice."

"Well, that's easily enough fixed by time. I'm glad we still had some of your supplies left from... well, before." Emily signed her name with fat, bold brushstrokes to the ruined tabletop. "There, that's the best this table has ever looked. If you can stand the sight of the beastly thing, then you must have it for your own use while you paint. Surely we can find a studio for you somewhere in the house. You could even keep painting here in the morning room if you don't mind rolling back the Axminster, of which I'm rather fond."

Henry looked at the heavy carpet guiltily. A splotch of warm red paint marred the fine sepia pattern of scrolls and bouquets. "I should have done that first thing. I'm sorry, Em."

She waved a hand. "I understand artists are remarkably forgetful creatures. Once the creative mood seizes you, you cannot be responsible for your actions."

"Are you giving me an excuse to be an aggravating guest? This could be entertaining."

Emily's mouth curled into the cunning smile that meant she was plotting something. "You're much more than a guest, as you know. But you're right. I should demand that you pay me a favor for spilling paint all over my possessions."

Henry took the brush from her and laid it carefully across the palette, atop the newly adorned table. "Let me guess. You already have a favor in mind, and you are delighted I have ruined your carpet, since now you can be sure I'll agree to whatever you ask."

Emily looked prouder than ever. "Excellent! We shall slip you back into polite society more easily than I could ever have hoped. Already you are speaking its secret language again, for you are correct in every particular of your guess."

"I'm overjoyed to be such a prodigy. What, precisely, have I guessed?"

"Tonight, I am going to introduce you to your future wife. What do you think?" She beamed at him, as though she expected him to jump up and start applauding. Which was, of course, impossible.

Henry gripped the edge of the fussy little table tightly. It was difficult to imagine feeling comfortable amidst the *ton* again—as difficult as it had seemed to leave it three years ago.

But he was just as determined on the former as he'd once been on the latter. Choosing the right wife could be exactly the key he needed to unlock London.

Emily passed a hand in front of his face. "You didn't answer me, Hal."

Henry blinked; stalled. "Don't call me Hal, please."

She raised her eyes to heaven. "You know perfectly well that I shall never be able to stop calling you Hal in my lifetime, just as you cannot stop calling your brother Jem. We are all far too set in our ways. But that's not the answer I wanted. What do you think of my idea about finding you a wife? Actually, it was Jemmy's suggestion, but if you like it, I shall claim it for my own."

Fortunately, Henry's elder brother Jeremy, the Earl of Tallant, poked his dark head into the doorway at that moment, saving Henry from a reply. "Em? Aren't you ready yet? I've already had the carriage brought around."

In his sleek black tailcoat, mathematical-tied linens, and waistcoat of bronze silk, Jem looked every inch the earl. Every inch, that is, except the one between his forehead and nose. His eyes—a bright lapis-blue, the only feature the brothers had in common—held an ignoble amount of doubt just now. "Hal? Are you sure you're ready for this?"

Henry decided on deliberate obtuseness. "For Lady Applewood's ball? No, I still have to change my clothing."

"I'll send my man up to help you," Jem replied too quickly.

Emily crossed her arms and regarded her husband slowly, up and down. "You look very elegant, Jemmy. But why are you ready? We aren't leaving for an hour."

Jem's expression turned puzzled. "An hour? But I thought—"

"We must make a grand entrance," Emily said in a hurried hush. "I told you we shan't leave until nine."

Jem shrugged, squeezed by his wife, and came to stand next to Henry. "It's too dim in here," he decided as he regarded the painting. "I can't tell what you've painted."

Henry swept his arm to indicate the baroque table. "This table, for a start. And your carpet. And my breeches a bit." He regarded his garments ruefully.

Jem nodded. "Rather ambitious for your first effort."

"Yes. It's served me well to be ambitious, hasn't it?"

Jem managed a smile as his eyes found Henry's. "I suppose it has. Well, best get ready. Em's told you about our grand plan, hasn't she?"

"If you mean the plan to marry me off, then yes. I can't say I'm shocked. I'm only surprised it took her two weeks to broach the subject."

"She's been plotting it for weeks." Jem sighed. "Quite proud of the scheme."

"I'm still *right here*," Emily said from the doorway. "And I *am* proud of it. It's just..."

When she trailed off, both brothers turned to her. Emily's merry face looked sober all of a sudden. "We think you'd be happier, Hal. If you were married."

Henry pasted a smile across his face. "Don't worry about me. I'm quite as happy as can be expected."

Emily studied him for a long moment, then nodded. "One hour, Hal. Jemmy, do come with me. You may help me decide which dress to wear."

The earl followed his wife. "It doesn't matter, Em. You always look marvelous. Besides which, you never wear what I choose."

"That's because you'd send me out with no bodice. Honestly, Jem!"

Their voices quieted as they moved down the corridor, and Henry allowed the smile to drop from his face. He could guess what they'd begun talking about: just how happy *was* he?

He'd given them a truthful answer on the surface of it. He was as happy as could be expected. But a man in his situation had little enough reason for happiness.

Still, he had determination. Surely that was even

more important. With enough determination, happiness might one day follow.

He dragged his easel to the edge of the morning room and gave his painting one last look.

Just as horrible as he'd thought. But in time, it would get better.

With a rueful shake of the head, he left behind his first foray back into painting and went upstairs to prepare for his first foray back into London society.

Frances Whittier was too much of a lady to curse in the crowded ballroom of Applewood House. Barely.

But as she limped back to her seat next to Caroline, the Countess of Stratton, she found the words a gently bred widow was permitted to use completely inadequate.

"Mercy," she muttered, sinking into the frail giltwood chair. "Fiddle. Goodness. *Damn*. Oh, Caro, my toes will never recover."

Caroline laughed. "Thank you for accepting that dance, Frannie. The last time I danced with Bart Crosby, he stepped on my toes twelve times. Oh, and look—I think I've cracked the sticks of my fan."

Frances wiggled her feet. "He's improving, then, for I'm sure he stepped on mine only ten." She exchanged her own unbroken fan for Caroline's. "And if you would quit batting everyone with your fan, it wouldn't break."

"I can't help it," Caroline said. "Lord Wadsworth puts his hands where they don't belong, and the only way to remove them is by physical force."

"In that case, we should have a new fan made for you of something much sturdier than ivory. A nice rosewood should help him remember his manners."

"Or wrought iron, maybe?" Caroline replied, and Frances grinned. Caroline was in quite a good humor tonight and more than willing to share it.

The role of companion to a noblewoman was often seen as thankless, but except when her toes were trod upon, Frances found her position quite the opposite. Maybe because her employer was also her cousin, or maybe just because Caroline was cheerful and generous. The young countess had been locked away in the country for the nine years of her marriage; now that her year of mourning for her elderly husband was complete, she collected admirers with the deliberate joy of a naturalist catching butterflies.

Frances enjoyed helping Caroline sort through the possibilities, though she knew her cousin was as determined to guard her independence as Frances had once been to fling hers away.

"What's next, Caroline? Are you of a mind to dance anymore?" Frances leaned against the stiff back of her chair. It was not at all comfortable, but it was better than having her feet stomped on.

"I think I will, but not just yet." The countess leaned in, conspiratorial under the din of hundreds of voices bouncing off a high ceiling. "Emily has told me she's bringing her brother-in-law tonight, and she intends to introduce us. He's a war hero, just back in London after three years on the Continent."

"A soldier?" Frances said faintly. The hair on her arms prickled from a sudden inner chill.

Caroline shot her a knowing look. "Yes, a soldier. That is, a former soldier. He should be intriguing, don't you think?"

"I have no doubt of it." Frances's throat felt dust-dry. "At any rate, he won't be one of your tame puppies."

"All the better." Caroline adjusted the heavy jonquil silk of her skirts with a practiced hand. "They're so much more fun when they don't simply roll over, aren't they?"

Frances coughed. "I can't really say. I haven't *rolled over* since I was widowed, you know."

Caroline raised an eyebrow. "Maybe it's time you changed that."

"Believe me, I've thought of it."

Caroline chuckled, though Frances's smile hung a little crooked. Any reference to her brief, tempestuous marriage that ended six years before still trickled guilt down her spine. Which was probably why she hadn't *rolled over* in so long.

"How do I look?" Caroline murmured. "Satisfactory enough?"

Frances smoothed the dark blue crape of her own gown, then cast an eye over Caroline. With quick fingers, she tugged one of the countess's blond curls into a deliberate tousle, then nodded. "You'll do very well, though I think you've lost a few of your jeweled hairpins."

Caroline pulled a droll face. "Tonight's casualties: one fan, an undetermined number of hairpins. I don't suppose a soldier would regard those as worthwhile, but I rather liked them all."

"They were lovely," Frances agreed. "I saw Lady Halliwell hunting the same hairpins on Bond Street after you last wore them five weeks ago."

"Oh, horrors." Caroline frowned. "She'll remember that I've worn these before."

"If she does, it won't matter, because she admires you greatly. Besides, she wasn't able to get any for herself. I'd already put the remaining stock on your account."

Caroline looked impressed. "You do think of everything, don't you?"

"I do. I really do." Frances permitted herself a moment of pride before adding, "But if Lord Wadsworth calls on you again, he'd better bring you a new fan."

"And himself some new manners," murmured Caroline. "Oh, look, I see Emily now."

Frances squinted, picking out Caroline's good friend Lady Tallant pushing through the crowd. The countess wore a grin on her face and her husband on one arm. A tall, fair-haired man followed a step behind. The war-hero brother, no doubt; his taut posture was military-perfect, his handsome face a calm cipher.

Caroline lifted her—well, Frances's—fan as soon as the trio were within a polite distance. "Emily! You look beautiful, as usual. How do you keep your silks from getting creased in the crowd?"

Lady Tallant did a quick pirouette to show off her indigo ball gown. "Jemmy uses his elbows to keep the crowd away. Isn't he a wonder?"

"Elbows, Caroline," muttered Frances, "would

work much better than your fan the next time Wadsworth becomes too free with his hands."

Her cousin gave a short cough of laughter. "Ah—yes, he is indeed a wonder. Jem, never let it be said there's no place for chivalry these days."

"I won't," said the earl gravely. "After all, I sacrifice the tailoring of my coat each time I drive out an elbow."

His wife rolled her eyes, then inclined her head to the man at her side. "Caro, Mrs. Whittier. We're here to make an introduction."

Frances could have sworn Caroline wiggled a little, though she managed to keep her face calm. "Oh? To a friend of yours?"

"Much better than that." The earl bowed. "To my brother, Henry Middlebrook. He's quite a war hero. Perhaps you've heard of his adventures on the Continent?"

The fair-haired man shot his brother a look so filthy that Frances made a little *ha* of surprise. He cut his eyes toward Frances and quickly composed his expression.

Lady Tallant must have noticed her brother-in-law's glare, because she swatted her husband with her fan. "Jemmy," she hissed.

Lord Tallant blinked. "Er, ah, forgive me. Er, Hal has been recently traveling on the Continent. For, ah, personal enrichment."

Another filthy look from the brother, another swat from the wife's fan. Lord Tallant looked positively discombobulated now. Next to Frances, Caroline was beginning to shake with suppressed giggles.

Frances grinned. The cipher of a soldier was actually

rather entertaining. Interest crackled through her body, the fatigue of the long evening seeping away.

"What, Emily?" said the earl in a beleaguered voice. "God's teeth, stop hitting me. You'll mar my coat if you keep that up."

"Well, you'll mar my fan," retorted his wife. "Never mind, Jemmy. You are hopeless. Caro, here is Henry. He is positively salivating to meet you. You too, Mrs. Whittier."

The man stepped forward with a wry smile. This close, he proved to be just as tall and well made as he had appeared from a distance. His eyes crinkled with good humor; his hair glinted as gold as Caroline's under the hot light of the chandeliers.

"Do forgive my salivation," he said. "Having been away from London, I suppose I've forgotten the proper manners."

Caroline shrugged. "Have you? Well, if you're living with Emily, you won't need manners."

Lady Tallant smirked. "And if he spends more than a minute with you, Caro, he'll need smelling salts."

"I doubt that," Mr. Middlebrook said smoothly into the middle of this friendly volley. "I rarely get the vapors."

"Nor do I." Caroline gifted him with a sunlit smile and extended her hand. "I'm delighted to meet you, Mr. Middlebrook. Perhaps we shall be good friends."

He returned the smile and bowed over her hand with impeccable military bearing.

And his right arm swung down, down, loose as the limb of a puppet.

When he straightened, his face pale, Frances noticed what she had failed to see before: his right arm hung stiff and wasted within its sleeve, facing painfully backward.

Two

Damn it.

Henry straightened as quickly as he could. He had forgotten again. This gentleman's uniform he wore tonight, the finely tailored black coat and breeches, made him look and feel like his old self again. When really, he was the only broken-winged blackbird in the flock.

Lady Stratton—a guinea-gold vision, as painfully beautiful as Emily had told him—simply stared, dumbstruck.

The woman at her side recovered first. Dark-haired and olive-skinned, she had a roguish look as she extended her left hand to shake his. "I'm pleased to meet you, sir. I am Lady Stratton's cousin and companion, Mrs. Whittier, and I am generally thought to be terrifying."

For an instant, warm fingers clasped his. Henry looked at his left hand as it released hers, feeling as though it belonged to someone else. "Thank you, Mrs. Whittier." His shoulders unknotted a bit. "I am accustomed to obeying my superiors. I shall do my utmost to be terrified."

"You shall be, Hal," interjected Jem in a relieved babble. "God help me, the woman never forgets a thing. She can tell me what I wore to a ball, say, last summer. Me or anyone else."

"That is no trick, my lord, as you always wear black," Mrs. Whittier said. "As for any other feats of memory, I can assure you, they are grossly exaggerated. I am well aware that a too-good memory is unforgivable in a friend."

Lady Stratton had recovered her aplomb, and she dimpled. "It is far worse in an enemy, Frannie, which is why we keep you as a friend. Mr. Middlebrook, would you care to sit with us, or do you intend to dance?"

Now it was Henry's turn to stare. "I'm not precisely suited to dancing, but I'd be glad to sit with you."

"I'll fetch lemonades all around, shall I?" Jem was already poised to battle through the crowd again.

"Two for yourself," Henry said, knowing his brother's love of sweets.

"Wine for me, Jemmy, if you can find it," Emily said, shoving a nearby chair into position next to her friend, then another. "Lemonade will give *me* the vapors."

Jem dropped a quick kiss on her forehead and set off.

"Use those elbows!" Emily waved at Jem, beaming when he shook his head at her before disappearing into the crowd.

She plumped down into one of the light giltwood chairs with a sigh. "It is rather fun discombobulating Jemmy, isn't it?"

"I've always thought so," Henry agreed, taking the other empty seat.

A silence fell as they all smiled at each other. Henry's thoughts unrolled swiftly:

I cannot stand it if they speak of it. But I cannot bear it if they don't.

Surely Lady Stratton must want a man who is whole.

But after living through the hell of Quatre Bras, surely I've earned the right to pursue whatever—whomever—I desire.

Surely no four people have ever sat in silence this long within a full-crammed ballroom.

After an endless few seconds, Lady Stratton spoke. "As you are a soldier, I must thank you for your service, Mr. Middlebrook. All London has been celebrating because of men like you. To have Napoleon vanquished at last—can it really be true?"

She waved her fan as she spoke, a fluttering gesture that drew his eye to the clean lines of her gloved fingers, her arm. The effect was rather marvelous. She could sit for a painting, just as she was.

Henry gathered his stiff right arm into his left hand, wishing it could paint that picture. "It can indeed be true. But please don't credit me with any significant contribution."

Too bleak. He summoned The Grin, a blithe expression that had eased his way through society in former years. "Though I thank you for your kind sentiments. It's very good to be back in London, and this is where I intend to make my mark. Emily and Jem are allowing me to stay with them as long as I care to, even though I have already ruined Emily's favorite carpet."

His soldiering had done him some good; he was adept at parrying and shielding, even in conversation.

Lady Stratton nodded her fair head and accepted this new topic. "You've made a mark on London already, then. That is admirably quick work. I've been trying for years to ruin Emily's carpets, as I am terribly jealous of their fineness. Were you roughhousing with the boys?"

Jem and Emily had two young sons, good-natured boys who were abominably full of energy.

"If only it had been that," Emily sighed. "No, he spilled paint on it. But he did also help me ruin a table I hate, *and* he came with Jemmy and me tonight. So I suppose I'll forgive him eventually."

"Spilled paint? You are an artist, then?" Mrs. Whittier's tilted hazel eyes grew bright, lending her features a glow.

Henry nodded. "I was, once. I hope to be again. Though today's effort was, shall we say, not sufficient to get me into the National Gallery."

Lady Stratton shrugged. "I've never had a painting accepted there, either, so that is nothing to be ashamed of."

"Do you paint?" He felt a quick flash of yearning.

She shook her head, smiling. "No, I don't. But that is nothing to be ashamed of either."

It took him a moment to sift her words; then he laughed. *Flirtation.* Just as in the old days, before he had left.

He settled into his too-small chair and regarded this widowed countess, this friend of Emily's who seemed to have wrapped all London society into a ball and put it in her pocket. "I wonder, Lady Stratton, if you consider anything worth being ashamed of."

She tilted her chin down and fixed Henry with the full force of her blue-green eyes. "Oh yes. But nothing that I'd admit to such a recent acquaintance." Her mouth curved in a secret half smile. "If you wish, you may call me Caro, and perhaps I'll tell you more."

"Outrageous, isn't she?" Emily murmured in Henry's ear. Mrs. Whittier covered a grin with one hand.

Henry rather suspected Lady Stratton was less so than she seemed, that she had carefully honed her act on all the suitors who had come before. When one had wit and wealth enough, the edge of propriety could prove astonishingly flexible.

He was more than willing to tread that flexible line with her. With such a woman at his side, he could walk anywhere—and eventually, the *ton* would follow along.

It was time to employ a little strategy; he would set the pace. "You do me a great honor, my lady," he said, "but as I cannot yet be *Caro* to you, I shall not ask that you be so to me." Not yet *Caro*; not yet dear. Someday, though. Maybe.

She was surprised by this small rebellion, because her eyes widened before she smiled again, slow and appreciative. "You keep me at a distance, Mr. Middlebrook. How am I ever to learn anything of you?"

"Simply ask me, Caro, and I'll tell you all his secrets," Emily said. "For one thing, he's a rotten caretaker of a carpet."

"That's one fact," Mrs. Whittier agreed. "And we know he has two occupations: soldier and painter."

Lady Stratton coaxed her fan closed with careful fingers. Her golden hair glinted, pale fire under the crystal-spun light of the chandelier. "I'll grant that," she said slowly. With a quick snap, she flicked the fan open again. "Very well, you've revealed three inconsequential facts about yourself. Perhaps you'll call on me tomorrow and share a fourth?"

"Inconseq—" Henry's brows shot up. "My lady, you are hard to please indeed if you think I've revealed nothing of consequence."

"I'm not always hard to please," the widow said with another of those veiled smiles. "It simply depends on what's being revealed."

"Honestly," said Emily *sotto voce*. "It almost makes me wish to be widowed so I could be such a scandalous flirt."

"She's got a rare gift," Mrs. Whittier replied. "I *am* widowed, and I couldn't possibly manage it."

The mischievous Mrs. Whittier seemed entirely capable of managing a scandal if she wished, but Henry dutifully pretended not to hear her aside. He considered her words, though. Yes, Lady Stratton did have a rare gift. She had already conquered society; if he could conquer her, then her triumphs would be his as well.

Emily thought they would suit one another; after all, she had said he would meet his future wife tonight. And Emily was usually fairly astute about such matters.

Very well. "Lady Stratton, I'd be honored to call on you and reveal as many inconsequential facts as your heart desires."

She pursed her lips in a cherry-ripe bow. "Excellent.

Perhaps I'll reveal a bit more about my heart's desires when you do. After all, a woman can't live by facts alone."

The hairs on Henry's left arm prickled. Possibly on the right too, though he couldn't tell. It only hung numb and useless at his side, as it had since Quatre Bras six weeks before.

Jem shoved his way back through the pressing crowd just then, trailed by a red-faced footman in a crooked wig. The footman hefted a tray of beverages, which Jem handed around their small party.

Emily held up a glass of cloudy, pale liquid. "If this is wine, there was a serious problem with the grapes."

"It's orgeat," Jem stated proudly. "Delicious."

Henry took his own cup and gave it a sniff. It smelled syrupy, like almonds boiled with sugar. Emily looked faintly nauseated as she handed the glass back to her husband, who drained it in one swallow.

Just then, a young man with a determined expression and a still more determined cravat, striped and starched up to his cheekbones, poked his face into their little gathering. "Lady Stratton? Our dance is about to begin."

Lady Stratton—*Caro*, as she would have it—turned to him. "Oh, Hambleton, thank you for fetching me." She stood and shook out the heavy silk of her gown, sunny and bright as gamboge pigment. "I must leave you all now. I've enjoyed our little tête-à-tête very much."

Henry received a proper nod as the countess accepted the arm of her new suitor. "It was a pleasure to meet you, Mr. Middlebrook."

And with a parting smile, she allowed her escort to pull her into the crowd.

So. She was a strategist too, as determined as he to set the pace for their flirtation or… whatever it might become. She would have him know she was quite willing to exchange his company for that of another. Even with Emily's encouragement.

It was time he formed another alliance, then. The companion, Mrs. Whittier—she would be best, if only he could remove the audience to their conversation.

Emily sighed and stretched out her arms. "Jemmy, care to have a seat? If you aren't going to bring me wine, you must amuse me in some other way."

"Why not have a dance?" Henry encouraged. "I know you'd like to, Emily." Indeed, the toe of her slipper was peeping from under the hem of her gown, wiggling in time to a sprightly scrape of strings.

Jem and Emily both regarded him with that bizarre expression he'd seen so often on their faces lately: half hope and half apprehension, with a seasoning of worry. "Are you certain? You won't mind if—"

"Go on, enjoy yourselves. I'm sure Mrs. Whittier won't eat me," he replied.

"Don't assume too much," that lady said with a shrug. "All the world has told you how terrifying I am." Her cheeks darkened from rosy madder to velvety alizarin, Henry's favorite reddish pigment. A lovely effect with the fair olive of her skin and the stark, earthy brown of her hair, the ink-dark blue of her gown.

He regarded her closely as the chairs around them

emptied, as the cream of London society crammed onto the dance floor.

"Mrs. Whittier, you might be surprised by what terrifies me."

Acknowledgments

This book took the Romance of the Turf trilogy to some new places, and for impeccable guidance, I must thank my editor, Deb Werksman. My thanks, too, to the Sourcebooks experts in art, production, publicity, and marketing who create such beautiful books and get them out into the wild.

As always, deep gratitude to my agent, Paige Wheeler, for her advocacy, to Amanda for her critiques, and to my husband and daughter for their loving support. And to you, dear readers, for traveling with me—and with Kate and Evan—in this new story.

About the Author

Theresa Romain is "one of the rising stars of Regency historical romance" (*Booklist*). A member of Romance Writers of America and its Regency specialty chapter The Beau Monde, Theresa is hard at work on her next novel from her home in the Midwest. *Scandalous Ever After* is the second book in her Romance of the Turf Regency series. For information about her other books, please visit her online at theresaromain.com.

Nothing Like a Duke

You'll fall in love with each one of
The Duke's Sons

Lord Robert Gresham has given up all hope that the beautiful and independent Flora Jennings will ever take him seriously. He heads to an exclusive country house party to forget about her. When Flora shows up, Robert is nothing short of shocked. Their attraction flares, until someone sinister arrives and threatens Flora. Every fiber of Robert's being says to step in and save her…but some damsels in distress insist on saving themselves.

"Fabulous series…every bit is a joy to read."

—*Fresh Fiction* for *What the Duke Doesn't Know*

How to Train Your Highlander

A foolproof plan to avoid marriage:

1. Always carry at least three blades.
2. Ride circles around any man.
3. Never get caught in a handsome duke's arms.

Wild Highlander Mary Elizabeth Waters has managed to dodge marriage up to now, but even Englishmen can only be put off for so long…and there's one in particular who has her in his sights. Harold Percy, Duke of Northumberland, is enchanted by the beautiful hellion who outrides every man on his estate and dances Scottish reels while the ton looks on in horror. The more he sees Mary, the more he knows he has to have her, tradition and good sense be damned. But what's a powerful man to do when the Highland spitfire of his dreams has no desire to be tamed…

"Grace Burrowes and Amanda Quick fans will enjoy the strong ladies in the latest fun read from the ascending English."

—*Booklist*

"With its quick and engaging characters, here's a pleasurable evening's escape."

—*RT Book Reviews*

For more Christy English, visit:

www.sourcebooks.com